JAN 1 8 2019

REMITTANCE MAN

Center Point
Large Print

**This Large Print Book carries the
Seal of Approval of N.A.V.H.**

REMITTANCE MAN

S. I. SOPER

CENTER POINT LARGE PRINT
THORNDIKE, MAINE

The text of this Large Print edition is unabridged.
In other aspects, this book may vary
from the original edition.
Printed in the United States of America
on permanent paper.
Set in 16-point Times New Roman type.

ISBN: 978-1-64358-066-1 (hardcover)
ISBN: 978-1-64358-070-8 (paperback)

Library of Congress Cataloging-in-Publication Data

Names: Soper, S. I., 1929- author.
Title: Remittance man / S.I. Soper.
Description: Center Point Large Print edition. | Thorndike, Maine :
    Center Point Large Print, 2019.
Identifiers: LCCN 2018045869 | ISBN 9781643580661
    (hardcover : alk. paper) | ISBN 9781643580708
    (paperback : alk. paper)
Subjects: LCSH: Large type books. | GSAFD: Western stories.
Classification: LCC PS3569.O666 R46 2019 | DDC 813/.54—dc23
LC record available at https://lccn.loc.gov/2018045869

REMITTANCE MAN

CHAPTER ONE

The man eased his lathered bay gelding tail-first into a tiny cul-de-sac in the boulders, dismounted silently and slid his Sharps single-shot buffalo gun from its scabbard before he fished binoculars out of his saddlebags. Gun and 'scopes in hand, he climbed the rugged side of one big buff-colored sandstone rock and bellied down onto it. He lay the rifle beside him before he took off his flat-crowned Stetson and balanced one edge of its brim atop his head, the other along the binoculars' length to shade lenses from the heavy yellow sun heating his sweat-stained blue-shirted back—he didn't want chance light flashing from glass to betray his position to his pursuers.

His mount was weary, nearly on its last legs. He was also exhausted, but his hands were steady and fingers careful. The glasses picked out a tiny town perched on the banks of a wide river oddly busy for this part of the wilderness, but that wasn't what interested him at the moment. He shifted position slightly to move the binoculars and threaded sight into finer focus to bring the two men far down on the flat into better view.

Yes, it was them, the skinny one all in rusty black as though mimicking a dime novel gun-fighter, the heavier man looking like a snake-oil peddler without his show wagon, dressed as he was in a yellow-and-black plaid jacket and dented black bowler. Damn them! They had dogged him across the Territories for over two years, weren't they ever going to give up? Old Liam Hardesty must have offered a mint for his head to make it that worthwhile!

There had been more of them at the start. He'd first seen them in St. Louis when he'd gone to the Overland Stage stop to pick up his mail. That had been in 1871; he had been merely a boy then—if not in body, at least in experience—and he hadn't thought to be cautious. As he tucked the money his father sent him into his inner jacket pocket and stepped out of the station, he'd found himself confronted by four men.

The one in the medicine-peddler's jacket and bowler hat had said, "Mister Sean Hood, ain't yeh." It hadn't been a question.

He had looked at the six-shooters pointed at him, had abruptly known Hardesty had sent these men after him to kill him or to bring him in, could not for the life of him recall how he'd escaped them but somehow had, and that was the beginning of his long run.

It was now 1874. Over the years, he had joined a group of trail hands for the trip from St. Louis to Sedalia, Missouri—as an eastern tenderfoot, he had barely completed the journey alive. That, he could recall. In '72 and '73, while he had traveled from Kansas City down through the Oklahoma Indian country and on into the New Mexico Territory, he had consciously transformed himself into what he was today, an itinerant, a killer of man and beast but not a hardened murderer, for underneath his tough sun-browned exterior still lurked the boy he had once been.

He was now in the Arizona Territory, and still running. The money he assumed his father regularly sent to him probably still awaited his pickup in what few sizeable towns there were here, but with hired killers relentlessly dogging his every move year after year, he didn't often have the opportunity to pick up his remittance.

Over time, his pursuers had been reduced from four to two, those two riding westward toward the town below and far to his right. It abruptly came to him that he was very tired of this, and that he was about to shift the odds into his favor. He told himself it would be self-preservation, not murder . . . you were chased by wolves, you killed them to keep yourself alive. At this point, in his need to stop running, he would believe anything.

He put the binoculars aside and picked up the Sharps. The buffalo gun was accurate for at least a mile and had such a range it was sometimes called the "shoot today, kill tomorrow" gun. It was no good in a close fight where rapid fire was required, but for distance shots such as this one . . .

He resettled his hat, shouldered the Sharps, braced elbows on the stone beneath him, adjusted the scope, drew a bead on the skinny man out there, and squeezed the trigger. The shot echoed over the desert and bounced from rocky outcrops and rises around him, but the inch-long bullet outraced sound.

He lay the Sharps aside and again took up his binoculars. One man was motionless on the ground. Bowler Hat leaned low over his mount's neck, racing for cover while the riderless horse, reins flaying and bit in its teeth, followed.

Grimacing bitterly, Hood eased himself down off the boulder, returned the Sharps to its saddle scabbard, the glasses to their case, mounted up and guided his bay toward the low desert. Bowler Hat was now alone, as *he* was alone, and now they were on even terms. He was going to end this once and for all. Two-and-a-half years of running was enough. He wanted to settle down somewhere in this new land, get himself a patch of ground, maybe a wife, and be able to live each day without having to watch his back every second of the time.

He hadn't always been alone, hounded by bounty hunters. While he guided his mount among the rocks, a certain night (what seemed to be a lifetime ago) played back into his mind as it had so often over these past years that sometimes he wondered if he was still sane. It was as though he stood outside himself, viewing himself like a spectator at a stage play as he had watched the vaudeville comedy he and Elaine had gone to that last night in New York. He could see himself riding in the carriage after he'd seen Elaine home . . .

. . . gas street lights at each intersection casting golden shimmers across wet cobblestones out beyond the drive-through lane . . .

He had paid the carriage driver before he turned toward the wide curving white marble steps fronting the mansion. A light rain pattered against bare branches edging the building. It was the cold misty-between-droplets drizzle of late Winter, not yet heralding Spring or the long hot muggy Summer to come.

He'd tipped a finger to his hat brim and smiled up at the driver. "Have a good evening and stay dry."

"Thank you, sir." The man slapped reins to move the carriage onward.

He clutched his opera cape more tightly around him, took the steps two-at-a-time, and had just reached for the knocker when the butler opened the door for him.

"Good evening, Mister Stormy. I trust the musical was entertaining?"

Hood grinned, handed his hat to the man and shook water droplets onto the thick Turkish entry-hall rug before he slipped the cape off and also passed it over. Soft flames behind frosted globes in the chandelier showed him to be a slim young man elegant in evening clothes. His gleaming black hair and obsidian eyes could have placed him along with the carpet as mid-eastern or perhaps even Indian, except that his skin was very fair, with cheeks blushed by the outside chill. The Hoods were Black Irish, only a generation absent from the "Auld Sod," but in that generation, had risen from famine to fortune in the New World.

"Yes, Burkhart, the play was fine." There was no trace of Irish brogue in Stormy's speech; he was a born American.

"And did Miss Elaine enjoy it, sir?"

"I hope so. I confess, Burkhart, I wouldn't know if she didn't. Miss Elaine has such a bubbly nature that it's hard to tell whether she likes something or not. Invariably cheerful and pleasant. That's part of what makes me love her so." He leaned toward the butler. "Tell you something in confidence, Burkhart—I'm about to pop the question."

Burkhart's nose pinched (Stormy often thought the man had practiced before a mirror for years to hone that expression to perfection—or perhaps, had Burkhart gone to some butlers' college in his youth, they trained their students to that). Burkhart didn't comment on the proposed betrothal; merely said, "Sir, Mister George

Senior and Mister George Junior are waiting for you upstairs in the library."

Stormy's straight black brows rose. "Waiting for me *now?* At this time of the night? It's well after ten! Is there a problem?"

"I wouldn't know, Mister Hood. But they have been closeted all evening. My instructions are that I send you up to them the moment you arrive home."

"Don't give me that: *You wouldn't know,* Burkhart! You know everything!" But then, Stormy's heart squeezed. "Mother's not ill, is she?" His mother had never been strong, especially not after his arrival during a raging December blizzard that had given him his nickname. Though four miscarriages had preceded his birth, he'd always felt somehow responsible for her frailty and loved her passionately for the sacrifice she'd made to give him life.

"No more than usual, sir," Burkhart answered. "Please, Mister Stormy, your father and brother are waiting."

"Thank you, Burkhart." Sean turned to run up the carpeted, portrait-edged stairway—like the steps out front, he took them two-at-a-time. Half-way up, he paused to frown back down at the butler. Burkhart had done his duty and had presented the message he'd been ordered to deliver, yet Stormy got the impression that

13

there was more the butler wanted to say. There had been an almost: *Don't go up there!* whisper hanging in the air around the man.

He snorted and shook his head sharply. Imagination. The butler had vanished now, presumably toward his own quarters. He turned again and proceeded more slowly on up the stairs.

The library was in the center of the second-story hall snuggled between bedrooms at the back of the house. It was expansive and lined to the fifteen-foot-high ceiling with leather-bound books. Here and there, casement windows broke the shelving. A graystone fireplace pierced the outside wall. Heavy mohair- or leather-upholstered wingback chairs scattered around the room atop a thick oriental rug. When Stormy entered through polished carved oaken doors, he saw his father sitting in one of those chairs, and his brother—head in hands supported by elbows braced against spread knees—seated in another facing The Old Man. An empty third chair seemingly waited for him.

They rose at his approach, and Stormy noticed both were pale and haggard—in fact, his brother looked like death warmed over—and again, his heart jumped. He breathed, "What's the matter, Father . . . Georgie . . . what in God's Name has happened!"

George Senior cleared his throat. Stormy had inherited the elder Hood's black eyes and hair;

George Junior's eyes were their mother's blue, his hair also dark but with ruddy highlights. George Senior shoved a hand stiffly toward the vacant chair. His brogue heavier than usual, he said, "Please, Sean, be seated."

Stormy's name was Sean Evan Hood, but no one ever called him that unless the occasion was exceedingly formal or he had done something to incur a parent's wrath. He knew he had done nothing offensive recently; therefore . . .

Again, he asked, "What is it, Father? What's the matter?"

"We . . . have a family crisis, son. Please sit and listen. *Georgie, sit down!*" George Junior had lurched to the fireplace to lean his face on forearms crossed over the mantle.

Stormy scowled at his older brother . . . it appeared that tonight, more than ten years separated their ages. Good God, but Georgie seemed to have the weight of the world on his shoulders! He gasped, "Has something happened to Gertrude? Is your wife ill, Georgie? Or one of your children? George Three? Matthew? Maggie? Are they well?"

Wordlessly, George Junior nodded.

The senior Hood snapped, "Georgie's family is fine . . . *so far*. Both ye boys sit. *Sit!*" He sighed heavily. "Boys. No, neither of ya are boys any longer, an' as men, ya must face family responsibilities." He shook his head grimly—it was fascinating to Stormy to be able to see what he would look like when he, himself, reached his mid-fifties; still tall, slim, and black-eyed, his hair gone brilliantly white . . . But tonight, his father's features sagged with . . . weariness? . . . dismay? . . . defeat?

"The business, Father? Have some of our ships been wrecked? What . . . ?"

"No, no, our shippin' is boomin', lad. Best Georgie tells ya himself." Now, Hood's features went taut as he firmed his resolve, and the expression erased years. *"Tell him, Georgie."*

Young George had sank back into his chair. Barely above a whisper, and not looking at Stormy, he said, "I've been . . . indiscreet, Sean. My God . . . my God, how could I have done such a thing?"

Stormy frowned as he lowered himself into that third chair. "What does *indiscreet* mean, Georgie?"

"I've had an . . . affair. An illicit affair."

"With a woman not your wife?" Stormy didn't know whether to laugh or be outraged.

"Of course with a woman not my wife," George flared. "What else did you think I could have meant!"

Stormy lifted both hands, palms outward in a placating gesture. "I meant nothing as offensive as what you've done, Brother. So . . . ?"

"So, the girl became with child," the elder

16

Hood snapped. "She tried to . . . remedy the . . . situation. Found a slimy hag in some back alley, and it . . . killed her."

Stormy's scowl deepened. He began, "That's tragic . . . for the woman, but . . ."

"The girl was Melissa Hardesty!" Georgie gasped. "Melissa Hardesty. You know . . . knew her, Sean." He glanced briefly at their father.

Stormy's mouth fell open. He stiffened in his chair; nearly stood. "Liam Hardesty's daughter? *Little Melissa?*"

"Aye," the father nodded.

All Stormy could think of was: *At least Georgie has good taste.* He knew he couldn't say that, so said nothing as the elder Hood went on.

"She was just a child, herself . . . and Hardesty's *only* child. He was here while you were out this evenin', Sean. He doesn't know which one of my sons was the . . . culprit. His little girl spoke to him as she was dyin', but only said Mister Hood was the father. Hardesty knows t'was not me who dallied with his daughter's affections; therefore, it had to be one of my sons. He has promised to kill the villain. He has threatened to ruin me should I not turn one of you over to him by tomorrow's dawnin'. And he can do it, y'know. Hardesty Drayage an' our shippin' business are too closely tied . . . we need him to cart goods to our ships . . . from our ships . . . You know he's a personal friend of High Sachem Boss Tweed an' has long-standin' friends an' colleagues in Tammany Hall and 'mong the dock workers and long-shoremen. . . . Aye, but a few words from him, and our cargo would set rottin' in port or our ships lay empty."

Stormy sat back. He knew everything his father said was true—Liam Hardesty was a powerful man. He had Hood Shipping by the short hairs. He glanced at Georgie. Or, in this case, by the balls. He said, "But, we're not the only family in New York named Hood, Father."

"True. But we're the only ones Hardesty knows of in the right social status. He knows t'was one of us. He'll not hear no."

"So, what are you going to do? You can't turn Georgie over to Liam! He'll . . ."

"No." It seemed now that neither of the older men in the room could meet his eyes. "No, Sean. Georgie is my eldest heir. He's long wed to a fine woman. Think what it would do to Gertrude. To their children. Trudy would have every right to divorce George. With Hardesty's support, even the Church would back her claim of adultery. Georgie would be ruined. And because of the scandal . . . oh, sure, an' there would be *such* a scandal . . . *I* would go down with him. That would kill your mother, aye, t'would."

Stormy felt a chill sweep through him that even the fire on the hearth couldn't combat when a heavy silence descended into the dim room. And

18

still, neither his father nor his brother would look at him.

Finally, George Senior whispered, "It's not the money, Sean. God knows, we've plenty of that. The early days in America . . . here in New York . . . were hard an' cruel, me gettin' the business started an' all. I could live with poverty should it come to that, aye. But for the family name, Sean. Hardesty has sworn that should he get his hands on the culprit, this whole thing will remain secret . . . for his Melissa's reputation, yes. But for Georgie's *wife an' children,* innocents that they are who would be crushed by the scandal . . . an' for your *mother,* who must never know for t'would kill her sure as had some lowlife took an ax to her. . . ."

Suddenly, Stormy knew what his father and brother were asking of him. "You want me to . . . take the . . . responsibility." He could hardly force those words past lips stiffened by horror. *"But, I'm innocent! I've done nothing wrong!* It was *Georgie* who . . ."

Hood's voice was stronger when he agreed. "Aye, I know you're innocent, lad. But for Trudy and the children . . ."

Stormy leaped out of the chair. He looked wildly from his father to his brother and back before he choked, "But, I'm only twenty years old, Father! You're ruining my whole life! I only have one more year at the university before I graduate! Even next week, I had planned to ask Elaine to marry me! What will she think? *What will Elaine believe of me, Father!* And Hardesty will *kill* me, and . . ."

"No! No, he won't! You're not yet twenty-one, merely a lad! You have no ties, no responsibilities like Georgie has, and you don't need to stay around to face Liam!" George Senior delved frantically into an inner-jacket pocket before he thrust a sheaf of paper bills at Sean. "Here, look, here is money! Before tomorrow mornin', buy a ticket west by train or coach or ship . . . I don't want to know how you go, but go! When you get to Denver or San Francisco or wherever it is, there'll always be money waitin' for you. You'll never want for anythin', son, and it'll only be for a few years, y'see, till this whole thing blows over. We'll write you when y'can come home, son, an' . . ."

"You're making me into a Remittance Man, aren't you!" Stormy felt rage surge into his throat. "And by the time *those few years* are over, *my* reputation will be ruined. Elaine will have thrown me aside in disgust. She will have married someone else, and should we ever meet again, she'll spit on me if she wants to waste the effort! And *Mother!* What will my mother think of me! No! No, I . . ."

Hood nearly shouted, *"For* your mother's life, Sean! For Trudy and the children!"

"No!" Stormy cried.

But in the end, he did it.

Regardless of passed time, the scenario still played back into his mind, over and over as it had all across the wilderness into which he thought he'd vanished. True to his father's word, money always waited for him wherever he stopped, when he stopped, but he had quit picking it up because it appeared that Liam Hardesty had believed Father and Georgie's story that he, Sean, had been the primary cause of Melissa's death.

Men hunted him to take him back to New York so Hardesty could have his revenge . . . or perhaps Hardesty didn't care whether he came dead or alive. But it had been a long run. A damned long run . . .

Once clear of the rocks, he urged his bay gelding into a hard gallop after Bowler Hat. The horse had no name; Hood merely called him "horse." That was another defensive ploy on his part. He had lost count of the mounts he'd had to ride into the ground since St. Louis. The first few had had names and personalities, but he'd become fond of them and their deaths had hurt too much. Now, he tried not to think of them as friends and companions—his only friends and companions. They were merely transportation. Or so he said to himself. Some niggling little voice deep inside told him he lied.

He was worried now about this one, for it had nearly come to the end of its line. Still, he urged it to use whatever reserves it could muster, because he rode at a slant across the uneven cactus- and joshua-tree-clogged desert toward Bowler Hat and he would catch the varmint if it killed this horse, too.

No, he wouldn't. His mount was failing. He could feel muscles straining beneath him and hear the bay's labored breath. No, this one had too much heart to let it destroy itself trying to obey its master's orders.

He urged the horse to the ridge of a low rise and reined him in. Fingers now shaking with urgency, he reloaded the Sharps, and still in the saddle, sighted on Bowler Hat's mount. He would rather fire on the man than the horse, but he needed Bowler Hat alive and as undamaged as possible, at least until the critter answered some pertinent questions.

He breathed, "I'm sorry . . . ," and once again pressed the trigger.

Both Bowler Hat and his mount vanished in a cloud of dust and spray of sand when the buffalo gun brought the horse down. Hood jammed the Sharps back into its scabbard and urged his stumbling bay into a trot. He pulled his side-arm from its tied-down holster and pressed the trigger to rotate the cylinder past the empty chamber—it was a six-shooter, but he commonly carried only five bullets in it in order to keep the hair trigger from accidentally firing and shooting either his mount or himself—and eyes sweeping the countryside, eased toward where Bowler Hat's horse lay.

The man, himself, was up and running. He cast wary looks back over his shoulder while he tried to catch his fallen partner's spooked horse. He saw Hood's approach and flung himself behind a mesquite.

Under a warning instinct honed by his years of escaping his pursuers time-after-time, Hood yanked the reins to the side and kicked the bay hard in the ribs. The horse collapsed as if shot, and Bowler Hat's bullet sang harmlessly past where Stormy had been. Hood stepped clear to keep from getting a leg trapped beneath his horse. He landed on his feet, and crouching, began a zig-zag run from mesquite to cactus to rock—he knew the bay would stay where it was until he whistled for it.

Bowler Hat seemed torn between continuing to chase his partner's horse and snapping off shots at Hood whenever he saw his target. Stormy smiled mirthlessly; he'd been counting bullets. Bowler Hat had fired four. Unless the man carried multiple irons or had a derringer in his boot top, there was one, or at the most two, bullets left before he had to reload.

Hood cast a quick look back toward his gelding.

The horse still lay on his side as he'd been trained to do and was out of sight. Good.

Rather than holding an outright gun battle with his pursuer, keeping low, Stormy circled around behind the man and slipped silently toward where the riderless black horse had now halted some quarter-mile to the south, but then sank quickly behind a four-foot-tall cactus when he saw the black bowler rise from among the bushes.

His cold grin broadened. He wasn't going to fall for that. Bowler Hat had evidently lost sight of him and was trying to goad him into firing at the lure. He watched the hat bob momentarily as though supported by a stick before it vanished again.

Carefully working his way southward, he kept one eye on Bowler Hat's location, the other on the black gelding. When he got close enough for the horse to hear him but felt fairly sure his voice wouldn't carry back to his pursuer, he straightened his crouch slightly and began talking quietly to the animal.

It had recovered from its spook. It tossed its head and rolled eyes, but the reins had fallen and it seemed to think it was ground-tethered. It let him approach.

Hood wanted this horse for himself to be able to give his bay a rest, and also to keep Bowler Hat from using it. He knew his pursuer was desperate to catch it. Bowler Hat still had a bullet or two in

24

his gun, or maybe had a full cylinder now—he'd certainly had plenty of time to reload. Instead of mounting up, Hood took the black's reins in his left hand, kept his unfired iron in his right, and almost on his knees to keep his head below brush level, slowly led the horse to the nearest thicket. He tied the reins together; then, looped them over a branch to keep the gelding from running off but tried to make it look like leather had merely tangled there. Then, he stepped back to another mesquite, burrowed deep into it, and hunkered down.

His own horse was hidden, and its fall could have appeared to be that of a wounded or killed animal rather than the practiced plunge it was. He doubted that Bowler Hat would waste time on the bay. That left the black as the only horse in sight. Now, all he had to do was wait for the bounty hunter to take the bait.

He watched the horse's ears rather than trying to depend on his own. He had no idea how adept Bowler Hat was at moving silently over pebbles, twigs, and gritty sand—once, he, himself, had been an urban dweller noisy in the wastes, but he had long ago learned how to be quiet. Bowler Hat had been chasing him nearly as long as he'd been running; maybe the man also had the skill, but the horse would let him know when someone .approached.

It was a long wait. The hot sun slipped into

afternoon, and though in the shade, Hood's mouth was so dry it tasted of ashes. Even his palm was no longer sweaty against the six-gun grip. He could see a canteen hanging from the black's saddle ties; he needed water, but didn't dare try for it because Bowler Hat could be only a few feet away. He had waited this long. To betray himself now would ruin everything. He worried about his own mount still lying on its side under the sun. That was an unnatural position for a horse to hold. The animal was undoubtedly suffering—how much longer until discomfort overrode training and the bay rose?

But then, the black snorted. His ears pricked before he turned his head to the left. Hood stopped breathing; didn't move when Bowler Hat—gun in hand, face heat-flushed and running sweat, and yellow-and-black jacket monochromatic with dirt, his narrowed eyes darting at every shadow or moving leaf—stepped out from behind some greasewood and sidled carefully toward the tethered gelding.

Stormy waited until Bowler Hat had almost reached the black. The man's back was to him. He had a clear shot if he wanted to end this here and now. He *did* want the long chase over with, but not that way.

Bowler Hat was just reaching for the reins when a voice behind him said softly, "Grab sky and hang on to it!"

CHAPTER TWO

July 1, 1874
To: Mrs. Fredrick Cooper
     Philadelphia, Pennsylvania
My Dearest Mother . . .

I know that by now you have despaired of ever hearing from me again and believe that my corpse lies decaying in some uncharted morass, but I assure you, I am very well, am involved in the most amazing adventure, and am having the time of my life! And yes, before you ask, this is my first correspondence to you since I left, for though I keep a regular journal, I've not essayed to write you because there has heretofore been no port from which to post a letter.

After my tiff with Charles (I trust the scoundrel promptly hung himself—yes, yes, very un-Christian of me, I know, Mother), I went to Chicago, obtained employment, and once my training was completed, appealed to my new employer for a wayward assignment. Ask, and ye shall receive! I confess, I never expected anything quite like this!

Under my employer's orders, I took

the train to New York; thence, obtained passage aboard the packet ship, *Apollo*, from New York harbor to Port Chagres on the Isthmus of Panama. My employer provided a first-class cabin for me (at, I believe, considerable expense, bless him). Though there were two bunks in the cabin, I was the only female aboard at the time, so had the quarters to myself.

At Chagres, we travelers disembarked and went by canoes (called *bungos*) for about seventy-five miles up the Chagres River to a place called Gorgona, where we then rode mules overland to Panama City on the Pacific coast of the Isthmus. The land journey was arduous, pestiferous with flies, mosquitos, and deluging rain, but also incredibly beautiful with flowered jungles replete with birds and monkeys and simple harmless natives; still, I confess that I took to wearing men's clothing merely to survive!

At Panama City, I boarded the barque, *Ina*, for a leisurely voyage northward up the Mexican coastline. The *Ina* docked at the quaint Spanish harbor of San Diego established, as I understand it, here in the Californias only a hundred and five years ago in 1769, where I again disembarked and was transported by freight wagon across the inhospitable southwestern desert land (you have never imagined such animals—prairie wolves, poisonous snakes, spiders the size of one's hand, scorpions . . . ugh!).

But survive, I have. I am now in a dreadful town called alternately Arizona City and/or Fort Yuma, which seems to be only a few sticks and mud-brick hovels perched upon the blazing breast of Hades, but hopefully, things can only get better. I am taking a paddlewheel steamer (the *Gila*) up a river called the Colorado (I hear the word means "red" in Spanish, and the water is so silt-filled it certainly earns its name) to an army garrison and port town called Ehrenberg. Thence, I shall proceed to Graniteville (or Prescott). I do wish these wilderness locals would pick a name and settle on it, because one never knows whether or not one is betraying one's alien-ness by erroneously naming a stop. And, Mother, since—despite my best efforts—the wind, sea air, tropical voyages, and desert passages have turned every portion of my exposed anatomy to a horrid terra-cotta color, I could, indeed, pass for a pioneer instead of an Eastern lady!

I understand that Graniteville (or

Prescott) is up in the mountains some hundred-and-sixty miles afield across the wastes—that means more unremitting sun, wind, and exposure, so I doubt you'll be able to tell me from a Californio when I return home unless you look at my hair, which has been sun-bleached into streaks of white!

I'm sorry this letter is so short. I have many stories and adventures to tell you, but I don't have the time to do it now as I understand the *Gila* will cast off within the hour and I must find a place here in Fort Yuma to post this; then, complete my report to my employer. I don't know when I will reach another semblance of civilization, but as soon as I do, I will write to you again. Suffice it to say, I seem to flourish under these strenuous conditions. I am <u>very</u> well. I hope this finds you the same.

All my love . . .
Your daughter, Veracity

Veracity folded the note, addressed the envelope, hastily pulled her hat down more firmly over her hair and rose from where she sat in the shade cast by the *Gila*'s double-decker cabins. She needed to find someone who knew how to start the letter on its way. *And,* perhaps buy some new clothes. She hadn't told her mother that her trunk had fallen over the side of the bungo in transit across the Isthmus and was still at the bottom of the Chagres River. Her parasol had been whisked out of her hands by heavy wind off the Mexican coast and probably was nudging oriental shores by this time. Now—except for her reticule to which she had clung tenaciously because it contained her credentials, her business cards, her journal, her credit voucher to fund her trip back to the east coast, and her remaining eighty-seven dollars cash—what clothing she wore had been purchased either in Panama City or San Diego.

Her employer's "General Principles" dictated that operatives should dress somberly at all times, a rule she was certainly breaking, but she did the best she could with what she presently had to work with. The tightly-woven tan straw hat with chin-string and wide floppy brim had replaced her bonnet hopelessly snagged by a branch during the mule ride from Gorgona to Panama City. A man's blue-and-white-checked calico shirt replaced her white chambray blouse soiled beyond any cleaning prior to San Diego. She had exchanged the man's pants she'd worn since the Isthmus crossing for a Spanish lady's heavy brown split riding skirt, and her mud-ruined shoes with knee-high riding boots.

In her reticule beside a pair of handcuffs Mr.

Pinkerton had insisted were part of her "necessary equipment" (she hadn't the slightest idea what she would ever do with them) nestled what she understood was called an "Avenging Angel"—a revolver pistol with the barrel cut off to shorten it for easy concealment. She had bought that item from a Mormon missionary fallen on hard times in strongly Catholic California.

A loaded derringer was tucked into her right boot top, and she had strapped a heavy-bladed hunting knife in its sheath to her wide brown leather belt.

All-in-all, she definitely did not appear to be the lady her mother believed her to be . . . *and,* she had carefully refrained from disclosing in her letter that she was now a Pinkerton detective in pursuit of a target, else Mother suffer palpitations!

Face burnished with sun and heat, she yelled, *"Captain, sir!"* Captain Bolton turned crow's-feet-edged blue eyes her way. A long-time employee of the *Colorado Steam Navigation Company*, he had begun as a deck hand in 1851 and had been captain of the *Gila*, the largest and best sternwheeler on the river, for the last six years. In his time, he'd seen freight and pioneers come and go, but rarely anyone like this fair-haired, wind-frazzled little woman traveling alone. He sighed, "Yes, Miss Cooper?"

Veracity flourished the letter. "Is there a place here in Fort Yuma where I . . ."

"Not here, Ma'm, but when we get to Ehrenberg upriver, the Butterfield Overland Stage passes through. You can post it there."

"Oh! Does the stagecoach go to Prescott?"

"Yes, Ma'm. The stage passes through Ehrenberg regular on its run from San Bernardino to Prescott, but I don't know its schedule. You miss it, you'll have to wait a week or two in Ehrenberg, but if you're in a hurry to leave, you might take passage with the freight wagons."

Her hazel eyes narrowed. "How long does a freight take, Captain? How long now until I reach Prescott? I was three weeks on a barque to the Isthmus, two weeks crossing that, another three weeks from Panama City to San Diego, and another near two weeks crossing California. Am I ever going to reach my goal?"

His eyes popped. "Izzat all? You made real good time, Ma'm. Took some of them Forty-niner gold fiends more'n six months to get to Californee."

Her lips firmed. "I am not an argonaut, Captain. Excellent arrangements from coast-to-coast had been made for me. How much longer?"

"Well, Ma'm, we should be in Ehrenberg 'bout two Pee Em t'morra afternoon, we don't hit no sandbars or nothin', an' the Apaches don't attack. But for as to how long it'll take you to git to the uplands, well, depends on catchin' a stage, no storms, no *bandidos*, no cholera, an' so on. I wouldn't hazard a guess, 'cept meby you could make it afore the month is out."

"But this is only the first! I . . ." Veracity looked worriedly around at the forbidding landscape.

"You got a pressin' timetable or somethin'? You a schoolmarm whose gotta be in Prescott to start learnin' young'uns?"

"No. Well, thank you for your information, Captain." Veracity tucked the letter into her reticule and returned to her seat in the shade to absently watch what ensued ashore.

Bother! Had she known she had until tomorrow to finish her letter, she could have written more! Oh, well, *any* news from her would be welcomed at home, she supposed.

She grimaced when she wondered if Mother would share the letter with Charles. She hoped not—let the opinionated, bigoted, hidebound, nearsighted bounder be forever in the dark about what had become of her! Watching raven-haired white-cotton-clad natives carting and carrying under the careless eyes of blue-uniformed soldiers from the army garrisoned here in Fort Yuma, and feeling the *Gila* rock beneath her as its load increased, she thought again of Charles Poindexter Brandenberg.

Old Philadelphia money. Old Philadelphia family with Old Philadelphia ideals. Not that she, herself, had been brought up on the wrong side of the tracks, but she considered herself to be worth more than merely an heir-producing ornament to Charles's arrogant posturing!

She was the eldest of four daughters; there were herself, Faith, Hope, and Charity. Lacking a son, her father had chosen her to fulfill that role. During her whole childhood and before his death, he had taken her sport hunting with him, had taught her to ride and shoot. . . . She smiled at that. How amazed her employer had been when she'd demonstrated her skills with horse, rifle, pistol, and casting knife, but why should he have been? After all, some of the most successful Revolutionary and Civil War spies and soldiers had been women! He had hired Kate Warne, his first female employee, prior to 1861. She had been deeply involved in foiling what was called the "Baltimore Plot," the scheme to assassinate President-elect Lincoln, and *that* was more than ten years ago!

Charles had treated her with great respect until the moment they'd become officially engaged, and then, in an almost "go to your room, little girl, women should be seen and not heard" attitude, he began to act as though she had degenerated into some brainless child he owned lock, stock, and barrel! Not that she was a member of the National Woman Suffrage Association or a personal friend of Elizabeth Cady Stanton or the like, because she had been too comfortable in her easy relationship with her father in 1869 when that movement was begun. But abruptly, she'd realized she had never really known Charles. And when she'd had her dressmaker create that absolutely lovely ball gown for their engagement party and he had forbidden her to wear it . . .

He'd said, "I see I shall have to teach you correct etiquette, Vera. Young brunettes may wear red. Young redheads may wear green. Young blondes wear blue, Vera, my dear. With your hair coloring, red is inappropriate. You simply cannot wear that."

She wasn't blonde . . . well, she hadn't started out that way until all this sun had bleached her hair . . . but it was more *how* Charles had said it than his words, themselves. Besides, the dress wasn't red, it was maroon, and she'd told him so. One thing had led to another. Mother, of course, sided with Charles . . . Mother *always* sided with Charles.

Suddenly, she'd known she didn't want to be Mrs. Charles Poindexter Brandenberg. Besides, she hated *Vera,* and hated even more that Charles called her that simply because he said the words *Veracity Louise Brandenberg* had more syllables in them than was proper for a female name to contain!

The clod!

A heightened hissing and a lurch beneath her announced that the *Gila* was ready to begin its voyage upriver. There was a flurry of activity dockside as mooring lines were cast off; then, an energetic thrash of water when paddles at the boat stern beat water into beige cream. The *Gila* moved slowly away from the dock and out into the river but not to the midstream current, and Veracity pondered how she would go about fulfilling her mission out here in the great desert wastelands.

It all seemed so huge! Pockets of humanity were so few and far between! Still, as one of the Allan Pinkerton Agency's few female detectives, she had to make good, didn't she. It was locate her quarry or crawl back to Charles in defeat, wasn't it!

She dug a creased envelope out of her reticule, unfolded it, lifted the flap and extracted a two-by-three-inch daguerreotype of a dark-haired dark-eyed young man about nineteen or twenty. He was dressed for his formal portrait in a white wing-collared shirt and wide silk tie beneath an elegant light-colored suit and vest. Sean Evan Hood had been a nice looking boy—she wondered how the Agency had obtained the picture? Well, however they'd done it, they obviously had their ways. But were *her* ways skilled enough to find him?

She sighed, returned the picture to its envelope, the envelope to her reticule, cinched the bag top, spent the remainder of the day watching the banks pass as the *Gila* plowed its way upriver, and occasionally wondered how a land adjacent to so much fresh water could be so arid, rocky, and inhospitable.

This time, unlike her sea journey west, she wasn't the only female passenger—a family consisting of husband, wife, and four children ranging in ages from infancy to perhaps ten, had hurried up the gangplank at the last minute to also make the trip. While the three stair-step boys tried to take over the ship much to the deck hands' amusement, the mother sat on a box across from Veracity, nursed the baby, and eyed her cheerfully.

"Good afternoon, Miss. You travelin' alone?"

Veracity smiled politely, nodded, and returned her stare to the landscape.

The mother—plump, pleasant, only in her late twenties but already tanned to leather from her life out here—wasn't deterred. "Goin' far?"

"To Ehrenberg, then overland to Prescott. And you?"

"Ah! We live up by Fort Mojave. My man is a blacksmith there. Come down here for supplies and to visit his brother and fambly." The wife lay her infant over her shoulder and burped the baby before she closed her dress. "You got fambly in Prescott?"

"No. My . . . work . . . takes me there."

"Ah!" For the second time, Veracity's response seemed to be a revelation to the woman. "You a schoolmarm?"

"No." That was twice she'd been asked that. Teachers must be in short supply out here. "Though I suppose I could teach music, if I had to."

"*Ah!* And what d'ya play?"

"The pianoforte."

"Ah-*ha!* Only piannas we got out here, if the poor things survive the trek, are either in churches or in saloons. You play churchy music?"

"Oh, yes. But . . ." now Veracity smiled, warming to the woman, ". . . they would never allow me to play in church at home in the east. They said my . . . *attack* . . . was too frivolous."

The woman threw back her head and laughed. "Well, then, Miss, welcome to Ar'zona. We like a li'l life in our hymns out here . . . both in the two-legged kind and the church-singin' kind!" She chuckled at her own wit, rose and thrust the baby at Veracity. "Here, hold Clara for me for a minute. I gotta go corral them boys else one falls overboard and poisons the fish." The young mother turned and shrieked, *"Soooooeeee! Sooooeeee! Got vittles here!"*

My word, she's calling the hogs! Veracity frowned to herself while she rocked the baby. But the yell got immediate results. The three little boys scurried across the deck to their mother and were rewarded with indefinable items from a covered basket.

The woman grinned at Veracity as she retrieved

the baby. "Food's the only thang that gains their 'tention." To the boys, she ordered, "Now Frank, now Sam, now Joe, you set a while! Set! Set, else I gotta take a switch to ya!" She lifted a brow to Veracity. "Whoppin' comes after food to make 'em set up and take notice."

Somehow, without her quite knowing how it happened, by the end of the day Veracity had become part of the "fambly." They didn't ask her name or give her theirs, but shared their food with her and chatted warmly as though they'd known her for years.

At sunset, the *Gila* dropped anchor out of the central current but not too near the shoreline, and Veracity retired to her tiny cabin to escape mosquitos that formed clouds thicker than fog over the river and to write her progress report to Mr. Pinkerton. At dawn the next day, the *Gila* proceeded, and since they struck no sandbars and met no Apaches, they in fact reached Ehrenberg around two that afternoon.

The wife hugged Veracity, and with a tear in her eye, wished her safe journey. Veracity returned the embrace, agreed that if she ever got as far north as Fort Mojave she would look them up; then, addressed the land.

Ehrenberg seemed to be a solid adobe town with an oddly ramshackle air about it, yet it was certainly larger and more substantial than Fort Yuma. It sported the Goldwater Mercantile Store, a church, a dressmaker, two saloons, a meat market, a bakery, a livery stable, the stagecoach office, and an army quartermaster's corps post supplying food, uniforms, and arms to the various forts and military *campos* scattered around the territory.

As she walked the gangplank over to the dock, Veracity said good-bye and thank you to Captain Bolton; then, shifted her mind to her own business. First item now was to post her report to the head office and the letter to her mother, and simultaneously purchase a coach ticket to Prescott at the stage office.

Ehrenberg's main street was of dirt whose surface had been churned by wagon wheels, horses' hooves, and passing boots while wet, then the mud sun-baked into iron-hard ruts and knobs. It was the roughest surface Veracity had ever tried to walk across, and she headed as quickly as she could without breaking an ankle toward the narrow boardwalk fronting the buildings.

She paused when passing Morris Goldwater's Mercantile Store to look in the window and considered purchasing more feminine clothing to replace the bits and pieces she presently wore, but then shook her head. She had only eighty-seven dollars left. Until she found out how much the coach fare was to Prescott and how much a hotel or boarding house room cost (if there *were* any such amenities there), prudence dictated that she make-do with what she had on.

The inside of the Butterfield Overland Stage depot was cramped, relatively cool, dim, and sported four small wooden benches for waiting stage passengers. At the far end, a barred window broke the wall fronting a counter reminiscent of an eastern banking establishment. A mutton-chopped mustachioed man in a gray-and-white-pinstriped shirt, detachable collar and cuffs, red sleeve-garters, and dusty black vest, his sweating bald pate far outshining his round wire-rimmed grime-coated glasses, stood beyond the grill. He was backed by a multitude of mail pigeonholes. Most were empty, but some of them contained letters and others were stuffed with packages. Truly, this was a major postal stop.

Well, now, she was supposed to be a detective, wasn't she! She had attended three weeks of classes taught by Mr. Pinkerton's instructors prior to receiving this, her first assignment, hadn't she? Now was the time to begin trying to locate the subject of her search, and it seemed that a postal servant and stagecoach clerk should be a prime source of information, didn't it!

She approached the cage and cleared her throat; smiled at the man when he nodded to her. "How much to mail this letter, please?"

"Where's it goin', Ma'm?"

"Philadelphia, Pennsylvania."

The agent plucked the envelope from her

fingers, weighed it on a small scale by his right elbow, and said, "Three cents, Ma'm."

She handed him the second envelope containing her progress report to Pinkerton. "And this one to Chicago?"

He weighed that, also. "Heavier. Six cents. Total, nine cents."

"My, but mail is expensive!" She opened her reticule, dug past the Avenging Angel hidden there, and found her coin purse.

The agent agreed; added, "But yer correspondence is goin' a long way, Ma'm."

"True." She handed over the coins. "And, I'd like a ticket on the next stage to Prescott, please. When will that be?"

"Oh, Ma'm, it come through day before yeste'day. You got near a week and a half till the next one. I can recommend a nice boardin' house for you while you wait, if you'd care to."

Bother! Wouldn't you know it! Well, so far, everything had seemed to move along like clockwork. This was the first hitch in her progress—and there were still those freight wagons out there to fall back on.

She sighed; said, "Very well, I'll make other arrangements. Ummm . . . I've just come upriver on the *Gila* from Fort Yuma. Mister Sean Evan Hood is there incapacitated at the moment with a broken leg. His horse fell on him. He will travel overland to Prescott when he recovers, but in the meantime, since this is such a major post office, he asked me to pick up whatever mail is waiting for him here. *Is* there anything for him?"

The clerk frowned. "Mister Hood send written permission with you?"

Veracity put on her most innocent smile. "I'm sorry, sir, but Mister Hood doesn't read or write. I usually read any correspondence to him."

Illiteracy was so common among the ranch hands, itinerant miners, and desert rats, that the agent saw nothing unusual in that. Still, he hesitated; began, "No, I don't recall the name. I don't . . ." But then, he brightened. "Wait! By golly, Ma'm, I believe I do!" He turned, stepped to the pigeonholed wall and fished around in the top left-hand space. Presently, he brought out a thick envelope covered by at least an inch of dust. He blew its burden from it before he passed it through the grill to Veracity. "I usually only hold a letter a year before I send it back as unclaimed, but I confess, this has been here so long I plumb fergot it." He squinted through hazed glasses at the date. "Damn near two years! I swear! Lucky for yer Mister Hood it's still here!"

"Thank you, sir." Again, Veracity smiled at him. "I'm sure Mister Hood appreciates this." She moved to one of the benches, turned her back on the agent, sat, and only hesitated briefly before she tore open the envelope. After all, snooping was now her business, wasn't it.

Inside was a sheaf of paper money and a letter. She counted the money. One thousand dollars in mixed bills had waited to be picked up by a man who had never come for it. Biting her lip, and firmly subduing the feeling that she invaded someone else's privacy, she opened the letter and began to read what was written there in a strong but simultaneously uncertain male hand:

To my beloved son, Sean . . .

It grieves me deeply to have to tell you that your mother passed away Monday this week. I know she died of grief at your disappearance—you were her "baby," her last child, and she could not survive your loss.

Sean . . . son . . . I have come to realize that I made a terrible error when I let your brother talk me into coercing you into taking the blame for Miss Hardesty's untimely and tragic death. I know now that I wasn't thinking clearly then—to learn of what George, Jr. had done and the result of his perfidious actions confounded my brain at the moment. What then seemed the only logical way around further catastrophe only compounded the tragedy.

Come home, son. Though some of these packages have already been returned to me as unclaimed, I have sent money to be held for you at St. Louis, Salt Lake City, Denver, Sacramento, San Francisco, Prescott, and Ehrenberg. Use the money for your return. I plead with you, if you read this, come home, and together, we will rectify the terrible mistake I have perpetrated upon you.

Come home, son . . . please come home.

Your loving and repentant father . . .

George P. Hood, Sr.

Veracity gnawed her lip as she looked up from the letter and out through the open doorway into the blazing adobe-yellow street beyond. Sean Hood was innocent! She was pursuing an innocent man! From what she gleaned from this letter, it was his older brother, George Hood, Jr., who was the culprit. Oh, she knew all about the family; had studied them thoroughly as was required before proceeding on a case. She had known, of course, that Sean's mother had long ago passed away, but what this plaintive missive didn't communicate was that George, Senior, had himself perished of a heart seizure not a month later, and that George, Junior presently ran Hood Shipping.

Stormy was innocent—this writing proved it— and if he would only return home to shout that innocence, he would become an immensely rich man.

On sudden impulse, she tucked the letter and all that money into her reticule and returned to the agent. "Sir, may I purchase a sheet of paper and an envelope from you . . . and may I also please borrow your pen?"

The paper and envelope cost her another four cents. Using the shelf before the cage as a desk, she wrote quickly:

> Mr. Hood . . . I have your money and a letter from your father. Come to Prescott to get it. I will be at the local hotel for three months from this date.

She signed: *V. Cooper, July 2, 1874*, folded the paper, tucked it into the envelope, sealed it, and addressed the outside to: *Stormy Hood*. She said to the agent, "Mister Sean Hood's brother. I've left him a note to advise him that I've picked Sean's mail up for him. Just put this away in the same pigeonhole the other envelope was in, and if Stormy appears, please give it to him."

She went back to the dock where the freight wagons were being loaded and asked to buy transportation to Prescott with them. The wagon master was agreeable, but inquired how much she weighed.

The question flustered her. "Why . . . uh . . . about a hundred and ten pounds, I believe, sir. Why?"

"Drayage charges, Ma'm. Cost three-quarters cent a mile. A hunnert an' sixty miles is . . ." His eyes glazed while he mentally computed that, ". . . three-quarters cent times a hunnert sixty miles is . . ."

"A dollar twenty cents," Veracity prompted.

He nodded. "Times a hunnert an' ten pounds . . ."

"I think that's thirteen dollars and twenty cents."

"Yup. An' you provide yer own food an' tent."

On her journey between San Diego and Fort Yuma, she'd learned that the first wagon there hitched to a twenty-mule team was called a "Deck Wagon"; the other three, each pulled by a twelve-ox team, were "Trail Wagons." All had tall sides, their cargoes covered with tied-down canvas tarpaulins. She'd seen them being packed with mining equipment, army materiel, liquor barrels, food and mail. They were further burdened with water barrels, team fodder, and the driver's provisions and camping equipment, and she eyed the high, hard, un-shaded wooden seat on the nearest wagon. She had perched long-term on one of those before, and her bottom had only recently recovered. "I would ride up there?"

"Yup."

"For how many days?"

"We make some ten miles a day lessen we meet trouble. Them oxen is sturdy but deliberate. Then, we got the escarpment to consider. Steep up. Three miles a day only. Takes two days. May take sixteen to Prescott, but safe to say takes eighteen days."

Eighteen days on that hard board! She asked, "Had I a horse and rode with you on my own transportation, how much for your protection?"

"Nothin'. The pleasure of yer company's free, Miss. But you gotta stay with me, Miss. Come the split, part of this train goes straight on to Wickenberg. An' best you hurry. We're leavin' shortly."

"Fine. I'll be right back."

At the livery stable, for ten dollars, she bought a reasonably sound sorrel mare with a white mane and three white stockings, whose name the stable owner said was Goldie. She added a saddle, bridle, and saddlebags for another fifteen of her remaining money.

At the mercantile store, she purchased a meager bedroll, a canteen, canned beans and peaches, grits, a bandana, and of all things, six fresh apples. Total cost, $4.65.

She checked her resources. What with postage, paper, envelope, and this, she'd spent $29.65 of her $87.00. She had only $57.35 left.

Well, at least she now had her own transportation. She tied her bedroll and the filled canteen on behind her saddle, mounted Goldie, and with the strings of the reticule containing the Avenging Angel, what remained of her money, and Sean Hood's thousand dollars secure on the saddle horn beside her right knee, rode to meet the freight wagons.

She'd paid two cents for a bandana at Goldwater's and smiled with satisfaction. While she waited for the freight wagons to pull out, she tied the bandana around her neck over the collar of her checked shirt. That cloth was bright red. She'd made sure it was the brightest *reddest* bandana in the store.

If Charles could only see her now . . . *ha!*

But then she sobered, thinking of what she'd read in George Hood's letter to his son. She knew now that Sean Hood was innocent of any wrongdoing, which heightened her urgency to find him—he had to be told that he could go home as a free man. Her own need to prove herself as a viable Pinkerton detective paled beside that other need, didn't it.

She wondered what Sean Evan Hood, whom family and friends had nicknamed *Stormy,* was really like, especially now after his years of running from blame for something he hadn't done?

The wagon master yelled to move out. The unbidden feeling of excitement that bubbled within her shoved her thoughts from Hood for the moment as she kneed Goldie into a trot to follow.

CHAPTER THREE

Before he proceeded with this, Stormy whistled sharply through his teeth. He was relieved to see from the corner of his eye that his bay gelding stumbled upright and shook himself free of a cloud of dust. He let the horse begin to crop at grass growing in tough stubby bunches amid brush and cactus while he concluded business here.

Bowler Hat, wall-eyed and wary, stared back over his shoulder at him when he asked, "Who are you and why have you been doggin' me for years?"

"I ain't trailin' yeh!" Bowler Hat looked desperately around at the landscape. "Youse got no call fer dis . . . I ain't done youse no harm! Youse shoot me partner, den me horse. . . ."

"I hear by your accent that you're from New York." Sean cut the man short. "What's your name?"

"Oscar Pratt! Me name's Oscar Pratt . . . and . . ."

"If you aren't tagging me, how come I've seen you in Missouri, in Kansas, in Texas, in New Mexico, and now here, Oscar?"

"Uh . . . jus' . . . goin' d'same way?"

Stormy's lip curled in his two-week beard. "Not likely, Oscar. Fling that gun aside and turn

51

around real easy. You make one false move and you're as dead as your friend back there."

Pratt tossed the iron a short distance off into the dirt. Hands again high, he turned to face Sean. "Now, Mister Hood, youse don' have to be so hard-nosed 'bout dis! We can talk here, y'know, sir. . . ."

Stormy barked a short, harsh laugh. "*Mister Hood,* is it? I didn't tell you my name. How do you know me unless you've been tailing me? . . . I have my signature printed on my forehead? *Down on your knees, Pratt!*"

Slowly, Bowler Hat obeyed. He panted as though he'd run a mile; Hood saw abject fear there. "All right, who do you work for, Oscar?"

"N-Nobody, Mister H-Hood. I swear to de Lord . . ."

"Don't blaspheme, Oscar. How big a price is on my head? Must be a lot for you and those others to spend *years* trying to bring me in."

Pratt shook his own head violently. "I don' know wot youse is talkin' 'bout, Mister H-Hood. Uh . . . yeah, I knows yer name. Uh . . . yes, I seen yeh in St. Louis couple of years back, but . . ."

Stormy aimed his iron at the space between Pratt's thighs and pulled the trigger. The bullet dug into soft sand a fraction of an inch from Oscar's crotch.

"Five t'ousan' dollars!" Pratt howled. *"Five gran', Mister Hood* . . . Jesus Christ . . ."

Sean was surprised. So much! "You legitimate law enforcement or working for yourself?"

"I . . . was workin' on de docks . . . Noo Yawk, sir. Me an' tree of de boys took de job. Splittin' five gran' four ways . . . dat's more'n twelve hunnert bucks each . . . more dan what we could make in two years' time, longshorin'. B-But we never expected it to take so long. Ferd an' Bill went home 'bout a year ago. Said bein' gone from wives an' families dat long wadn't wert it. Rabin an' me let 'em. We got no families, an' . . ."

"And dividing five thousand two ways is more profitable than by four." Stormy shook his head slightly. "Now, there's only you, right, Pratt? That five thousand is all yours now, isn't it, if you can just get at it." Again, he shook his head. "How old Hardesty must hate me to put up five thousand dollars for me. I know he's wealthy, but . . ."

Pratt frowned. He almost lowered his hands before he blurted, "Who's dat?"

"What? Who is Liam Hardesty?"

"Yeah. Who's he?"

"The man paying you! God, has the sun fried your brains? How does he want me . . . dead or alive?"

Pratt licked his lips. Still on his knees, he darted a look from Stormy to the weapon lying in the

53

dirt a few feet away, then back to Hood. "No, I ain't addled. And I don' know no Liam Hardesty. De one what hired us wants youse dead, an' *proof* youse is dead . . . like a picher of yer body or yer head or somethin', yeah, but his name ain't Hardesty."

Stormy was taken-aback. He blurted, "If Hardesty didn't contract with you to kill me, who did?"

"G-Got the same name as yers, M-Mister Hood. S-Said his name was G-George H-Hood. Offered five t'ousan' fer yer head. W-Wants youse dead, sir."

Sean's mouth fell open. For a moment, it felt as if a horse had kicked him in the gut. His eyes went wide, his face white as he gasped, "My . . . my father? . . . or my brother, Georgie? *My father or my brother want me dead?*"

Pratt saw his prey frozen in disbelief. His moment had come; it was now or never. Before Sean could recover, Oscar flung himself toward his own discarded weapon, seized the grip, flipped over onto his back with the agility of a younger much more athletic man, and snapped a shot off at Hood.

The bullet was half-wild. It plowed along Sean's ribs instead of through his heart, but it ruined Hood's own shot. Pratt's bowler hat sprang from his head and rolled on its brim until it lodged against the black gelding's forefeet.

Sean had been knocked flat by the bullet's impact. Even as he lurched back to his knees, Oscar fired at him again, but the hammer clicked on an empty chamber. Pratt saw Stormy trying to clear his sight enough to draw a decent bead on him, knew his own gun was empty, that he didn't have time to reload, panicked, leaped to his feet and at the black horse, yanked the reins free of the mesquite and grabbed the saddle horn to vault into the saddle.

Hood's next shot took a hunk out of Oscar's left buttock and nicked the horse's chin. The black squealed in pain. With Pratt clinging to the horn and only one foot in a stirrup, the gelding wheeled and bolted into the desert.

Stormy started to fire again, but stopped himself. Brush and cactus made the shot too iffy; besides, his mind reeled both from the wound and from what he'd heard from Pratt.

It was a lie. It had to be a lie. Father . . . or Georgie . . . wouldn't do that to him! Or would they?

No, no, it was a lie. Why would Father or Georgie hire someone to kill him after he, Sean, had fled New York to take the blame for Melissa Hardesty's death? He had written a "confession" that night before he'd gone. He had assumed responsibility. It was what they'd wanted. . . .

No, it *had* to be a lie.

But what possible reason could Oscar Pratt

have for making up such a story? Surely, if Liam Hardesty hated enough to send hired killers after his daughter's violator, the man would want his victim to know who had the final revenge before his men slaughtered their target . . . anonymous killing held no satisfaction for a man seeking retribution.

So, it *had* to be George Jr. Or Father.

"Why?" he whispered. He holstered his iron, and still on his knees, looked at his side. His shirt was soaked with blood. The flow was lessening though the wound burned as though a hot iron pressed there, and when he tried to take a deeper breath, a rib cracked or broken by the bullet's passage bit at him.

"Not Father. No. Can't be Father." He stumbled upright and headed at a slow, uneven walk back toward where Horse still waited.

What should he do now? Should he stay out here in the Territories waiting for word that might never come to tell him that he could return home? He had given up everything for his family . . . the woman he loved . . . his education . . . his future . . . *surely,* they couldn't . . . *wouldn't* do this to him!

Should he not wait for word, go home to New York and find out what the hell was going on? He knew that if Pratt didn't ambush him first, the next time he and Oscar met, one of them would kill the other, but . . .

No, he couldn't kill Oscar now. He had to somehow capture the man and take him back to New York with him to point out the one who'd hired him. He, Sean, *had* to know for sure whether Liam Hardesty, or his father or brother—each named George Hood—offered five thousand dollars for his life, because now that the question had been raised, he had to know the truth.

Not Father! Not Georgie . . . not Father . . .

He seized the bay's bridle but didn't mount up—Horse couldn't bear a rider at this moment. Reins in his left hand, his right pressing bloody cloth over the long gouge across his ribs, and mind swirling from weariness and shock, he walked until he came to the well-defined ruts that announced the wagon road leading to that town far at the west on the banks of a slow, muddy river.

He started to follow the tracks west, but it abruptly seemed that someone kicked his legs out from under him and he found himself sitting on the dirt without quite knowing how he got there. It took him a long time to discover tears drying on his face; he wasn't sure how those had gotten there, either. He was still sitting on hot sand clutching at the wound when six freight wagons labored up and over a slight rise.

The lead driver leaned against reins to halt the twenty-mule team and jammed a foot down on the wooden brake lever before he scowled at the man seated by a drooping horse. "Git yer ass outta the middle a' the gawdamn road, ya idjit! Whaddya doin' just sittin' there like a horney-toad on a cold rock!"

Beside the driver, the shotgun guard pressed hammers back on his weapon. His eyes swept the desert for signs of ambush.

"He's hurt! Can't you men see the blood on his shirt?" Veracity guided Goldie up beside the lead wagon and frowned from the driver to the motionless man in the middle of the road.

"Ain't necessary true, Miss," the guard cautioned. "Could be he's bait for outlaws or . . ."

"Oh, phoo! I know blood when I see it!"

"Miss! Miss, now you wait a minute, dammit!" the driver yelled when the girl kicked her mare forward. To his guard, he snapped, "Gawdammit, Jonsey, git that piece of calico back here! No tellin' what that varmit's got up his sleeve!" When he finished with the burst of profanity that had given mule skinners their reputation for creative cursing, his team flicked ears as though the words were flies assaulting them.

Veracity paid no attention—she was fresh from months among sailors and the mule drivers from San Diego to Fort Yuma. With the shotgun guard scrambling to catch up to her, she reined Goldie up beside the exhausted bay gelding, leaped from the saddle and knelt on one knee by the wounded stranger. She opened her mouth to talk to the man, but found herself staring down the barrel of a six-shooter. She would have been frightened except that when she looked at the young man's face, she saw where tears had washed streaks through sweat-caked dust, and thought: *Bandits don't cry.*

"You're not going to shoot me, my friend. We're here to help you."

Sean blinked twice to make sure what he thought he saw was real and not merely a heat- and pain-generated mirage. When the light-haired, hazel-eyed girl gently pushed his gun aside and reached to pull his shirt up out of his belt so she could examine the bullet wound, he felt solid flesh and bone pressing his side and knew he wasn't hallucinating. The round black eyes of a double-barreled shotgun staring at him from the hands of a sturdy, scowling guard were also very real, and when the man growled, "Who be ya! You alone? What ya doin' here?" he knew he'd better answer.

Voice hoarse from thirst and strain, he said, "My name is . . . John . . . Evans. I'm alone . . . now. Got bushwhacked out there a while back, but he . . . they're gone. I . . ."

"Enough!" the girl snapped. She looked up at the guard. "Mister Jones, can he ride atop your wagon cover? Though not mortal, that wound is long and deep, and his horse looks worse than he does."

It seemed to Stormy that he didn't have strength left to argue. It was as though the few words he'd had to say had used up his last ounce of energy. He sat and watched the shotgun guard vacillate. Finally, the man said, "I dunno, Miss. I'll have to ask Leroy."

"Then, do it, please, Mister Jones. Poor Mister Evans is perishing here for lack of care."

Jonsey hurried back to talk to the driver. Presently, he returned; said, "Leroy says no, not 'less he can pay the freight, Miss."

"Oh, for goodness sakes! Tell Mister Axt that *I'll* pay!" Veracity rose, stepped to Goldie, grabbed her canteen from the saddle strings, uncapped it and started to offer water to the man who called himself John Evans, but found he had fallen over onto his side, unconscious.

Sean came awake suddenly. He reached for his side-arm only to find the weapon gone. He also discovered that he was half-naked and lying on something jarringly hard—his fingers told him it was canvas stretched over boxes, barrels, and crates—and that the young woman sitting cross-legged beside him with her back to the sunset fanned him with his own hat.

He made a grab for the hat, failed to snag it, and tried to sit up, but both a tearing along his side and the girl's palm on his bare chest kept him where he lay.

She smiled, "Well, welcome back, Mister Evans. You certainly slept a long time. You must have been worn as thin as a sinner's soul. Would you like a drink of water?"

His tongue was dry enough to stick to the roof of his mouth, but he managed, "Yes, please. Wh-Who are you?"

She reached aside for a canteen, uncapped it and offered it to him. "My name's Veracity Cooper. And you are John Evans?"

He had taken the canteen from her. He kept drinking while he nodded.

Presently, she pried it out of his hands. "Not so much at once. You'll make yourself sick."

He let her retrieve the canteen without argument before he looked down at himself. His ribs were wrapped with torn blue cloth bandages. "My shirt?"

"Well, you wouldn't expect me to use my own, would you?" He could see more of her than merely her silhouette when she turned her head to glance northward briefly before she looked back at him. "*Now,* I believe you can sit up. You owe me twenty dollars."

"What?" He got an elbow under him, and with hands braced behind him, legs sprawled out in front, did sit. "How do I owe you twenty dollars, Miss Cooper?"

"I talked the wagon master into hauling you along as freight, but he charged me for your transportation and weight."

"I didn't ask you to do that, Miss Cooper. Where is this train headed?"

"Prescott. We should be there in about sixteen or seventeen days."

He flared, "Dammit, I don't want to go to Prescott! How long was I out?"

"I believe you were truly unconscious for only about five minutes. I'd got you bandaged, and your eyes opened when I washed your face, but then you sort of sighed, shut them again, and slept for nearly four hours. What about my twenty dollars?"

"Give me my hat! Where's my horse!" Pratt was getting away; the bounty hunter now had a four-hour head start and he had to catch him because the man held the answer to the *why* that plagued him.

But she whipped his hat behind her before he could get it, lifted herself and slid it beneath her. "Your horse is tied to the rear of the wagon along with mine, Mister Evans, and you're welcome for your thanks for my help. I'm holding your hat as collateral. No money, no hat. Who is Georgia?"

That stopped him. He gritted, "Where'd you hear that?"

"You talk in your sleep. A lot."

"And you listened to every word."

"Of course. Rather interesting, if somewhat disjoined. You spoke of Oscar Pratt . . . some ladies named Georgia and Eileen . . . and you kept asking why . . . why. Why, what, Mister Evans?"

He slid her a brief, cold look that she found disconcerting, but she forced herself to meet those black eyes. Their expression was sharp and hard, not the kind to shed the tears she'd noted when she had first seen him. She had studied him as he slept, and relaxed, he seemed merely a boy rather than the grim man perhaps nearing thirty he now appeared to be.

It was his expression. The black hair windblown over his forehead couldn't soften it, and the short but heavy black beard and moustache only added harshness to his appearance. There was also a bitterness and an almost desperate determination to survive about him that camouflaged his true age—he could be anywhere from twenty to thirty-five. Now that he'd had water and had rested, his voice seemed to be back to what was normal for him; low, crisp, educated, and with a faint eastern flavor. All in all, she found him to be very good looking in a dark and dangerous manner.

His mouth quirked to a slight smile. "Well, what's the verdict?"

"Wh-What?"

"You've been studyin' me like I was some kind of rattlesnake. What did you decide?"

"That regardless of your . . . pain . . . you're a basically decent man in your twenties . . . originally hailing from somewhere near New York."

Even the glaring crimson sunset painting his face couldn't hide from her that he went very pale. He seemed about to return a sharp retort; obviously caught himself and said instead, "I'm sorry you spent money on me that I can't repay. I have only three dollars, more or less. If you'll give me my hat, I'll leave now, and perhaps the driver will refund most of what you paid him."

"Mister Evans, you're not up to . . ."

"This freight came from the west?"

"Uh . . . yes. From Ehrenberg."

"You know that town?"

"Only slightly. But Mister Evans, you . . ."

"Is there a postal stop there? A stage stop?"

"Yes, but . . ."

"How far are we from there now?"

"Well, we made four miles yesterday afternoon, and about nine so far today, I believe. Not more than fourteen or fifteen miles, but . . ."

"Please give me my hat, Vera."

She snapped, "Don't you *dare* call me that! *I hate Vera!* My name is *Veracity* Cooper. *Veracity, NOT Vera!*" She swallowed and tried to settle herself more firmly onto the hat; began again more calmly, "Really, Mister Evans, you're not well enough to . . ."

"Please give me my hat."

"No, you . . ."

"Then, I'll go without it, dammit, *Veracity* Cooper! Where's my gun belt?"

"On your saddle along with your rifle. Mister Evans . . ."

But he had gotten to hands and knees and was crawling down the length of the canvas-covered cargo. Gripping tie-lines, he swarmed over the end, held on with one hand while he reached the other to free the rope that tethered Horse to the tailgate; then, stepped from the wagon to the road and up into the saddle.

Veracity followed him. She sat on the end of the wagon with her feet hanging over the edge, and seeing that he was leaving despite her logical objections, flung the Stetson at him. "You are a most exasperating man, Mister Evans! Here's your darn hat! We're going to stop for the night soon, so if you want some supper, you're welcome!"

He caught the hat in mid-air, punched up the crown and jammed it on his head; yelled back, "Thank you for your help, Miss Cooper. I hope you have an enjoyable time in Prescott!" He reined Horse aside, kicked him into a canter past the line of plodding oxen and on toward where the sun was halved by the horizon.

Veracity watched him go. She muttered, "Stubborn man," before she turned to crawl back across the wagon cover to see if she could talk the driver, Mr. Axt, into indeed giving her a refund.

Sean spent a cold and lonely night under a mesquite. He had gotten spare clothing from his saddlebags; dressed in a dark red shirt, black britches beneath brown shotgun chaps, and black hat, with his dark hair, eyes, and sun-weathering, he was merely a shadow in the night.

At dawn, he rose from his thin bedroll, drank from his half-empty canteen, poured the remainder into his hat crown and watered Horse as best he could. He used what little moisture was left to wash his face and smooth back his hair; then, mounted up and followed the wagon road westward toward the river. He reached Ehrenberg just before noon.

With bounty hunters relentlessly dogging him over the last few years, he had learned not to ride boldly down the main street of an unfamiliar town. Keeping a careful eye on his surroundings, he eased quietly toward the livery stable, dismounted at the corral, led Horse to the watering trough, removed the bit from the gelding's mouth, and while the animal drank desperately, looked around for the proprietor. He was about to do something he didn't want to do but felt was necessary.

Hy Claghorn, the stable master, was agreeable—he knew good horseflesh when he saw it, even in a cayuse as done-in at the moment as Horse was. Sean traded his mount for a light-footed sturdy black-and-white pinto and told the stableman to give Horse a rest before selling him. He transferred saddle, bridle, bedroll, and carry-sacks to the pinto Claghorn said was named Spot, and thus entered Ehrenberg's center wearing different clothing and on a fresh mount.

His first stop was at the Butterfield Overland Stage depot. He walked up to the window and nodded to the agent beyond the grill.

"What can I do for you, cowboy?"

"Are you holding any mail for Sean Hood?"

The agent's brows rose. "I swan! Years pass that letter sets up there with nobody claimin' it, an' now in a space of a couple of days, seems like traffic for it'll never cease. No, sir, the young lady picked it up for Hood . . . uh . . . 'bout two . . . three days ago, but I expect you're Mister Hood's brother, ain't you. She said you might be comin' by."

Young lady? *Brother?* Carefully, noncommittally, Sean nodded. The agent turned toward the pigeonholes, reached up and plucked an envelope from the box. He turned back and asked, "You Stormy Hood?"

A cold wash of surprise stiffened Sean. Only his family and eastern friends called him that. But again, he nodded.

The agent held on to the envelope. "You want me to decipher it for you?"

Sean reached through the grill. "Why would you think I can't read?"

"Oh, well, the young lady said Mister Hood didn't read or write, that she done all that for him, which is why I gave her his mail. But if *you* can read, well, good for you."

"I can." Sean took the envelope, saw it was addressed to *Stormy Hood*, nodded thanks to the agent and moved nearer the outside door for better light and privacy before he opened the flap. Frowning, he read the brief note signed by V. Cooper.

V. Cooper? He had heard that name before, hadn't he. Somebody named Cooper . . .

Vera . . . no, *Veracity* Cooper? The girl who had sat on his hat last evening and who traveled with the freight wagons? *That* V. Cooper? That sunburned, fair-haired, bossy little Veracity Cooper was, indeed, headed for Prescott, but . . .

He scowled back at the note. *I have your money and a letter from your father.*

Dammit all, if Veracity was *V. Cooper*, he'd been within grabbing distance of funds and word from home even yesterday if he'd only known they were there. Gritting his teeth, he tucked the note back, folded the envelope and shoved it into his shirt pocket. There was nothing left to do now but run Veracity Cooper down and demand his property from her, was there. Problem with that was, he would have to give her his correct name, and he wasn't sure he wanted to do that.

It seemed this Veracity Cooper—if she was *really* the one who'd appropriated his money and his correspondence—had asked specifically for any message waiting for Sean Evan Hood. Why? Who was Miss Cooper? How did she know his name if not his person, and why was she here? Was she another hired killer either Georgie, his father, *or* Hardesty had commissioned to hunt him down?

He could hardly believe that. He tried to visualize what little he'd seen of her yesterday, got a vague image of a small but sturdy girl about five feet three, with fine fair hair blowing about her face as it escaped from a single braid down her back. Dressed oddly in a man's shirt and a dark divided riding skirt. Floppy straw hat. Red bandana. Couldn't recall the color of her eyes. Still, along with the refinement of her Eastern-inflected speech, for all her forward snippyness, the total picture hardly lent itself to his mental image of some female who tracked men for pay.

Long-learned caution made him survey the street before he stepped from the shadowed security of the stage office. He didn't see Oscar Pratt anywhere around; walked swiftly toward

Goldwater's Mercantile Store to stock up on trail supplies, buy an extra canvas water bag, and more ammunition. He'd lied to Veracity last night; had more than three dollars in his pocket, but not much . . . only seventeen. Purchases in hand, he headed back to where he'd left Spot tethered.

The freight wagons had been some twelve or thirteen miles from Ehrenberg when he'd left them last night at near-sundown. If they had plodded another mile or two before they halted for the night, make it fifteen. If they had headed out again this morning at dawn, perhaps they could have traveled some four or five miles before noon. He cast a quick look at the sky. The position of the sun announced that it neared two o'clock. All told, the freights shouldn't be more than twenty miles out. In his better days, Horse could have caught them before dark, but Spot was an unfamiliar mount with unknown capabilities and failings. Nevertheless, he thought he could catch them at least by mid-day tomorrow.

He tied his equipment on behind his saddle, ensured that his side-arm and the Sharps buffalo gun were both fully leaded and ready to go, filled the water bag—it was unseasoned and leaked badly, but would have to do—tied that on also, and headed eastward. This time, he followed the wagon road toward Prescott.

A half-hour later, a stocky man wearing an obviously new shirt, vest, britches and Stetson, his gun belt draped over one shoulder like a bandolier, limped slowly into the stage office to ask if there was any mail for Sean Hood.

The agent gasped, "My Gawd! Near two years . . . nothin'! Now, in three days, a gawdamn stampede! No! The woman got the mail, an' Hood's brother, Stormy, picked up her note less'n a hour ago!"

Pratt leaned nearer. He cried, "Stormy? Stormy was here? Which way did he go?"

"Dunno. Don't care."

Pratt licked his lips. "Uh . . . de doll who picked up de mail. Wot'd she look like?"

The agent shrugged. "Purty little thing. Lots of fair hair. Brown eyes. Wearin' a queer getup . . . man's shirt . . . split ridin' skirt . . . some kinda straw hat the like of which I never saw before. Why, you know her?"

"Where'd *she* go?"

"How the hell should I know! I ain't no Granny Gossip keepin' eyes on every citizen's doin's!" The agent turned away to case mail.

Hurriedly now, Oscar limped back out into the street. His butt hurt fiercely from Hood's bullet, but it could have been worse, and for five thousand dollars, he could put up with a lot of things. *And,* he was too close to Sean Hood to give up now.

Look as he would, he couldn't see his quarry anywhere. Glumly, he headed for the livery stable. The thought of sitting a saddle again was almost more painful than the wound, but for five thousand dollars . . .

CHAPTER FOUR

Sean halted Spot and frowned at the split in the road. Wagon tracks, shod horses or mules, and cloven hooves followed each path—it seemed that the six freight wagons had split up, three taking one road, three the other. Damn! Which group had Veracity Cooper accompanied?

He squinted against the sunlight, searching the desert for a blossom of dust or any moving specks that might indicate the location of the freight wagons. The land around him appeared to be a bowl edged about at the north and south by jagged mountains and the vertical faces of painted cliffs, its bottom punctuated here and there with the broken spires of truncated ranges and lone buttes. He had discovered that July and August were the rainy months in the desert; a flotilla of purple clouds borne on gray pedestals of rain or futile virgas whose moisture evaporated before reaching parched soil scudded swiftly north to south.

Well, Prescott was north and east of here, wasn't it? He looked at the track to his left. That cut north, yes, but it seemed to him that the split was too far west to lead into the high desert. He couldn't be more than a few hours behind either segment of the freight train. So what if he picked

73

the wrong group? If Veracity Cooper wasn't with them, he could always backtrack to the other road and pursue those wagons. It didn't really matter whether he caught up to her today, tomorrow, or the next day, so long as he found her before she vanished into whatever population dwelt in Prescott . . . except that his need to know what the letter from his father contained was so strong it hurt. He starved for word from home.

And perhaps that letter would let him know the answer to the *why* that Oscar Pratt's words had raised in his mind and heart.

He chose to ride straight on. Spot was proving to be a strong, reliable easy-rider, well-trained and willing. He urged the pinto into a tireless canter and settled himself into the saddle to merely eat up whatever miles lay between him and the supply train.

An hour later, Oscar Pratt also came to the split. He, too, halted and pondered directions. As an easterner, he didn't read sign well—couldn't tell Spot's tracks from the hoof prints of the freight mules. Unlike Sean, he took the left-hand road.

Late in the afternoon, Hood reined Spot to a halt and frowned ahead. Gunfire echoed dully in the thin oppressive heat, but he couldn't see the problem or readily pinpoint its source except that it came from somewhere not too far ahead. Warily, wondering whether he wanted to get mixed up in whatever occurred there or not, he urged Spot forward at a slow walk. He halted the pinto at the brow of the next rise.

The freight wagons were down in a dip and surrounded by Indians whom Sean recognized by their cloth shirts and wide rolled-bandana headbands to be Apaches. Cochise and his Chiricahuas were riled-up these days; he'd heard the government was trying to get them to go to a new reservation somewhere in New Mexico and the Apaches resisted relocation. Now, a band of about ten or fifteen attacked the freight wagons. A driver and a guard attended each wagon, plus there were two outriders, eight Whites in all. While the two sides were pretty evenly matched in numbers, the Apaches had more mobility than wagoneers forced to stay with their teams.

He searched for a female figure in the melee but didn't see anyone resembling Miss Cooper. If she was there at all, she was hidden.

Well, maybe he should help. He urged Spot to a more advantageous location, turned the pinto sideways to the fray, unlimbered the Sharps, shouldered it and sighted on an attacker. He squeezed the trigger, but abruptly found the horse at least four feet up off the ground with himself some three feet in the air above the saddle. The Sharps still in his right hand, he flailed arms and legs, desperate not to land on his head and break his neck. Spot wasn't underneath him when he came down; the pinto had bolted.

Somehow, Sean managed to hit the dirt and roll up onto his feet without more damage than a sharp pull at the wound along his ribs. He caught his stagger, jerked around to see his mount bucking like an unbroken mustang, and before he thought, yelled, *"Woah, Spot!"*

The paint came to earth stiff-legged, trembling and wild-eyed but otherwise frozen. Sean's mouth fell open. He gasped, "Well, I'll be damned!" Spot was the most gun-shy horse he'd ever seen, yet totally trained to stop on command. Then, he noticed that his single shot had gotten the Apaches' attention. While the majority still concentrated on the wagon, four headed his way.

"Oh, shit!" He scrambled toward Spot, grabbed the pinto's reins and tied them securely to a close bush, whirled and dashed as far away from his mount as he could get in the time he had—he didn't want the paint to kill itself trying to escape the sound of his heavy rifle firing but wasn't going to let himself be shot, punctured with arrows, or tomahawked because of consideration for a spooky horse.

Panting, he fell to one knee behind a rock, jammed another shell into the Sharps, sighted, and fired. The big bullet almost blew one Apache apart and stopped the other three in surprise. Quickly, Sean reloaded, fired, killed a second and then a third Indian. When the fourth made a desperate dive for the nearest boulder, Hood shifted his attention to those still attacking the wagons and downed two more Apaches before those left alive gave it up, whirled and vanished into the desert.

Carefully, Sean shifted the Sharps to his left hand and drew his side-arm. That same crawling instinct that made him wary of a strange town's main street told him that the one Apache he hadn't killed in the group that had advanced on him was still around close by waiting for him to move to a more exposed location. He had lost sight of the redskin. Tense, he held his breath and listened hard around. He could hear the wagoneers' voices faintly from down where they cussed over a wounded oxen, the wind in dry leaves, a distant grumble of thunder, and a hawk crying from somewhere high and to the left, but . . .

Spot squealed. Hood jerked around to see the pinto rear and stamp stiff forelegs against the hard earth. His ears were flat, and his eyes rolled white.

Sean shouted, flipped over onto his back and simultaneously pulled the trigger on his weapon twice in rapid succession. The first hammer-fall was only a click, but the second sent a bullet dead center of the Apache's breastbone. Without a sound, the Indian plunged face-down over his intended victim's feet. The knife in his right hand drove hilt-deep into the dirt beside Hood's left thigh.

Sean leaped up and away. Crouching, and watching for any sign of life, he pointed the iron at the Apache. There was no movement. Finally, he straightened slightly and used his boot toe to shove the redskin over onto his back. The man was dead.

Again, he said, "Well, I'll be *damned!*" This time, it was in appreciation. It seemed that Spot hated guns and Indians equally; the paint may have bolted when the Sharps fired, but he stopped on command and had for all intents and purposes saved his new master's life by warning him that the Apache crept up behind him.

Hood let the Indian lay and walked back to where Spot still trembled. Smoothing the paint's forehead and neck, and talking quietly to him, he thanked the horse for his help before he mounted and rode at a slow walk down toward the wagons.

The drivers saw him coming and waited as a group for his arrival. When he got close enough, one yelled, "Holy Jesus, you the *hombre* blastin' away with a gawdamn Big Fifty? Shit-by-golly, I seen one of them bullets take out two of them varmits at a time! Went clean through one an' blowed the brains outta the one behind him! Scared them varmits right outta their red hides, you did. We owe you a big vote of thanks, mister, that we do! Y'all want a job? We could sure use you an' yer buffalo gun 'tween here an' Wickenberg, I'll tell ya that!"

Sean frowned. He asked, "You're going to Wickenberg? I thought this freight was bound for Prescott."

"T'others went up north. Got supplies an' the like fer the town folks, an' arms an' the like fer them pony boys at Fort Whipple beyond. They cut off a ways back. Why?"

"There was a young woman with the train that . . ."

"Oh, yeah. Miss Cooper. She went with Leroy Axt an' Jonsey." The mule skinner took a closer look at Hood. "Say, ain't you the *hombre* we found sittin' in the middle of the road just east of Ehrenberg?"

"Yes, I am," Sean grinned. "I left the train rather abruptly and didn't get a chance to . . . properly thank Miss Cooper for her help. Besides, I owe her twenty dollars and was lookin' to pay her back."

"Well, sir, it's too late in the day now fer you to catch 'em an' what with them Apaches slinkin' 'round the brushes out there, I suggest y'all stick with us tonight. We're only goin' 'bout 'nother two miles to Tamarisk Springs. Ain't safe fer a man go roamin' 'round the desert alone at night with them Apaches skulkin' 'round. You come spend the night with us. Least we can do is feed ya dinner. Yep, we sure 'nough owe you some vittles. Now, we won't hear *no* fer a answer!"

Hood bowed to logic, and much to his amazement, ate one of the best meals at the wagoneers' campfire he'd enjoyed in months—venison steak pickled in a barrel of pepper-laced watered-down molasses, piñon nuts roasted over the coals, tortillas, whiskey-spiked coffee, and for dessert, a foot-long licorice twist.

Still sucking the candy, he unsaddled Spot and rubbed him down with a handful of grass growing by the spring. Abruptly, he nearly lost two teeth when without warning, the pony reached around and nipped what was left of the licorice twist from his owner's mouth.

Sean laughed. He watched Spot wallow the candy around enough to blacken his tongue before spitting it out. As he led the pinto to drink at the tiny clear pool below a fountain of bright water gushing from a crack in the cliff face, he said, "I think we're going to get along fine, you and me, Spot."

"Spot! Spot?" One of the teamsters had come up behind them. "Yer horse's name's *Spot?* That's a gawdamn *dawg's* name, Mister Evans. Downright degradin' namin' a good horse *Spot!*"

Again, Sean chuckled. "I agree, but the name came with him and he seems to know it, so who am I to change it?"

He watched the drivers dig a bullet out of one of the oxen's flanks then sear the hole with a coal from the fire. They posted night guards, but he wasn't among them; he was almost an "honored guest." He spread his bedroll under one of the wagons, lay staring at sheet lightning flickering over the far mountains, and thought about home.

About New York. About a dead girl and a vengeful father. About Oscar Pratt, and about a *George Hood* who offered five thousand dollars for his life. Again, he pondered the possible whys of it all.

Then, his mind drifted to Veracity Cooper, and the questions multiplied. Who was she? Why had she claimed his letter and his remittance, then left him a note telling him what she'd done and where he could locate her?

He was still wondering *why* when he drifted off to sleep.

The north-bound arm of the road had made a bend that seemed to lead nowhere, for though hazed by distance, the sheer, apparently impassable carmine faces of a geologic shelf lowered dead ahead.

Axt's three wagons toiled at an oxen-pace all day. They didn't halt for lunch; munched trail jerky and water on the plod, and even following that meager meal with an apple left Veracity feeling hollow and unfulfilled.

She was hot, and irritated by the slowness of their pace. The day dragged on like a snake hitched to a rock—they didn't seem to make any progress at all. The stands of mesquite, greasewood, and cactus appeared to be the exact same stands of mesquite, greasewood, and cactus they'd passed an hour ago . . . or two or three hours ago. Once, she urged Goldie up beside the mule-drawn Deck Wagon and asked, "Mister Axt, is there no possibility of moving on faster?"

Leroy—elbows on knees and reins lax in his hands—spit a stream of dark tobacco juice to the side before he shook his head. "No, Miss. Oxen is deliberate. They tread as they tread. Ain't no chance a' rushin' 'em. We'll git there, don' ya fret none. We'll git there. Ya git bored, whyn't ya git down an' walk a spell. Jaunt'll do ya good."

Well, she thought, if this was their pace, no wonder it took six months or more for pioneers to trek across the plains to their new home in the west. Once again, she appreciated Mr. Pinkerton's foresight in securing passage for her by ship rather than on other transportation. Had she used this method, she doubted she'd have passed the Mississippi River yet!

Jonsey stood on the Deck Wagon seat and squinted at their back path. He said succinctly, "Rider comin'." The click of a pulled-back shotgun hammer was loud in the baking quiet.

Veracity also turned to look back over her shoulder. A thick-set man had slowed his lathered black horse to match the freight train's pace, and she noted that while the newcomer's clothes were sweat-stained and trail-dusty, they not only seemed new but uncomfortable on him, as though his garb was a costume for effect rather than accustomed daily wear. And he sat the saddle gingerly; he obviously was not an accomplished rider.

The stranger guided his horse off to the side, worked a smile to his lips, and tipped a finger to his hat brim at Veracity before he looked up at Axt. "Afternoon."

"Yup, 'tis," Axt observed.

"Youse guys just come from Ehrenberg?"

Leroy nodded once. Spit. "Yup."

"Where ya headed?"

"Prescott. Fort Whipple."

"Mind if I rides along? I don' like to be out here by meself."

"Road's free."

"Much obliged." Pratt kicked his black to beside Goldie and whipped off his Stetson. Under the hat, his hair was graying-brown and sweat-stringy—it appeared to Veracity that it hadn't been laundered in months.

Pratt squinted at the girl. By damn, he'd bet anything it was her, wasn't it!—the petticoat that stage agent had said had picked up Hood's mail. He thought back over the near past. Couldn't be that Hood had her stashed away all this time, because he, himself, had been trailing Stormy

83

since St. Louis. He had rarely seen Hood with a woman except for the occasional one-night poke with some calico queen in some pity-poor desert town, and *this* female sure didn't look like a whore to him. So for whatever reason she'd had to collect Hood's mail, however she'd known Stormy's name, it could be she didn't know his face. And he, Pratt, wanted to see what was in that envelope, because it might tell him where Stormy would head next since—for all practical purposes—he'd lost track of Hood at Ehrenberg.

He put on his best smile and with an unaccustomed burst of imagination, said, "A good afternoon to youse, Lady. Me name's Sean Hood. Who d'I have de pleasure of accompanyin'?"

Veracity almost choked. She quickly turned her face away so her expression wouldn't betray her incredulity . . . *in no way* did the man riding beside her resemble the picture of Stormy she carried in her bag. Not even two years of the worst kind of hard living and privation could have altered the slim, black-haired, black-eyed twenty-year-old of the portrait into this graying, blocky, brown-haired, pale-blue-eyed creature. She would have laughed except that a warning chill stopped it in her throat. *Who was this man to know Hood's name and who accosted her here and now?*

She urged Goldie a little nearer Leroy Axt's wagon for protection before she cast a cold look at Pratt and snapped, "You do not *accompany* me, Mister H-Hood, you merely proceed along the same road." She didn't give him her name.

Undeterred, Oscar asked, "Youse goin' to Prescott, Missy?"

Veracity made no response.

He tried, "I just come from Ehrenberg on de Colorado River. Stopped by de Butterfield office dere to get me mail, but de clerk said some skirt'd awready picked it up. Youse wouldn' be dat lady, now, wouldja?"

Veracity's chill deepened. Who *was* this man! She darted him an unsmiling look. "Do I appear to be the kind of person who goes around absconding with a stranger's personal mail, Mister . . . Hood?" *Could he be another agent? No, surely, Mr. Pinkerton would have told her had he intended to send a back-up man.* She hadn't yet given him her name. Perhaps she should. If the man was a Pinkerton operative, he would be likely to know it, and then perhaps he would confide his real name to her.

He was saying, "Well, no, yeh don't, Missy, but . . ."

"My name is Veracity Cooper, sir. I'm sorry . . . your name again?"

Pratt beamed that she'd gone so far as to introduce herself. He repeated jovially, "Hood. Sean Evan Hood."

Not hardly! her mind told her. That John Evans

they'd picked out of the dirt the other day was more likely to be Sean Hood than . . .

Her mouth open in shock, she reined Goldie in abruptly. In her mind's eye, she saw John Evans—hair shaggy and nearly as sun-streaked as her own but nevertheless black. Eyes so dark brown they almost appeared black. Several days of beard covering his chin and cheeks. Tall, trail-hard . . . The image superimposed itself over the portrait of Sean Hood at nineteen or twenty, and if she imagined a beard on that boy . . .

Pratt also reined in and looked back at her. "Anything wrong, Missy? Was it somethin' I said?"

She pulled herself together, nudged the sorrel back into motion and shook her head. "No, Mister . . . Hood . . . I just had a . . . thought. But it has nothing to do with you." *She would bet anything she and Sean Hood had met a few days ago, but she hadn't recognized him!*

Sean Evan Hood?

John Evans?

If she remembered correctly, *John* was the Anglicized version of the Irish *Sean*.

It *had* been him, and she'd been too stupid to realize it!

She bit her lip. What should she do? Should she turn around and try to find him *back there* somewhere? He'd seemed to be headed west toward Ehrenberg . . . had appeared to be in a hurry. Suppose he had caught a sternwheeler north to Fort Mojave or south to Fort Yuma or had merely crossed the Colorado on the ferry! If so, she would never find him.

No, she had left him a note. Her best course was to merely continue onward with Mr. Axt and the freight wagons to Prescott, gain lodging in some local establishment there, and wait for the *real* Sean Hood to appear to retrieve his money and his letter.

In the meantime, what was she going to do with the unsavory man beside her who claimed Stormy's identity? Put up with him. It may be safer to travel with him so she could keep an eye on him than to have him lurking around among the cactuses somewhere preparing to leap out at her unawares.

She forced a smile and said, "I hear from your accent that you're from the east coast, Mister . . . Hood. Have you been here in the west long?"

That opened up a tedious day-long narration of adventures, narrow escapes, and escapades the like of which Veracity felt belonged in lurid fiction rather than to real life. After an hour, her mind blurred from "Hood's" constant blathering. She no longer really heard him, and only responded with an "Ummm," or an "Oh, my!" as appropriate. She was profoundly relieved that when Mr. Axt reined his mules off the road and toward a sheltered nook among some boulders to halt for the night, "Hood" transferred his mouthings to the men and left her alone for a while.

She bedded down that evening beneath one of the wagons, and tied her reticule strings securely to her left wrist (after all, the real Sean Hood's thousand dollars was in there beside her own money). With her Avenging Angel clutched in her right hand, she lay her head on her bunched blanket and slept—very lightly, indeed.

Pratt eyed the cold glint of the sawed-off side-arm in the girl's hand and decided there might be a better time to find out whether or not Stormy Hood's mail was in that bag. There was always tomorrow or the next day, and *one* day, Miss Veracity Cooper might get careless. He also went to bed.

The next day and the days after that were repeats of the days before—heat, dust, an occasional downpour—except that Pratt's repertoire of adventures appeared to have been exhausted. After his initial outburst, Oscar mostly kept his mouth shut and his eyes on the girl. It took eleven days of slow plodding from Ehrenberg through the desert to a tiny village called Congress Junction where the road took a turn for the worse. They had finally arrived at the base of those towering cliffs they'd seen from afar for so long.

"Camp here rest of today and t'night, Miss,"

Axt informed her. He nodded toward the cliffs. "That's some seven miles up. Want the teams fresh. Make three-an'-a-half miles t'morry, camp at The Flat, then three-an'-a-half miles day-next, an' we'll be up top the hill. From there on, it's less 'n thirty-five miles on to Prescott. Different country up there, Miss. I think you're gonna like it."

Veracity thought that anything would be an improvement over what they'd just traveled through. She watched the man who called himself Sean Hood watching her, and pointedly removed the Avenging Angel from her reticule. She slipped the weapon under her belt as she nodded to the wagon master.

Neither she nor Pratt, nor even the teamsters, realized that they had been followed for the last eight days. Sean had spotted the train far ahead of him when it once topped a small rise. Under the hard-learned caution that was now habit, he'd approached to within binocular sight, halted Spot in the shadow of a tall broken saguaro cactus, and unlimbered the glasses. He studied the freight wagons and tagalongs carefully. Though he didn't know the man's name, he'd recognized the wagon master driving the twenty-mule team, and the other teamsters walking beside the oxen. Then, he studied the off-riders.

There was the girl, but who was that beside her? Without his black-and-yellow medicine-show jacket and bowler hat to identify him, it took Sean a few minutes to recognize Oscar Pratt.

Hood's fingers tightened on the binoculars while he scrutinized the pair. It appeared that Veracity Cooper and the hired killer rode side-by-side. He could see Pratt talking animatedly to her. Did Miss Cooper and Oscar Pratt work together? If so, and Veracity truly had the letter from Father and his remittance money as her note said, was this a plot she and Pratt had cooked up between them to lure him into a fatal trap?

He didn't know. It seemed to him that his only choice was to trail the freight wagons rather than to join them as he'd intended to do, and to wait until he might be able to catch either the girl or Pratt separately in Prescott.

So it was that he continued to travel alone. He followed far enough behind the freights not to be seen but close enough to be able to keep regular watch on their progress.

Damn, he thought more than once. He was sorry to see that Miss Cooper was in with Pratt . . . he had thought she was a nice girl. Looks could sure be deceiving, couldn't they!

CHAPTER FIVE

The freight wagon drivers halted their teams for a half-hour every half-mile going up the steep grade, a total of nearly four hours rest time in three-and-a-half miles, and Veracity thought she would go mad at the snail's pace. All-in-all, it took eight hours to negotiate the narrow switchback climb from Congress Junction to "The Flat" where they would set up a dry camp, water the animals from barrels carried on each wagon, and spend the night.

After dinner (such as it was), Veracity sat on a rock at the edge of the escarpment and watched night race across the lowlands—the flaming crimson, orange, cerise, and gold sunset at the west cast distant serrated un-forested mountains into shades of molten metal above the wide dust-misty blue valley. In the east, the sky already shaded toward night, and almost before she knew how it had happened, so many stars appeared seemingly so close above her that she nearly reached a finger to touch them.

Behind her, wagoneers chatted and laughed around their small fire, their faces as craggy as those far peaks and likewise flame-painted with gold. Their animals stood grouped beyond; mules and oxen; leisurely transportation comfortably safe in the wilderness . . . until one noticed shotguns and six-shooters close at hand among the drivers.

She was weary from travel; felt quiet yet somehow uneasy. Almost absently, she opened her reticule, took out George Hood Sr.'s letter, unfastened a button and slid the thick envelope inside her shirt above her belt. There. Her bag seemed too insecure, and the belt was tight enough that she wouldn't lose Stormy's money and correspondence.

She had just re-buttoned her shirt when footsteps behind her announced that someone approached. She stifled a groan when the man said, "Can I join youse, Missy?" It was that irritating character who called himself Sean Hood.

She rose and stepped aside. "You're welcome to my seat, sir. I'm going to bed."

He reached to grab at her wrist, but she jerked away. "Wait a minit, Missy. I din't come out here to look at de scenery, I come to talk to youse."

She sighed. "What is it you want, Mister . . . Hood?"

Pratt shuffled feet for a moment. Finally, he said, "Youse is a fine lookin' petticoat, Missy. Ain't right youse should be travelin' alone out here, y'know. Now me, I can offer yeh de protection of me strong manly arm, an' . . ."

"Thank you for your offer, sir, but I'm . . .

already spoken for." Veracity again tried to step around him.

Once more, Pratt moved to intercept her. "But yer man ain't *here,* Missy. He in Prescott? Dat why youse is headin' dere?"

"Where he is at the moment is none of your affair, Mister . . . Hood. Kindly step aside and let me . . . *oh!*"

He had reached to snag her reticule from her. She jerked back, a stone turned under her foot, she fell and slid over the precipice. Only Pratt's hold on the strong bag cord wrapped around her wrist kept her from plunging a hundred feet or more to the next out-jutting shelf below. Her scream startled the wagoneers from around their fire and brought them running. Together, they knelt, seized her arms and pulled her back to level ground.

Pratt began immediately, "I seen her fall an' grabbed at her, but . . ."

"Lie!" Veracity out-shouted him. "He attacked me! He tried to steal my reticule, and when I resisted, *that's* when I slid over the edge!" She moved closer to the wagon master.

Axt's scowl was clear even in the twilight. He had known Miss Cooper longer than "Sean Hood"; he said gruffly, "We don't need no shenanigans like that goin' on here, Hood. The Miss is a respectable lady. Git yer gear t'gether, saddle up, an' git out."

Pratt shook his head. "No, now lissen, Axt, I din't attack de petticoat. She mistook me tryin' to save her fer . . ."

"*Oh, no, I didn't,*" Veracity flared. "The only reason I stepped back was because you grabbed my purse *first!* What are you, some kind of slimy preyer upon women? Mister Axt . . ."

Leroy nodded. "I'd believe the Miss over you any day, Hood. Jonsey, run him outta camp on the end of Ol' Scatter, wouldja?"

"Old Scatter" was the shotgun guard's weapon. Hammers clicked ominously in the evening air before Jonsey's teeth flashed in his beard and he murmured, "Sure 'nough, Leroy. Ya wantta move on, here, Hood?"

Oscar flung arms wide. "But it's *dark* out dere! I don' know de trail! I'll fall off d'edge and get *kilt!*"

"Moon comin' up shortly," Axt observed. "Be plenty of light then. Ya walk an' lead yer horse, you ain't gonna fall. It's only a li'l over three miles, then you'll be on the flat."

"No! No, dat ain't human! Don' make me go alone! Uh . . ." Pratt reached toward Veracity. "Come wit' me, Lady. I'll pertect youse, an' togedder, we . . ."

"You are a total twit, sir, if you think I would go anywhere alone with *you!*" Veracity pulled the Avenging Angel from her belt and jammed the end of the snubbed barrel against Pratt's nose. "Furthermore, I don't need your protection! Mister Axt said leave . . . *leave!*"

Mule skinners and ox drivers chuckled when Oscar flung his hands up, said in a wounded tone, "An' here I tawt youse was a discriminatin' lady!" and Veracity snapped, "I am. That's why I choose my companions carefully!"

Swearing, but under the threat of one pointedly-aimed shotgun and one Avenging Angel, Pratt hastily gathered his bedroll, saddled his black gelding and mounted. Still within the circle of firelight, he tried once more to get the freight drivers to let him stay. It wasn't the men he should have worried about; the bullet from Veracity's weapon fanned his ear as it passed, ricocheted from rock faces behind him and nicked the gelding's hock on the way back before it dug into the dirt between Jonsey's feet. Pratt yelled, grabbed for the saddle horn, and vanished into the darkness when his mount bolted up the trail.

The teamsters were in hysterics. When he could talk, Axt gasped, "I swow, if that wouldn't surprise the bloomers off a schoolmarm! Best carom-shot I ever seen! You play pool, Miss Cooper?"

"Of course." Veracity calmly shoved the Angel back beneath her belt. She had to work hard to hide her trembling; didn't want the men to know that so-called "carom-shot" had been pure accident. "I'm really quite good at the game. But I believe we may have made a mistake here, Mister Axt. It might have been safer for us had we allowed that man to stay here where we could keep an eye on him."

"Ya know we post guards of a night, Miss. He ain't gonna git t'do us no harm." Leroy shook his head. Still chuckling, he repeated, "Best gawdamn carom-shot I ever seen. Wait'll I tell the boys down Ehrenberg-way when we git back!" He bowed Veracity toward her bedroll. "Ya gowan an git some rest now, Ma'm. Y'can sleep easy. We'll guard. Made a name fer yerself t'night, ya did. That carom-shot'll be knowed all over Ar'zony by this time next year."

Grim-lipped, Veracity nodded and bedded down. She thought that it was all well and good that she had "made a name for herself" by accident, but if that scurrilous scoundrel whom she was certain was *not* Sean Hood kept using Stormy's name, he would ruin Sean's reputation all over the territory!

She patted the envelope. It was still safe next to her skin beneath her shirt. Nevertheless, she slept too lightly for true rest.

Three miles below, dry-camped at the foot of the hill, Sean tensed and lifted his head to look northward when the single pistol shot resounded from ungiving cliff faces before racing off into the southern valley. He could have stayed in the meager town only a half-mile to the south, but his funds were down to fourteen dollars, and he needed to save as much as he could until he reached Prescott. He had spent the day in Congress Junction, waiting for the freight wagons to near the crest of the escarpment before he, himself, headed up.

Only one road bit into the cliffs, and it was open and without cover. He'd heard in Congress Junction that it was seven miles to the top. He knew that he and Spot could make that in at least half the time it took the wagons. He intended to start out early in the cool of the morning tomorrow, hoped to bypass the freights atop the cliffs at a decent enough distance aside that neither Oscar Pratt nor Veracity Cooper would recognize him, and thus reach Prescott ahead of the train. Once in town, he would go first to the stage stop to see if any mail waited for him, secondly to a mercantile store for some fresh clothes, then to a local barber and bathhouse to get cleaned up. And then . . .

Well, he wasn't quite sure what he would do then. Meet events as they came, he guessed.

He stared at his campfire—so small it barely produced three flames but large enough to heat his fatback, grits, and coffee—and wondered what that pistol shot up there in the cliffs had been all about. He also wondered what kind of a town Prescott would be.

It took Sean and Spot four hours to climb the seven-mile upgrade. He rested his mount several times en route, and even then, almost overrode the freights at the top of the hill. He had to linger another hour in the shade of a roadside boulder until his binoculars told him the wagons had vanished onto the flat.

He discovered a different world atop the escarpment, one of lush grass and evergreen trees tall among huge rounded tan rocks. There were still some cactus groves around, but all-in-all, the greenery, even in mid-July, amazed his eye. Yesterday, he had estimated it was over a hundred degrees in the valley now behind him. Here, he doubted it reached ninety. Though the actual temperature variance wasn't that great, the air almost seemed crisp.

He guided Spot off the beaten road and out into the flat at the right. He wanted to pass the freight wagons and arrive in Prescott far enough ahead of them that he had time to accomplish what he needed to do before Veracity Cooper and Oscar Pratt arrived (he hadn't checked the train closely enough recently to realize that Pratt no longer traveled with it).

On the Deck Wagon seat, Jonsey said, "That rider that's been doggin' us is comin' on."

"Yup," Leroy agreed.

Presently, Jonsey muttered, "Here he comes."

He automatically thumbed shotgun hammers.

They watched a man on a black-and-white pinto gallop by some half-mile to the right.

"There he goes . . . in a hurry," Jonsey said.

"Hell-bent," Leroy nodded.

"What he think he is, a pony express rider?"

"Looks like."

Sean had let Spot run just for the fun of it, and the paint seemed to enjoy himself as much. Some mile or so on, Hood returned to the road, slowed his mount to an easy canter, and looked forward to entering a real town again. He thought it was a relief to know that he probably had at least a day's grace before he had to be watchful for Pratt.

He watered his horse where the road crossed a swift creek; then, rode on. He camped for the night beneath tall fragrant trees at the west of the open valley he traveled through, then at dawn the next morning, again headed out.

The southern city limits of Prescott seemed to be marked by a single pine incongruously left growing in the middle of the road. Prescott, itself, appeared to be a mountain city surrounded by thickly forested peaks and guarded in the distance by the brooding basalt heart of a long-vanished volcano. It was the largest, most bustling town Sean had been in since he'd left Santa Fe in New Mexico.

Though the town sported the usual necessities in a tidy conglomeration of stone or wood buildings fronted by pillar-supported porch roofs over boardwalks—hotel, meat market, haberdashery, mercantile store, dressmaker, doctor's office, and so on—it was centered by a large grassy tree-shaded gazebo-graced city park. The main street by the park was wide and dusty; on one side was the plaza, on the other sat at least five or six saloons, the largest an imposing two-story broad-windowed and balconied building called "The Palace." It was his first view of Prescott's Whiskey Row that not only catered to local ranchers, cow punchers, and gold, silver, and copper miners in the area, but also to the infantry and cavalry men stationed at Fort Whipple—but for Ft. Leavenworth, Kansas, the largest army installation west of the Mississippi and one of the few stockaded military posts in the southwest—that was situated only two miles northeast of town on the banks of Granite Creek.

Blue uniforms were everywhere, picks of dusty color among even dustier, drabber miners and ranch hands. Women bustled along the boardwalks, shopping and hesitating to gossip. Horses' hooves raised dust in the unpaved streets; Prescott appeared to Sean to be a real going concern.

He thought his first order of business was money. He squinted around at the buildings edging the park-side streets and finally located the stage depot. During his scrutiny, he also checked for anyone resembling Oscar Pratt, saw no one suspicious, and nudged Spot toward his goal. He braced his feet in the stirrups before he murmured, "Woah, Spot," in front of the office. The pinto froze, and grinning, Sean shook his head. He wondered who had owned Spot before he'd acquired him, and why that previous owner had chosen to part with such a strong, reliable, well-trained mount? The pinto's only failing seemed to be that the horse was incredibly gun-shy.

The inside of the stage depot here was almost a duplicate of the one in Ehrenberg except that the clerk was a laconic woman whose black moustache nearly rivaled his own. He asked, "Are you holding any mail for Sean Hood?"

The woman's brown eyes raked him from head to toe. "Hood, yes. John Hood, no."

"Not John . . . Sean. S-E-A-N."

"That, I got." She whirled, reached for a cubby-hole, plucked out an envelope, and handed it through the grill to him.

Sean took it, nodded and touched his hat brim in thanks as he started to turn away, but then hesitated. "Do you have a public bathhouse here in Prescott?"

The woman said yes. "On Cortez Street, over there. Fitty's" She brayed a sharp laugh that didn't disturb the rest of her face. "Mister Fitty also owns the meat market. Careful you don't pick the wrong Fitty's, or the townfolk'll be havin' you for dinner." Chuckling, she leaned elbows on the counter to watch Hood grin in acknowledgment of her joke, again nod, then head for the door.

Before stepping back onto the boardwalk, he paused to open the envelope. Inside wrapped in a sheet of plain paper, were four one hundred dollar notes, three twenties, three tens, and two five dollar bills, five hundred dollars total.

Remittance Man, his mind said to him bitterly. *I am truly a Remittance Man paid to stay far away from home.* He folded the money and stuffed it into his front right-hand pocket beneath his gun belt; then, looked at the paper that had wrapped the bills. He was hoping for a letter written there; ached for some kind of personal touch from his mother or father.

There were five words. *Come home. George Patrick Hood.*

And they didn't seem to be written by Father's hand. He shut his eyes briefly, trying to recall Georgie's pen—no, that wasn't his brother's scrawl, either.

What the hell?

Chewing his lip, he put the envelope into his shirt pocket, moved out and across the boardwalk to where Spot stood, then without touching the reins, said absently, "Come on, Spot," and walked down the street. Obediently, the pinto followed.

At Gurley's Mercantile Store, he again "woah'ed" Spot, and inside the store, bought two new shirts, another pair of pants, and some fresh underwear, including socks. All were plain and utilitarian, for he wanted to be clean, not spiffied-up.

He found *Fitty's Barbershop, Bathhouse, & Laundry* on Cortez Street, had his beard and moustache removed and his hair cut; then, spent the next forty-five minutes soaking in a tub of steaming, soapy water while he pondered the cryptic note that had come with the money. No news. No inquiries regarding his health. Nothing but: "Come home." Not signed, "Your father," but merely "George Patrick Hood," as if Father—or the writer—corresponded with a business associate or an absolute stranger.

Something was wrong here. Something was *very* wrong. He thought about the letter from Father that Veracity Cooper claimed to hold. Was it a real correspondence or merely another "come home"?

Much as he'd yearned to receive the call to return to New York, something about this "come home" raised the short hair at the back of his neck. That silent cautionary voice he'd learned so well to heed that it had now become instinct nearly shouted at him that something was deadly wrong back east. And, too, there were Oscar Pratt and Veracity Cooper to deal with right here before any of this went much farther.

He washed his hair, rinsed under a cascade of cool fresh water a bath attendant poured over him, dried with a stiff abrasive towel that nevertheless smelled of clean sun, and examined the bullet wound along his side. Coming along fine. Nearly healed.

He transferred his money and the envelope from his filthy trail clothes, and asked to have the old ones washed. He heard that they would be ready for pick-up day after tomorrow, and left to rent a room somewhere.

"Damn it!" Hastily, he stepped back into the barbershop. Oscar Pratt held his black gelding to a slow walk down Cortez, his eyes narrowly studying buildings, pedestrians, and other riders. Hoping that Pratt hadn't seen him, Hood watched the bounty hunter pass on down the street and rein in beneath a sign announcing: *Du Shane's Boarding, Rooms & Eats*. He'd expected to have a day or two to himself, but . . .

Why didn't Pratt still accompany the freight wagons? Did that mean that Veracity was also here? Whatever the implications, it did mean that he, himself, wouldn't be using *Du Shane's* for lodging. And, he'd better get gone before Oscar came out of the boarding house.

Keeping a wary eye on his backtrail, he moved out onto the boardwalk, snapped, "Come on, Spot," and headed toward the tallest building in town, the three-story hotel on the opposite corner. He again ordered the pinto to wait while he pushed through polished wooden doors inset with etched-glass ovals.

The inside seemed to have been transported straight from the very best New York City locale. Wainscotings of dark mahogany gleamed below discreetly-patterned forest-green gold-embossed wallpaper. At his left across the thick dark oriental rug, stood a waxed desk attended by two men in elegant suits; to the right, a wide carpeted ornately-bannistered staircase led up to the next floor. A green-and-gold-uniformed bellhop lounged against the Reception Desk, and Stormy was so startled by the *alien-ness* of the hotel lobby that he stepped back outside briefly to make sure he was still in the untamed southwest.

He was. Smiling wryly, he again entered the hotel and strode toward the desk. "Room available?"

The clerk behind the counter put on the same nose-pinched expression Sean could recall the family butler, Burkhart, often wore. (Hood thought there *must* be a class held to practice that look!) The clerk said, "At one-fifty a night . . . sir?"

Sean lifted brows at the man. He asked, "Is that one-dollar-and-fifty cents or a hundred-and-fifty dollars a night?"

"One-dollar, fifty-cents, sir." The clerk was not amused.

"And the accommodations?"

The clerk slid a look at the other man before he cleared his throat. "The one-fifty accommodations are on the second floor at the rear. They are furnished with bed, armoire, and commode stand. The communal relief station and water pump are behind the hotel. The boy can show you where they are."

Sean shook his head. "I'd like a room overlooking the street, if any are available."

"They are two dollars a night . . . sir."

"What floor?"

"Second. The three dollar and three-fifty suites are on the third floor." The man warmed to this task. "Of course, if you wish the Presidential Suite, that is twelve-fifty a day."

Sean chuckled. "No, I think one of your second floor front rooms will be adequate." He glanced around. "This is a fine hotel for such an out-of-the-way place."

Stiffly, the heretofore silent second man put in, "Prescott is *not* an out-of-the-way place, sir. It was the Arizona capitol until 'sixty-seven, and we hope it will be again soon! High-ranking Army officers from Fort Whipple have quartered here! Should President Grant take it upon himself to visit, he would naturally lodge *here!*"

"I meant no offense, sir," Hood said coolly. "May I sign your register now?"

Silently, pale-lipped with insult, the clerk turned the open book on its carousel, dipped a pen into a gold-based inkwell, and handed the instrument to Stormy. Sean wrote: *John Evans* on the last line of the page, and handed the pen back with a smile.

The clerk was expert at reading upside-down. Even before he turned to a fresh page in the register, he snapped, "Room two-oh-three, Mister Evans. That will be two dollars, sir."

Sean nodded, pulled the wad of bills from his pocket and peeled off one of the hundreds. "Of course, you can make change?"

The clerk kept a straight face. He carried the bill through a side door and returned shortly with ninety-eight dollars in mixed bills. He nodded to the bellboy. "Tom will help you with your luggage, Mister Evans. Would you care to check your weapons, sir?"

"No. Is there a stable nearby where I can put my horse?"

"The hotel provides complimentary stables in back on the other side of the creek. Merely identify your mount and Tom will see to its care."

"Thank you." Followed by the bellhop, Sean pointed out Spot; then, took his key and said, "Please bring up my saddlebags," before he reentered the hotel and headed alone up the stairs.

Room 203 held a double bed, the promised armoire and wash stand, and also two wingback chairs, one on either side of a small round table set before the lace-curtained window. He was looking out the window watching street activity below when a knock on the door brought him around sharply with his hand on his side-arm.

"Who is it?"

"Bellboy with your luggage, sir."

Sean said, "Come in." When the boy entered, draped the carry-sacks over the ornate iron foot of the bed, then lingered for his tip, Sean held up a dollar bill. "For taking good care of me and my horse."

"*Thank* you, sir!" The boy grabbed the bill. "If there's *anything* else I can . . ."

"There is." Hood held up two more dollar bills but kept them out of Tom's reach. "I want to know the moment a young woman named Veracity Cooper checks into this hotel and what her room number is, all right? When, or *if* she appears, these are yours, understand?"

Normal tip for saddlebags and to lead a horse to the stable was a dime. Tom had already received a more than healthy tip. He blurted, "*Yes, sir!* Miss Veracity Cooper, yes, *sir!* Can I bring you a bottle, sir? Name your poison, sir!"

Sean shook his head. "No, thank you. Who serves the best meal in town?"

Tom looked around warily. "Don't tell the management I said this, sir, but don't eat here in the hotel. Try the Palace, sir. Good food, good gamblin', good whiskey, and it's got the purtiest girls in Arizona, sir."

"All right, thank you. You see Miss Cooper come in, that's where I'll be."

"I'll come get you, sir, you can count on it."

"Then," Hood flourished the bills before he tucked them back into his pocket, "you can count on these." He headed down to see what he could see of Prescott and the Palace without being spotted by Pratt.

Veracity had also watched that unknown rider on the black-and-white pinto speed by yesterday, and envied him the freedom his maleness and perhaps familiarity with the country lent him. He raced headlong toward his destination while she was stuck to the slowly plodding oxen because as a woman alone in a strange land, she needed the wagoneers' protection.

When they halted for the night, she asked, "How much farther to Prescott now, Mister Axt?"

"Oh, twenty-five or so miles, Miss. We're near there."

Only twenty-five miles! If she left the freights tomorrow morning, surely she could make it to Prescott before dark. She said, "You have my undying thanks for your companionship on this journey, Mister Axt . . . Mister Jones . . . but I shall go on ahead in the morning."

Axt frowned. "But whut 'bout that there varmit, Hood, Miss? He may be layin' fer ya alongside the road. No, you'd best . . ."

"Mister Axt, I believe Angel and I can handle Mister . . . uh . . . Hood." She indicated the sawed-off side-arm in her belt. "Forewarned is forearmed, as they say. I'll keep a careful eye out for him, and I assure you, I'm a *very* good shot."

Recalling the "carom-shot" she'd nicked "Hood's" horse with the other night, Axt chuckled and nodded.

"Ummm . . . there is only one road, right?"

"Yup."

"Then, if I follow the road, I can't possibly get lost. If something happens to Goldie, I'll just camp till you catch up." She took a deep breath and looked around with admiration. "Besides, this climate, these surroundings, are so salubrious, to ride alone here will be exhilarating!"

Axt shuffled feet. "Uh . . . I . . . dunno what y'mean by sal . . . salu . . ."

"Salubrious? Healthful! Invigorating!" Again, she breathed deeply. "*Wonderful!* Oh, I could live here permanently!"

She started out shortly after dawn that next morning, kept her pace brisk but leisurely to enjoy her surroundings, wondered occasionally if it was unprofessional for a Pinkerton detective to be having such a good time, and arrived at the middle-of-the-road pine at the edge of Prescott about four o'clock that afternoon.

That was when her real problems began.

CHAPTER SIX

Veracity abruptly realized she'd never gotten back the twenty dollars she'd paid Mr. Axt to transport John Evans (Sean Hood?) as freight. That left her only thirty-seven dollars and thirty cents to her name. On the note she had left for Stormy, she'd told him she would spend three months in Prescott. That was ninety days. The note was dated July 2. Unless she miscalculated, today was the sixteenth—she'd cut almost two days off the trek by leaving the freights early. But that still left seventy-five or so days here in town—barely fifty cents a day to live on. Could she get by with that? She didn't dare try to cash her return travel voucher; if she spent that, she would never make it home. And to dip into Sean Hood's thousand dollars would be stealing.

She bit her lip as she looked around the town. Really charming here, with its quaint tree-sheltered stone, log, and wooden Victorian-style buildings, the cottonwoods shading the park and all . . . And out beyond the city was the most starkly impressive butte she'd beheld. Very interesting, but . . .

There! There was a boarding house. She guided Goldie around the central park to *Du Shane's Boarding, Rooms & Eats*, dismounted, tethered the sorrel to the ring inset in the boardwalk that seemed to be placed there in lieu of a hitching rail, and walked slowly into the interior of the building, but turned around immediately and hurried out—there was the most motley conglomeration of unwashed desert rats she'd ever seen gathered in what appeared to be the dining room. The table oilcloths were filthy and fly-blown. The stench of soapy lye water, decaying meat, old cabbage, sour milk and cheap whiskey nearly nauseated her.

Back on the boardwalk, she took three deep breaths and gasped, "Oh, my!" That was worse than anything she'd experienced on the Isthmus, aboard either ship, or in any of the towns she'd passed through.

Well, over there was a hotel. Dreading to hear how expensive it might be, she nevertheless retrieved Goldie and led her down the street toward the building. Her misgivings increased when she saw the elegant doors; crashed down around her as she entered the lobby. *Too* expensive, she could tell that immediately.

But then, she thought no. She could afford to stay here a couple of days at least, perhaps long enough for a bath, a night or two in a decent bed in a nice room . . . time enough to locate other more frugal lodgings. And, when Mr. Axt arrived with the freight wagons, she would try to get her money back, for that twenty dollars would help a lot. Otherwise, she would have to find employment somewhere to augment her funds while waiting for Hood to arrive (if he ever did).

She selected a dollar-fifty-a-night room. Her name seemed to glare accusingly at her, alone as it was at the top of the fresh page, when she signed the register. She allowed Tom to carry her bedroll and saddlebags up the stairs for her, tipped him five cents for the service and to stable Goldie, and when the door closed, sank onto the bed with a sigh.

She had to write to her mother. She'd promised to do that when she arrived in the next island of civilization. She needed to send another report to Mister Pinkerton. She wanted a bath, a good dinner, and then maybe a walk around town in this high-mountain air. What to do first?

Bath. It had to be the bath, even if she was forced to put her soiled clothes back on over her clean body. She availed herself of the hotel's facilities. They added the charge to her bill.

She ate sparingly in their dining room—unlike Sean, she hadn't inquired of other, cheaper places to eat—and she decided that her steak had been an old goat when alive, but ate it anyway. The establishment added the charge to her bill.

She thought about writing letters and reports but couldn't face those chores. Tomorrow. She'd do them tomorrow. She went for a walk in the Plaza across the street.

Prescott didn't die at five o'clock. Instead, what by day was an ordinary cowtown or mining center came alive at dusk. The many saloons lining the street opposite the park were alight with the sounds of laughter, the whir of roulette wheels, slap of cards, shouts, curses, a few gunshots, and from the balcony above the door to what appeared to be *the* major saloon in town, soiled doves shouted cheerfully down at cowpokes, miners, and soldiers on the street or boardwalk and leaned far over the ornate railing to show their cleavages to best advantage.

Veracity sat on one of the wooden benches in the park, watched the activity with some amusement, and considered ways and means of enlarging her funds. While two cowhands beat up a miner on the street corner, she thought perhaps she could become a cook in the hotel for a while. She was no great shakes at a stove, but even her cooking was better than what she'd eaten this evening. Or, could she become a schoolmarm? Ugh! No! A music teacher? That was better than perhaps becoming a laundress.

The miner had survived the cowboys; even as she watched, the cowhands lost interest and staggered back into the saloon, their victim lurched upright and stumbled off toward *Du Shane's* to lick his wounds, and Veracity winced when the piano player in the Palace hit a horrible clinker for at least the fourth time since she'd been sitting here. It finally got through to her that whoever tortured that poor piano in there played mechanically, without zest, without heart. At this moment, she thought the piece was intended to be *Annie Laurie*, but the rendition was so terrible she wouldn't have been positive had someone not accompanied the tune, singing the words in a beautiful, clear, tenor voice. But that *awful* piano playing ruined . . .

She said, "Ah!" and rose. And sat back down.

Oh, well, but no. She was a decent, well-bred eastern lady who . . .

. . . had ridden bungos and a mule across the Isthmus of Panama accompanied only by un-introduced men and savage guides, had sailed thousands of miles alone with the ships' male crews and passengers, had ridden with mule skinners and riverboat captains, and was supposed to be a Pinkerton detective. Even though Pinkerton operatives were not allowed to frequent disreputable establishments, *as* a detective, she should go where her best source of information lay. Where did men meet and talk fly around like mosquitos on a warm night? Where might Sean Hood stop first to wash away the low-desert dust? In a *saloon,* of course!

She stood again, took a deep breath, clenched fists, and strode purposefully across the street. At the swinging double doors, she hastily stepped aside when the bouncer flung a drunk soldier out onto the boardwalk (had time to notice that someone had repaired a bullet hole in the large side window with two washers and a nut-and-bolt) but then resolutely pushed through into the interior.

To her left was a long polished wooden bar backed by as-long a multi-segmented mirror. Stuffed elk, bear, and deer heads were mounted on the wall above that. To her right, many round tables and rickety chairs crowded the area. Straight ahead in the back were the gaming tables and roulette wheel; then, the stairs that led up to the brothel on the second floor. And *there* was the piano with a slim young man laboring at the keys.

Conversation hesitated when, looking straight ahead, Veracity squared her shoulders, marched down the narrow aisle between men packed at the bar's brass rail and the fully-occupied tables, halted beside the piano player, and cleared her throat.

His fingers hit another off-key chord when he looked up at her.

"May I?"

"May you . . . what?"

She waved a finger at him. "Let me try that for a moment, if you please, sir."

Totally astounded, the piano player stopped hitting keys, rose and stepped aside. Veracity put her reticule on top of the piano where she could keep an eye on it, sat, did a few square-dance chords to get the feel of the piano (maybe it wasn't the young man's fault after all, for the instrument was *horrible*), but then launched into Steven Foster's *Camptown Races*. She followed that with *Oh! Susanna*, and really, after she got used to it, the piano wasn't all that bad.

Her music teacher, her mother, and the choir director at church back home had always despaired of her "frivolous bent" with the keyboard—as she had told the young mother on the sternwheeler on the Colorado, they would never let her play in church because of it—but now, she let herself go. She didn't realize that much of the conversation had stopped until she had run through three or four of the more lively pieces, then asked the piano player, "Do you know *The Rose of Tralee*? That's made for a tenor."

At his nod, she began the piece. His fine voice rang in the silence:

"The pale moon was rising above the
    green mountain,
The sun was declining beneath the blue
    sea
When I strayed with my love to the pure
    crystal fountain
That stands in the beautiful Vale of
    Tralee. . . ."

Her own voice was low; she'd always sung alto parts, and while no soloist, she could harmonize with a tenor. She joined the piano player for the chorus, and when they were done, she was amazed at the cheers and applause . . . and at an audible sob from one particularly drunk old prospector.

"Do you want a job, Miss? You have one if you want it."

Veracity turned around on the stool to look behind her. A man who seemed to be her envisioned image of a Mississippi gambler—a leonine swoop of graying hair, an expensive black suit, silk vest, watch chain, cigar in hand—studied her with amused blue eyes.

She nodded. "Yes, sir, I do . . . but not at his expense." She indicated the piano player. "I will play only if he will sing. Who are you, sir?"

"Bart Reynolds, owner. Fifty cents an hour, six to midnight."

That was three dollars a night! That would pay her room and board. Still, she asked, "And *he* stays?"

"Mmm . . . I don't know."

The young man looked desperate. He blurted, "*Please,* Mister Reynolds, I always done my best here!"

Reynolds chuckled and nodded. "You can stay on as a waiter, Mike, and sing with her occasionally. What's your name, Miss?"

Veracity told him. "And I can start tomorrow, Mister Reynolds."

"Not tonight?"

"No, I have to get settled. I just arrived in Prescott today."

Again, Reynolds nodded. "Agreed. But starting tomorrow, wear something with a little more style, Miss Cooper. I like my girls to look . . . feminine."

"Fine." Veracity rose and extended her hand to shake his. "It's a deal, Mister Reynolds. See you tomorrow at six in the evening. But please remember . . . *I am not one of your girls!*" She jabbed a thumb upward toward the brothel, grabbed her reticule and eyes lowered and expression haughty, left amid cheers, howls, and more applause.

Because she refused to look at those around her, she didn't see the dark young man who rose from a far corner table and followed her out. She hadn't noticed Stormy, but he'd watched all this with interest. After turning Goldie over to hands there, the bellboy, Tom, had gone directly from the stable to the Palace to find Hood, had delivered his message and had received his two dollars. Sean had taken his time over dinner, for it seemed from what the boy said that Miss Cooper was staying the night at least, at the same hotel he, himself, lodged within. Therefore, he was still finishing the apple pie and coffee, and was not yet quite ready to leave when the girl appeared. He'd found what happened next more than a little curious. Who was this *lady* who could pound a piano like a practiced whiskey-mill entertainer?

The streets around the Palace were now lighted with flaming torches. On their balcony above the Palace, two calico cats sat silhouetted by the lighted open door behind them and shouted invitations down at passers—all male, for Veracity seemed to be the only woman out and about at this hour.

Beyond the wide street, the park was a pool of darkness. Sean saw the girl walk quickly at a slant across the un-cobbled dirt to the Plaza side; then, hurry along the park edge toward the hotel on the far corner. She had almost won to the boardwalk when two very young, very drunk soldiers stepped out in front of her.

Hood saw Miss Cooper try to bypass the soldiers; saw them move to intercept her. He quickened his own pace. By the time he reached the trio, one young man had snared Veracity with an arm around her waist and was trying to kiss her. The boy let go abruptly and doubled over. Her knee had found its target.

Sean didn't say anything. He merely walked up and flattened the second soldier with a well-placed punch. By this time, the first had recovered enough to straighten. Hood finished him off as easily as the first, for both were too drunk to be much of a challenge. Shaking his hand, he looked for the girl.

Veracity hadn't waited around to see the results. She had taken off running. Even as Sean looked, he saw her cross the next street and hesitate in front of the hotel a moment to gather her dignity before pushing through the door into the interior.

He glanced back at the soldiers on the board-walk. One stirred. The other was still out. But over there, four more blue-coats headed his way. He didn't want to get mixed up in a brawl—where was the sheriff or a few deputies to keep peace of an evening? The law office was over across the park, but other than lighted windows, he saw no evidence of security of any kind here in town.

Hurriedly, he turned on his heel and pursued the girl. The four soldiers followed him, but he made it to the hotel door ahead of them without rushing to the point of retreat. At the front desk, he asked what room Veracity Cooper was in, heard 204, and moved on up the stairs. It was time to talk to her.

Sean discovered Room 204 to be directly across the hall from his own quarters. The carpeted corridor was silent and unoccupied—this hotel was not your local rowdy boarding house. He stood for a moment pondering the best way to proceed. He needed his letter from home. Now that he had other funds, whatever money may accompany word from his father was incidental. But to do any of it, he would have to tell Miss Cooper who he was. *If* she would believe him.

He sighed heavily, lifted a hand, and knocked.

"Who is it?" Her voice muffled by the wood made her sound tired.

"John Evans, Miss Cooper. I came to pay you the twenty dollars I owe you."

There was a long silence from inside the room, so long that he finally asked, "Miss Cooper?"

"Just a minute, Mister Evans. I was preparing for bed." She hadn't been. She'd started her report to Mr. Pinkerton; now hastily gathered her papers and journal and stuffed them back into her saddlebags. As she withdrew her hand, her fingers met warm metal. She'd wondered what she would use those silly handcuffs for, and now she knew. She took them out, opened them and slid them beneath the doily under the lamp, then took a deep breath. She checked that Angel and the letter were back in her reticule and the derringer still in her boot, smoothed palms over her unbound hair and stepped to the door. She turned the key to unlock the panel and opened it to see a tall young man, his hat in one hand, leaning against the wall across the hallway, and her heart bounced. With his hair cut, and now cleanly shaven, she could tell that "John Evans" matched the picture she carried. Oh, a couple of years older, yes, but . . .

"Mister Evans! It *is* you! However did you find me!"

His teeth were very white in his sun-weathered complexion when he grinned at her and pushed away from the wall. "I was in the Palace tonight when you came to play. I didn't know you were an entertainer."

"I'm not, but I need to support myself, and playing the piano is much less strenuous than washing some cowhand's dirty clothes." She took a deep breath before—against all propriety—she asked, "Please, won't you come in?"

His brows rose. "Are you sure I won't place you in a compromising position, Miss Cooper?"

Now, she also smiled. "Recall that I am employed in a saloon, sir. I do believe my reputation is already ruined. You said you came to repay my twenty dollars?"

"Yes." When he stepped across the hall and into the room, she moved away, back toward the kerosene lamp lighted on a small table near a window that unlike his looked out into an air well rather than over a street. He dug in a pocket as he approached, produced a wad of bills, tossed his hat on the bed so he could use both hands, peeled off a twenty and a five and held them out to her. It was the first time he'd seen her without that strange floppy straw hat and with her hair unbraided. It transformed her into a young girl with a peeling sunburned nose spattered by freckles, virginally innocent and appealing. He finished, "The five is . . . interest and for . . . services rendered, Miss."

She didn't hesitate to accept the extra money, but said, "My, you must think I charge usurious prices, Mister Evans." She waved a finger at the door. "Come in, shut the door, sit and chat with me for a while. How is your bullet wound healing?" The bills in hand, she stepped to where her reticule sat to put the money away. Her fingers lingered on the Avenging Angel.

"Very well, thank you." Wondering how the hell he was going to tell her without scaring her to death that Evans wasn't his real name, he turned to close the door. He never got the chance to turn back, because something struck him solidly behind the ear and an instant blackness drove him to the floor.

Veracity wasn't accustomed to hitting people. Her heart pounded wildly while she stared at the man crumpled at her feet. Gasping, *"Oh, my . . . oh, my . . ."* she forced herself to move, shoved Angel under her belt, bent and seized Hood's shirt. Panting, she dragged him from the door, around the foot of the bed and toward its head, let go of his clothing and leaped to the table to get the handcuffs. Trembling with haste to get this done before he woke up, she closed one side of the cuffs around his right wrist, lifted his arm and locked the other band around the iron bedpost between the frame and the ornate metal finial at the top so he couldn't slide the circle free.

She pulled his six-shooter from its holster and knife from the sheath and put Angel beside them on the table. Next, she yanked up Hood's pants legs to make sure he wasn't hiding a derringer in his boots as she did. Finally, she lurched to a chair and sat down to compose herself before she rose again, picked the pitcher from its wash basin on the commode stand, and poured a small stream of water into his face.

She half-expected him to come to cursing, but while the smoldering snap in his dark eyes betrayed that he was furious, he said nothing, merely looked from her to where his right arm was tethered to the bed, then at his empty holster. Finally, he pushed himself up to sit leaned against the mattress and held his head for a moment.

Veracity had pulled herself together. She said, "Get up and sit on the edge of the bed, Mister Hood. If you struggle, you'll only hurt yourself, and if you somehow succeed in escaping, I could shoot you with impunity. A man who forces himself into a lady's room at this time of night expects to get shot."

Sean hadn't missed her use of his real name. Still, he barked a short, morose laugh while he eased up onto the mattress and nodded at the handcuffs. "Suppose *I* yelled for help, Miss

Cooper . . . how would you explain this to the management?"

"Don't be facetious, Mister Hood. I could shoot you and have the handcuffs gone and hidden by the time anyone arrived."

"Why are you calling me *Mister Hood,* Miss Cooper? I told you . . . my name's John Evans."

For an answer, Veracity dug two envelopes from her reticule, lay one on the table beside Angel, opened the other and extracted a small stiff rectangle. She offered it to Sean but made him stretch to reach it so he couldn't grab her hand.

A wash of surprise poured through Hood when he looked at the daguerreotype. It was a picture of him, a formal portrait taken several years back in New York. He scowled at the picture, then glanced at the girl, waiting to see what came next.

Again, Veracity sat down in the chair by the table. "I know who you are, sir. Sean Evan Hood, youngest son of George Patrick Hood . . . Hood Shipping Company of New York City. I have come a long way to find you."

Now, he asked, "What are you, law enforcement? Some kind of a hired killer?"

"No, I'm employed by the Allan Pinkerton National Detective Agency, Mister Hood."

This time, his laugh was disbelieving. "A Pinkerton agent? Pinkerton doesn't hire women!"

"Oh, yes, he does—there are four of us at this moment, but that's beside the point. The agency has been looking for you for almost two years, Mister Hood. Levi Jenkins was the first assigned to your case. He traced you from New York to Texas. Unfortunately, he met with a debilitating accident there. Adam Gleason took up the case. He started at San Francisco and was working his way east but came down with a fatal stomach ailment in Santa Fe. Before his death, he reported that you had been there and were headed even farther west. I started from San Diego, and . . ." She shrugged.

He sailed the daguerreotype back to her and tried, "I'll admit that the man in the picture does look somewhat like me, but . . ."

She interrupted gently, "Mister Hood . . . Sean . . . don't you want to see your letter from home? It holds information you need to know. And if you will work with me, *I also* have intelligence you must hear."

Much as he wanted to see the letter, caution and curiosity made him ask coldly, "Who hired your agency to chase . . . this Sean Hood?"

"Mister Liam Hardesty."

"Hardesty? Why!"

She sighed. "Mister Hardesty told us that he had thought Sean Evan Hood was the cause of his daughter's death. He said he'd threatened to kill you, but you'd fled before he could do the deed.

Then, he came to realize that Miss Hardesty's demise had been an accident. That she was as much at fault in the . . . affair as you were, and that while he still mourns his daughter, he wants you to know that you can return home with no threat to your life."

"Really. How much is Hardesty paying Pinkerton to deliver that message?"

She shook her head. "Mister Pinkerton didn't confide that to me. Suffice it to say, it was enough for the agency to pay the way for three representatives to search for you—one of whom died in the effort." She picked up the second envelope, but held it out of his reach. "Before I give this to you, I must make certain you *are* actually Sean Hood."

He tipped his head. "I thought you were already sure of that."

"It pays to be doubly cautious. Ummm . . . Sean has a nickname. Can you tell me what it is?"

Sean looked at the envelope. Somehow, he couldn't believe that Liam Hardesty had forgiven Melissa's death. But if Hardesty had hired Pinkerton agents to track him down, would he also offer five thousand dollars to other men to kill him? That wouldn't seem likely. He abruptly felt that things were making less and less sense. How many other unknown persons paid for his head? However many, there must now be an enormous amount of money out on him, and unfortunately, these present events only lent credence to Oscar Pratt's insistence that someone named George Hood had hired him.

Not taking his eyes from the envelope, he asked, "Then, you're not working with Pratt?"

Veracity frowned. "Who?"

"Oscar Pratt. He's not a Pinkerton agent?"

"I never heard of him."

"But, I saw you riding with him while you traveled with the freight wagons. Stocky man . . . florid faced . . ."

She laughed. "So, *that's* his name! He claimed to be you, but I knew he wasn't."

"And how do I know *you* aren't lying, Miss Cooper?"

She delved again into her reticule and handed him a business card and a fold of paper. "My credentials, Mister Hood."

He looked at the card, lay it aside, shook open the paper, perused the sheet briefly, saw it was, indeed, a formal introduction, also saw that it was notarized and signed by Allan Pinkerton, and tossed it back to her. "All right, you are Pinkerton."

"And let's be sure of who you are, Mister Hood. What's your nickname?"

He glanced again at the thick envelope she held. There was a letter from home. Real word from home, he knew it. It didn't matter that she had stolen it from him in Ehrenberg, it was here now. Almost before he knew he spoke, his mouth said, "Stormy."

She leaned forward and silently handed the envelope over but then rose and turned away to look out the window into the air well to give him what privacy she could manage. She stood that way until she heard his breathing change. When she looked quickly back over her shoulder, she saw him sitting bent over, his elbow braced on a knee, his left hand over his eyes. The money was scattered unimportantly on the bedcover beside his hat. The letter lay on the carpet between his feet. Even as she looked, a drop of moisture on his wrist caught the lamplight.

He gasped in a choked voice, "If she . . . if Mother ever heard why I . . . left, she died still believing me to be . . . to be . . ."

Softly, Veracity said, "Perhaps your father told her the truth before he also passed away, Sean."

He straightened with a jerk that rattled handcuff chain against the bedpost, and he was as pale as his rich coloring allowed him to be. "Wh-What?"

"Your father died less than a month after your mother passed on. His heart . . . I'm so sorry to bring you this news, but . . ." Again, she shrugged, this time helplessly.

Silently, Sean fell over onto his side, fists clenched and face buried in the crook of the arm tethered to the bed. Veracity knew grief when she saw it. She gave him another few moments to deal with his emotions before she said, "I know you're innocent, Mister Hood. I confess that I read your letter, and I know that your brother, George, is the . . . the culprit. Mister Hardesty has forgiven you. If you will return east with me, I'll help you if you want to see that the truth comes out."

He lay without speaking for a long time. She didn't know whether he'd even heard her or not until he abruptly sat up and she flinched from the ugly bitterness in his expression. Though his shirtsleeve bore a large dark spot where tears dampened it, his eyes were dry now, and his voice steady when he snapped, "Don't get involved with me, Miss Cooper. I'm a Remittance Man too unsavory to be allowed to stay at home. Do you know the whole story?"

"Probably not. But do I need to? I know you're innocent of complicity in whatever happened to Liam Hardesty's daughter. You may call yourself a Remittance Man, but you're not that. What you are is a scapegoat . . . what else is there to know?"

He told her everything. It had been such a long time since he'd had a sympathetic audience—the occasional prostitute didn't count—that once he got started, it seemed he couldn't shut up. He told her about Elaine whom he'd planned to wed, about the meeting in the library that night with his father and Georgie, about his "confession" to save his parents and George Junior's family from scandal and ruin, about his years of running, and finally about Oscar Pratt's assertion that he and the other bounty hunters had been hired by "George Hood."

Veracity listened to it all, commenting only occasionally until he was done. Then, she said, "When we first met on the road, you said you only had three dollars left to your name. Yet now, you're wearing new clothes. You have bathed . . . shaved . . . where are you staying?"

He grinned wanly at that. "Across the hall from you. My room is two-oh-three."

"Ah-hah! Now, you have lodging in the most expensive hotel in town . . . where'd you get the money, Mister Hood?"

"Please call me Sean, Miss Cooper. It has been so long . . . I would like to hear someone say it."

She smiled brilliantly at him. "Thank you, Sean. And remember . . . it's Veracity, not Vera. How'd you come by the money to fund all this?"

"I picked it up at the stage depot. Why?"

"Do you still have the envelope it came in? Yes? Let me see it, please."

He fished it out of his pocket and handed it to her. "And there's a note inside."

She took it nearer the lamp, put that envelope side-by-side with the one she knew had come from George Hood Senior, and breathed again, "*Ah-hah!* Come look, Sean. The handwriting isn't the same! And there's also a great difference in the ages of these envelopes, see? The one from your father has been sitting around a long time, it's yellowed and brittle, and . . ."

"Veracity . . ." Hood tugged at his handcuffed wrist. "You'll have to unlock this if you want me over there. Why'd you do this, anyway?"

She made a wry gesture. "Oh, I'm sorry. I needed to make sure you would stay put while I said what I had to tell you. Besides, I don't . . . *didn't* really know you. Your partial story, yes. Your person, no."

"And even though Hardesty has forgiven me, I still have the reputation of being a low-down skunk."

"Now, Sean, I know you're not that."

"Then, why'd you hit me?"

She was fishing in her reticule for the key. She laughed, "I didn't think that if I merely asked you please, Stormy, have a seat and let me put handcuffs on you that you'd do it."

"You're damn right about . . ." His voice died abruptly when the door burst open and Oscar Pratt, side-arm in hand, stepped into the room.

"Well, now!" Pratt's expression was a leer of triumph. "Ain't dis cozy!"

CHAPTER SEVEN

Sean's heart squeezed when he looked from Pratt holding a weapon on them, to Veracity frozen with her mouth open and one hand still in her reticule. He darted a quick glance back at his right wrist. He was weaponless and securely cuffed to the bed. Two irons and a hunting knife lay on the table beside the girl but he couldn't reach them, and with Oscar's own weapon pointed dead-on at Veracity, she didn't dare make a grab for something. Besides, women weren't usually gunfighters.

Pratt also noted the weapons in the pool of lamplight, the handcuff restraining Hood, and his grin broadened. He stepped farther into the room, hooked the door with his heel and pressed it shut behind him. "Well, now, look wot we got here. Yeh nabbed 'im, din't youse, Missy. Got 'im good an' proper. Not bad fer a petticoat." Then, his expression hardened. "But if yeh tinks youse can chisel in here an' gyp me outta de reward up on him, yeh got 'nother tink comin', see? *I* been trackin' him fer more'n two years, an' I ain't splittin' dat five gran' wit *nobody,* see! Step away from dat table, doll."

Veracity pulled herself together. She straightened and closed fingers into fists to hide that she

137

held a key in one hand when she lifted her arms. Sean could see her struggling to work a smile to her lips before she said, "Why, Mister Hood! I didn't know you were also after John Evans! Why didn't you say so when we rode with the freights? . . . we could have worked together to . . . uh . . . nab him."

Pratt's lip curled. "Don' give me dat shit. Dat ain't no *John Evans,* an' youse knows it. Hey, now, lookit all dat money layin' dere. Dis here's gonna turn out to be a big night fer me!"

"Pratt," Sean said abruptly, "leave the girl out of this. She's not part of it. You have me now . . . let her go and I'll leave quietly with you. I'm tired of running, Oscar. Let's finish this *now,* but just you and me."

"Oh, my, ain't dat *heroic* of yeh, I do declare," Pratt sneered sarcastically. "Youse ain't in no shape to bargain wit me, Hood."

Sean tugged against the handcuffs. They were solid. He licked lips and shot a look at Veracity before he said urgently, "Oscar . . . Oscar, listen to me. You told me G-George Hood offered five thousand dollars for my head. You know I hail from a wealthy eastern family. I've heard that my father and mother are both . . . dead, now. That means my brother, Georgie, and I, inherit Hood Shipping . . . split the inheritance.

"You've worked hard to get that five thousand. I'll pay you *ten* thousand to come east with

138

Veracity and me to find out who said he was George Hood and offered the five thousand. You can claim that bounty for bringing me in, *plus* receive the ten thousand I'll pay you for working with me. That's *fifteen thousand dollars,* Oscar, more money than you could make in your whole lifetime. You'd never have to longshore again. Live a life of ease. My ten thousand . . . George Hood's five thousand . . . fifteen thousand. Think about it, Oscar."

Both he and Veracity watched Pratt waver; both held their breath while the bounty hunter considered Sean's proposal. Presently, Oscar mused, "S'pose, when we got dere, we find out youse's been cut outta yer daddy's Will?"

"Then, you would still get the five thousand for bringing me in," Hood said quickly. "You can't lose, Oscar."

Pratt shook his head once and scowled, "It's one helluva long way from here to Noo Yawk. No, too many chances fer yeh to 'scape me."

"I give you my word I won't, Oscar. I want to find out for sure if my own brother put a price on my head. I *have* to know, one way or the other. Ten thousand dollars, Oscar. My word on that."

"Oh, sure! I wouldn' believe *youse* on a stack of Bibles!"

Veracity had been listening silently to all this, not wanting to interfere in what she knew Sean was doing, but now she said quickly, "Mister . . . Pratt? . . . your name's Pratt? . . . listen to me. I am a Pinkerton detective. My agency also wants Mister Hood back in New York. Liam Hardesty has paid Mister Pinkerton well to locate Sean and return him to the east. If you won't work with him, work with me. *True,* it's a long journey and you can't stay awake for weeks, but I could watch him while you slept, you guard him while I rested, and *together,* Mister Pratt . . ."

Oscar gawked at her. "*Youse* is a detective? A Pinkerton agent? No shit!"

"No . . . um . . . shit, Mister Pratt. Is it a deal?"

Sean tensed. He didn't know whether or not Veracity intended to work with Pratt or if it was a ploy on her part; decided to act as if he took her at her word. He jerked at the handcuff and growled, "Damn you, woman, I *believed* you when you said . . ."

She pointed to his six-shooter lying on the table beside her Avenging Angel and cut his words short with, "*There* are two fully-loaded weapons, Mister Hood. I could have made a try for them at any time, and Mister Pratt knows from past experience with me that I'm a very good shot. But I haven't interfered here, because it will be more profitable for me to work with *him* than with *you.*" She looked back at Oscar. "Is it a deal, Mister Pratt? You still get to keep your fifteen thousand dollars, and I get to make a name for myself with the Pinkerton Agency. *That* is more important to me than money, sir."

Oscar nodded. "Yeah. Yeah, youse got yerself a deal, Missy. But first, I need to pay Hood back fer shootin' me in de ass." Before Sean could fling up his left arm to defend himself, Pratt lunged at him and smashed the six-shooter barrel across his face.

The blow knocked Stormy off the bed and onto the floor. Still tethered to iron by his right wrist, he tried to ward off the second blow, but it never reached him because Veracity pulled her derringer from her boot top and shot the weapon from Pratt's hand.

Oscar jerked around to stare open-mouthed at her. Sean grabbed the edge of the mattress with his left hand to brace himself, hooked a toe behind Pratt's ankle, rammed the other foot against the man's kneecap and Oscar plunged to the carpet. It gave Veracity time to seize Angel from the table and aim it at Pratt.

She gasped, "*Don't move, sir!* Sean . . . Sean, here's the key to the handcuffs." She tossed it onto the bed beside the money. "Quick, free yourself. That shot will bring establishment representatives here in a hurry. *Don't move one hair, Mister Pratt!* The damage is already done . . . another shot cannot do much more!"

Pratt was swearing—the mildest thing he said was to call Veracity a lying bitch—but under

Angel's threat, he didn't move. Sean grabbed the key, unlocked the handcuffs from both his wrist and the bedpost, and staggered up. He sidled around Pratt to retrieve his own gun and his knife, then with the pistol in one hand, used the other to hoist the ex-longshoreman upright and fling him onto the bed.

He panted, "Keep a tight bead on him, Veracity," while he holstered his own gun, pulled Oscar's arms up and used the cuffs to lock Pratt's wrists to the ornate head of the bed.

Veracity whispered, "They're coming!"

Sean looked around for something to use to gag Pratt. There was nothing handy but the money still lying on the foot of the bed. He grabbed bills, wadded them, stuffed them into Pratt's mouth; then, knelt beside the bed, drew his six-shooter, and with the weapon pressed hard against Oscar's temple, ordered, "Quick, douse the lamp. When they knock, you heard nothing . . . you were asleep!"

Veracity leaped to the lamp, turned down the wick, cupped her hand at the chimney and blew hard. In the instant darkness, she rushed toward the faint streak of light below the door. She reached it just as a fist beat on the wood.

She let them pound again before she asked, "What? Who is it?"

"The manager! We heard a gunshot from up here. Are you all right, Miss?"

"Yes. Perfectly. I was sleeping . . . didn't hear a thing. Are you sure it was a gunshot, sir?"

"Yes. May we come in and look around?"

"You may *not,* sir! I am in dishabille! I assure you, if you heard something, it didn't come from my room! Have you checked the others?"

"There are only you and Mister Evans on this floor, and he doesn't answer."

"Well, maybe he is dead! Go check him again and let me get back to sleep, *please!*"

On the bed, Pratt made an urgent *"Mmmmphhh!"* past the money. Sean pressed a palm hard over the man's mouth and twitched his weapon ominously against Oscar's skull.

Beyond the thin door, the manager asked, "What was that?"

"My yawn, sir," Veracity answered instantly. "I appreciate your concern, but will you *please* allow me to go back to bed?"

"All right. Good night."

Hood and Veracity waited breathlessly while they listened to hotel employees use a key on Sean's door across the hallway. There was a lengthy silence while they assumed Room 203 was being searched, then a door closed, a lock clicked, and footsteps passed on down the hall. More doors opened and closed. Finally, the employees retreated to the ground floor.

"Light the lamp!" Sean hissed at Veracity. He fumbled in the darkness for Pratt's belt, located the buckle, and by the time the girl had re-lighted the lamp, had removed the belt from Pratt's pants. Working quickly, he pressed a forearm over Oscar's shins to subdue the man's kicking and wrapped leather around ankles.

"What are you doing?" Veracity frowned.

"Making sure he can't get loose until we're long gone." Hood ran the end of the belt through footboard iron and leaned to tighten it; tied it off. "Dammit, Veracity, why'd you have to shoot at him? I had him talked into coming back east with us, but now . . ."

"Well, I couldn't just stand there and let him hit you!"

"You should have! He would only have hit me a couple of more times." He scooped up the money remaining on the bed. "I don't need you to rescue me all the time—you ruined everything! Pack! We're getting out of here now!" He counted what was left of the thousand dollars, folded it and shoved it in his pocket.

"I can't leave!" Veracity waved a hand around. "I haven't settled my hotel bill! I promised to play the piano at . . ."

Sean groaned. "So what if you have a bill here . . . put a couple of dollars on the table for them if it'll make you feel better. And if you want to be a saloon entertainer, fine, but you'll only last until *he* is free, and then he'll have your head! *Pack,* dammit!" He retrieved his hat from the foot of the bed and snapped, "Goin' to get my saddlebags. Be right back."

Veracity muttered, "He's right . . . he's right," and hastily stuffed her possessions into her reticule and her own carry-sacks. On the bed, Pratt made indefinable sounds of fury while he squirmed futilely against the handcuffs and belt.

Sean was back, his bags over his shoulder, his Sharps in his left hand. He moved to Pratt and grasped the stubbled chin to focus the man's attention on him. "Now, listen to me, Oscar. I should just cut your throat here and now and be done with it, but I want you alive to identify the man who hired you, understand? I am going home. You have about three hundred and fifty dollars between your teeth . . . unless you're careless, that will finance your trip to New York City with a lot left over. You come back east, point out the man who hired you to kill me, and you still have the ten thousand I promised you.

"Now, when *I* get to New York, I'm not going to go directly to the family residence . . . if my brother did hire you, that would be walking right into his hands. I'll be staying at the . . . Hardwick Club. Yes, the Hardwick, you understand? You getting all this, Oscar?"

Pratt glared at him, but nodded.

"All right." Sean let go of him and asked Veracity, "You ready?"

She also nodded. Though her hair still hung

loose down her back, she had put on her hat. The Avenging Angel stuck in her belt; her reticule and carry-sacks were over her arm.

"Good. See you in New York City at the Hardwick, Oscar." Hood stepped to the door, cracked it and peered cautiously out into the hallway. Empty. He motioned to Veracity, saw her out, pulled the key from the inside of the door, closed the panel, turned the lock and slid the key back into the room through the crack between the floor and the bottom of the door. With another quick glance around, he took the girl's arm and hustled her swiftly down the hallway away from the lobby stairs.

He halted at the window at the end of the corridor, unlatched and opened it. Good. It was a fire escape, for a ladder was attached to the wall outside. He whispered to Veracity, "Down."

Without hesitation, she threw a leg over the sill, fished for a rung with a toe and began to descend. He followed, but paused long enough to close the window before joining her in the darkness below.

"Stable's this way." He led her blindly across a rough cobblestoned yard.

"How do you know? I can't see a thing!"

"Smell it." The abrupt flare of a lucifer wavered in the light breeze. He led her across the wide wood-plank bridge spanning the creek to where the stable sat on the other bank before he said,

"Door." He lifted the bar, and once inside, feeble light from a single lantern hanging over the head of a snoring stable hand seemed abnormally bright to them.

They didn't disturb the man. Sean found Spot, Veracity located Goldie, they saddled their mounts, led them outside and closed the door gently behind them. The guard never knew the difference.

"Where to?" Veracity asked.

"Away," he said, mounted, and quietly urged Spot toward Prescott's outskirts.

They rode northward in the night at a slow walk through the streets, then along a well-defined road until they were outside town. The moon was now up, the cleared area they passed through lighted silver and black. The outlines of that distant unnamed butte pointed a charcoal thumb at the stars. Beyond the rolling open area, mountain peaks rose in ebony, their trees absorbing all moonlight.

They came to what appeared to be a jumbled pile of building-sized boulders, and here and there, shacks—didn't know this was the remains of the old Granite mining camp—and as long as the moon lighted their way, pressed onward. They halted on the banks of Granite Creek a mile or so farther on, to make their own camp.

Hood hadn't spoken since they left Prescott. Neither had Veracity; she merely followed him until they halted. But over the small fire he built of grasses and twigs, she finally asked, "Why are we going northeast?"

His face burnished by flame, dark eyes blacker by contrast, he stared at the fire while he answered, "Because I told Pratt I was going home and he will expect us to head south down into the lowlands where there is more commercial transportation available. Secondly, I hear the trail to Raton Pass and Denver starts up here. In Denver, I hope to catch a stage or train east to New York."

She, too, looked into the coals for a moment before she shook her head. "He has been trailing you for a long time?"

"Yes. Longer, I think, than your agency."

"Then, he knows your moves well?"

"I suppose so. Why?"

"He'll know we didn't head south. He will come looking for us here. We should have gone back down the hill."

"Possibly." Another long quiet ensued before he said, "Get some sleep, Miss Cooper. If you intend to follow my dust, tomorrow will be a long, hard day."

She nodded and started to rise to lay out her bedroll, but hesitated. "Mister Hood . . . Sean . . . Stormy . . . I'm so very sorry about your parents. Sean, whoever hired Oscar Pratt to kill you, I know it wasn't your father. Recall that I read his letter to you . . . it wasn't your father who did that, Stormy."

All he said was, "Good night, Miss Cooper."

She asked, "Are you going to sneak out on me while I'm asleep, Sean?"

He breathed a short, morose laugh and shook his head. "No."

She took him at his word. "Then, good night, indeed, Mister Hood."

The massive silence that only the high desert can create fell over their tiny camp. In the dying fire, a stick lost its grip on form and collapsed, and in the quiet, its fall seemed as loud as a gunshot. Somewhere far off, a coyote cried in frustration, but its voice only added immensity to the vacancies around them. Almost subconsciously, Sean listened into those spaces, waiting for the distant tattoo of approaching hoof-beats to warn him that hired killers once again pursued him, expecting the barely-realized crunch of a twig or blade of grass broken beneath a stealthy foot, but heard nothing other than bats flittering on velvet after insects and the occasional nighthawk cutting the stars with black-scythe wings.

Once, he looked over to where the wan glow of embers faintly outlined the curves of the blanket Veracity had rolled around herself, the contours announcing *woman,* and wondered briefly who she really was, what her background was, but mostly why he felt nothing but irritation toward her.

Had his flight leached him of all humanity? He was twenty-three, a healthy male, if a bit weary at the moment, but not yet dead. There was a female, certainly pretty enough in her rather frazzled way; obviously intelligent and courageous—she hadn't collapsed into hysterics tonight when Pratt had appeared at the door with gun in hand—and unusually talented. She seemed to be a dead shot with a hand weapon . . . and could she pound the piano! Still, nothing came to body or mind except the thought that if he ever got her near a piano again, he would ask her to play *I'll Take You Home Again, Kathleen.*

Kathleen. His mother's name had been Kathleen, and that song had been . . .

Had been . . .

Kathleen Mary Hood was dead now, wasn't she. George Patrick Hood, Sr. was dead. And Georgie? Well, he would make it back to New York City. He would take Miss Pinkerton Agent Veracity Cooper with him, hopefully meet Oscar Pratt there . . . if he'd adequately bribed the bounty hunter . . . if Pratt survived the journey . . . if he and Veracity made the trip alive . . . if . . .

He stopped thinking about that and shoved his mind back to Veracity. He tried to envision a male-female relationship, even a hasty one-night-stand, and couldn't. Again, he thought that something was very wrong with him. That worry alarmed him, and it took him a long time to get to sleep.

Veracity, on the other hand, dropped off immediately and slept like a log.

It was a tossup who was angriest, the hotel management or Oscar Pratt. Oscar'd had the whole night for his fury to fester. By the time the maid let herself in to change bed linens, saw him handcuffed and otherwise bound to the bed and her screams brought both the desk clerk and hotel manager, Pratt had decided that greed had been his downfall. Five thousand dollars was enough to last him a long while—what he wanted more than money at this moment was *revenge,* both upon Hood and upon that Veracity Cooper. He had invested years on his hunt for Stormy Hood, he wasn't going to let them go to waste. And to be bamboozled by a petticoat . . . no, that would never do.

Hotel management called the local blacksmith who saw to removing Pratt from the bed. The front desk clerk seriously considered charging Pratt for the resulting damage to the headboard and for a night's lodging in their establishment. Only when Pratt dug saliva-soaked bills out of his mouth and belabored them with a barrage of New York City dock swear words that would have made Leroy Axt blanche, did they allow him to leave (almost forcibly evicted him) and transferred their outrage to Miss Veracity Cooper. The two dollars she'd left on the table helped some, but not a lot.

Oscar had also determined that what he needed here was backup. Muscle. He stormed over to *Du Shane's* boarding house and looked around at the miners, between-job cowboys, and general scruffy itinerants wolfing breakfast there, put on a smile and edged toward the toughest-looking of the lot.

"Boys," he said, "has I got a deal fer yehs."

Sean and Veracity rose early, ate lightly, and headed at a canter across the rolling flat ever-rising toward the seemingly impassable mountains ahead. Sean said once, "I think we have to go east around that peak to hit Raton Pass." He nodded to the almost cinder-cone blackness of Mingus Mountain at the north.

She asked, "How far is it?"

"How the hell should I know!"

"A little pleasantness on your part would go a long way in this situation, Mister Hood."

"We wouldn't be in this situation if you hadn't tried to rescue me yesterday, Miss Cooper."

"All right, all right!" she flared. "I apologize! Next time . . . if the occasion arises . . . I'll merely stand by and cheer your attacker on, for goodness sake!"

He slid her a grim sidelong look and urged Spot into a faster pace, but his conscience said to him: *She's right. I should be thanking her for her help, not complaining that she didn't just watch Pratt addle my brains with that pistol barrel.*

But he didn't say it.

They reached the banks of another unknown creek around noon, halted to water and rest their horses and to eat what little they had with them. Sean looked at Veracity trying without much success to chew the iron-hard trail jerky and follow that down with a few dry crackers and water, did attempt a little pleasantness, and said wryly, "That's the trouble with climbing out of windows and running for it in the dead of night. Short rations. We'll have to stock up on trail supplies . . . somewhere."

Veracity thought about her dwindling funds. The twenty-five dollars she'd gotten from Stormy helped, but her money was still limited and she didn't want to borrow more from him. Nevertheless, she nodded, filled her canteen from the creek, and again followed when Hood tightened Spot's saddle cinch, mounted, and once more proceeded northeast.

Only a half-hour on, they met a group of a dozen riders headed south. One of the strangers hailed them. "Ya hittin' north?"

Sean nodded. "Might be."

"Ya cain't go there. Got the cholera bad there.

Stay 'way from up north! We left so's not to catch it."

Hood scowled. "Uh . . . we're strangers here. Where would you suggest we go instead . . . west?"

The miner shook his head. "Huh-uh, Mister. Them ol' Hualapai Injuns joint up with the Apaches 'tween here an' Kingman, or Hardyville on the river. Ya come from Preskitt, best you an' yer missus head back thataway."

Sean didn't disabuse the miner of his assumption that Veracity was his wife, and for once, the girl kept her mouth shut. He asked, "Then east? What's east within riding distance of here?"

The miners shrugged. Presently, a different man said, "Fort Verde's 'bout twenny miles dead east on the Verde River. No road. A good hard ride over some rough country, yeah, an' since this day's worn on some, ya might have t'bed out t'night, 'specially with her missus ridin' with ya. With any luck, ya might make it afore sundown. But I shore wouldn' go north or west, just the two of ya alone. Cholera up north! Injuns 'tween here an' the Colorado. You ain't goin' back to Preskitt, nope, I'd hit fer Fort Verde, was I you."

"Thanks for the advice. Straight east, you say?"

"An' a hair south. Ya hit the Verde River, ya cain't miss it."

Sean tipped a finger to his hat brim, and without

speaking to Veracity, wheeled Spot off the road into the raw high-desert grass, kicked the paint to a gallop and pounded east. Veracity opened her mouth to protest but saw he wasn't waiting for her. She smiled tentatively at the miners before she yelled at Goldie and pursued Stormy.

The miners shook their heads grimly. One muttered, "Fool young'uns, just the two a' them out here alone . . . what they think they is . . . immortal?"

Another agreed. "Need a wagon train an' army guard these days. *Then,* ain't safe. I'll be powerful glad t'make it down t'Preskitt."

Three miles north of Prescott, the miners met two of the hardcases Pratt had hired. Oscar had sent two up the road north, two down south, and two east toward Fort Whipple to question any incoming travelers whether or not they'd seen a man, and a woman on a white-maned, three-stockinged sorrel mare, traveling the other way.

The miners said yup, damn fool young'uns. Headed to Fort Verde, they are.

When the men reported back to him, Oscar inquired where the hell Fort Verde was from here. His men said the miners told them it was about fifty miles past Fort Whipple; to go east following their noses to The Springs; then, angle northeast to the Verde River. Only a two-day ride, if they didn't stop to pan gold on the way.

Oscar gathered the rest of his men. He said to

them, "Right, now. Fifty bucks each after we catch dem bastards. But remember dat I gets Hood an' de petticoat first, take me meanin'?"

The six hardcases nodded, grinned, retrieved their mounts (a scrubby mix of mules and range nags) from *Du Shane's* back-lot lean-to stable, and followed Pratt's lead.

Half-way down the street, Oscar reined in and flung up a hand to halt the others. Grinning, he snapped, "Youse guys wait here a mo." He dismounted, passed reins to the nearest man and stomped across the boardwalk into the shop there—a lady's millinery.

Presently, a woman's angry voice issued from within. Pratt reappeared with a hatbox in his arms. The woman pursued him with outraged shouts while he tore open the strings, lifted the top, extracted a large green-feather-decorated hat and flung the bonnet at her.

"Shut yer face, woman, I ain't stealin' yer merchandise, all I want is dis here box it come in!" He stepped to his black gelding, tied the box strings to his saddle, remounted, and men trailing, thundered on out of town, leaving the milliner standing in the shop doorway with the hat clutched to her bosom and her mouth open in astonishment.

CHAPTER EIGHT

Though lengthening shadows preceding their progress assured them they were still heading due east, Sean reined Spot in and raised a hand to Veracity to signal a halt. Throughout the afternoon, the countryside had gradually changed around them, yet in the land's unique way, had stayed the same—wide grassy areas cut by dry washes interspersed among tall broken tan cliffs, stark stone monoliths standing alone, and now, ever-thickening trees—pine, juniper, tamarisk, sycamore, and cottonwood.

Veracity guided Goldie closer to Spot, pushed her hat back to let air dry her sweaty forehead, and asked, "How far do you think we've come, Stormy?"

"I would have thought at least fifteen or twenty miles. We've ridden hard all afternoon, but I don't see anything you could call a river anywhere, do you?"

She shaded her eyes to scowl around. "No, but they call some amazing dry ruts rivers in this country. The freight wagons crossed several washes and so-called rivers between Ehrenberg and Prescott, though there wasn't a drop of water in sight. *River* doesn't always mean water here."

"Ain't that the truth," he smiled. He worked

hard to be pleasant, not to let bitterness and anger rule him. He was trying to recapture what he felt was his lost humanity, because his thoughts last night had alarmed him. "We may have to dry-camp tonight if we don't find some kind of a river or at least a spring or creek. Let's go on a while longer." He urged Spot forward.

Ahead lay yet another jumbled pile of rocks the lowering sun painted in amber. Tall pines and a few graceful cottonwoods reared skyward among sycamores and shorter gnarled junipers. Abruptly, behind him, the girl gave a sharp cry of alarm. He jerked around in the saddle to see the mare down and Veracity on all fours, picking herself up out of the dirt. By the time he had hauled Spot in, turned the pinto and cantered back, the girl was standing by Goldie, arms spread and a look of horror on her face.

The mare didn't even try to get up. Her left foreleg was still trapped down in a hole with splintered bones sticking through bloody hide.

"Shit," Hood breathed. "Woah, Spot." To Veracity, he asked as he leaped to the ground, "Are you hurt?"

She shook her head. "No, but . . ." Her hand indicated the mare.

Sean took a firm hold on Spot with his left hand to keep the pony from bolting and pointed with his right to behind Veracity. He yelled, *"Oh, my God, look there!"*

Mouth open and frowning because his tone indicated Indians, rattlesnakes, or a stampede threatening her back, Veracity whirled to look behind her. Before she could turn back, Hood whipped his iron from its holster and put the mare out of her misery.

Veracity stumbled almost as wildly away from the gunshot as Spot did, and jerked around to stare wide-eyed at the dead horse. Sudden anger flushed her cheeks and blazed in her hazel eyes, but then her expression softened. She swallowed, and said, "That was . . . thoughtful of you, Stormy. Thank you."

He calmed the pinto before he tipped his head wryly. "You're welcome. Uh . . . we'll have to leave the saddle, I guess, but let's get the bridle, your bags, canteen, and bedroll."

"Yes." She moved to help him tug her possessions from beneath the carcass and watched him tie them on his own saddle.

He mounted, kicked his foot free of the left stirrup and held a hand down to her. "Get on."

"But riding double is going to slow you down a lot."

"Not as much as you walking. Get on."

She put a foot in the stirrup, grasped his wrist and swung up behind him. As Hood tapped Spot into a trot, she wrapped arms around Sean's waist and said, "Umph."

"What?"

"Oh . . . nothing."

He grinned into eastern distances. "You thought I'd take the first opportunity to get rid of you?"

"I wouldn't have put it past you."

He turned to scowl back over his shoulder at her. "My God, Miss Cooper, I wouldn't leave anyone out here miles from nowhere without a mount . . . except maybe Pratt! What kind of a man do you think I am?"

"I don't *know* what kind of a man you are . . . except innocent of the suspicions against you back east. I've heard that since you left New York, you've been a trail hand, have killed people, have become a brawler . . . uh . . . done just about everything except rob a bank. So . . ." She shrugged.

"Don't believe everything you hear, Miss Cooper."

Her brows rose. "Oh? Then, you *have* robbed a bank?"

"No, I've never robbed a bank, Miss Cooper."

"Veracity."

He had to work hard to return to his efforts at being civil, if not jovial. Presently, he asked, "Veracity what?"

"Louise."

"Tell me about yourself, Veracity Louise. What prompted you to become an extremely unlikely Pinkerton agent?"

She told him about her home in Philadelphia,

about her tomboyish childhood, about her engagement to that pompous ass, Charles Poindexter Brandenberg, and her reasons for breaking their engagement.

At that last, Sean chuckled, and Veracity's eyes widened. She murmured, "That's the first time I've ever heard you *really* laugh, Stormy. You should do it more often. Sounds nice."

His brief humor faded. "I haven't had much reason to laugh over the last few years, Veracity. So how many other times have you run your man down?"

"None. You are my first assignment."

"Really! I'm honored! You must be good at it . . . didn't take you very damn long to locate me."

"Others had paved the way. Narrowed the gap. And, I think maybe it was beginner's luck. Or accident."

Again, he laughed. "I won't tell Pinkerton if you don't."

They rode for another half-hour or forty-five minutes before Hood picked a place to camp for the night. He pulled reins to halt Spot, but the pinto tossed his head, strained against the bit and kept moving.

"Woah, Spot, dammit!"

The paint nickered, slobbered over the bit, and unlike the other times when he'd stopped on a dime at Sean's command, continued onward.

Hood put more force on the reins. *"Woah it, you dumb brute!"*

"Not so dumb brute!" Veracity tapped Sean's shoulder. "Stormy, look down there!"

Hood quit fighting Spot and turned his head to follow Veracity's pointing finger. Then, he whistled and eased-up on the reins. He gave Spot his head and just sat the saddle to let the horse pick his own way to and down the steep cliff-side into what appeared to be a huge sandstone sink bottomed by a broad sheet of water. The calm blue lake was edged-about with floating plants, and on land, a fringe of trees, bushes, and grass. Five ducks whirred skyward at their approach, but settled back to the water's surface before they left the sink.

Hood said softly, "Fresh water and lots of it. Sweet, too, not alkali or full of arsenic like other water holes I've seen."

"How can you tell?"

"Those plants growin' in it. Green plants, not slime or other scum. And there are trees crowding around to sip at it. Flowers over there. Birds makin' use of it. It was poison, this'd be barren all around with maybe a few skeletons of critters too thirst-desperate to take heed, who drank and died. No, that's good water. Besides, Spot, here, has too much sense to head for a death-trap. I have to agree with you, he's no dumb brute."

Again, she grabbed at him and pointed. "Look! Houses!"

"Where?" His hand dropped to his side-arm.

"There! See them there in the shadows under the overhanging rock?"

He relaxed. "Oh, yeah, but they're empty. I've seen their like before. Ancient Indians built them. The people are long-gone."

Spot had made his way to a narrow, grassy bank. He stretched his neck against the reins, needing to drink. Sean dismounted, lifted hands to Veracity and helped her down, then slipped the bit from the pinto's mouth so he would have an easier time watering.

Veracity turned around and around to study the sink walls. "Look, there are more dwellings there and there." When she turned back, she discovered Hood drinking from a tipped canteen. "Why don't you try *that* water?" She nodded at the small lake.

He grinned down at her. "Let's just say I don't trust Spot's taste or my own experience that much. Waitin' to see if he gets a belly-ache. I . . ." He let go of the canteen with one hand to seize Veracity's wrist and shove her arm up. She didn't fire Angel, but glared at him.

Simultaneously, each asked, "What are you doing!"

She said hotly, "I'm hungry! Starving! See

those ducks over there? . . . I was going to shoot one for dinner, that's all!"

"Oh, well, put the gun away. There's something you don't know about Spot—he's the most gun-shy horse I've ever seen. You'd have fired so close to his ear, he'd have ended up twenty feet out in the sink. But if you're that hungry, you just sit here and I'll go get your ducks for you."

She tossed her head. "And how are you going to do that, Mister Hood? Witch them into submission?"

His grin reappeared. "You might say that."

Veracity's mouth opened when he shucked out of his gun belt and hung it over the saddle horn, then sat on a rock to take off his boots and socks. When he stood and began to unbutton his shirt, she gasped, "What are you doing! You can't just undress right here in front of me!"

"I'm going swimming to get your ducks. You wouldn't want me to get my clothes wet, would you?"

"Oh . . . no . . . but . . ."

He shrugged off his shirt and lay it over the stone, dropped his shotgun chaps and began on his belt buckle. "You can leave if you want to, Miss Cooper."

She was flustered. She saw that the bullet wound along his ribs had almost healed now, but didn't mention it; tried, "I . . . uh . . . h-how are you . . . getting the . . . the ducks?"

"Watch." He was down to his underwear now—half-cut long-johns. He draped the pants by his shirt, chaps, and boots, took off his hat, lay it on top of his other clothes, stepped to a nearby bush and broke off a large, well-leafed branch.

Veracity watched him wade silently into the water, slide off a ledge into the deeps, and float the branch. Pushing his cover ahead of him, he began to swim slowly and without splashing across the sink toward the ducks.

The birds wagged tails but didn't take alarm. Some twenty or so feet from them, Hood let go of the branch and sank out of sight under the surface. Watching from the far bank, it seemed to Veracity that nothing happened for so long a time that she leaned forward, frowning. Had Stormy met with some sort of accident? Were there monsters hidden in the dark lake?—she wouldn't put *anything* past *this* country!

Abruptly, two ducks squawked, flapped, and were jerked beneath the surface. The other three began a panicked run across the water away from where their flock-mates had suddenly vanished. Veracity saw Sean come up for air, and sink again. The next time he appeared, he was a good thirty feet closer to her with a drowned duck in each hand.

At the ledge, he wrung the birds' necks for good measure before a wet fowl hit Veracity in the chest when he flung it at her. Holding the second by the legs, he climbed out of the water, dropped the duck at her feet, squeezed his hair back with both hands, and smiled, "Dinner, Miss Cooper. I've done my part, you can clean 'em."

Veracity stared hard at the ducks, partly because Sean's wet underwear clung too revealingly to his body. She began, "Uh . . . I . . . uh . . . you s-seem to have me at a disadvantage, S . . . S . . . Mister Hood. We always h-had a cook at home. I don't know what to do with those birds in their . . . present condition."

His brows rose. "Really! I thought all females were born knowing how to cook."

She flared, "Were you born knowing how to shoot and ride?"

He recalled the terrible trek from St. Louis to Sedalia, Missouri, that had almost killed him. Certainly, he'd already learned to sit a horse, but as a city dweller accustomed to team-drawn trolleys and hansom cabs, his riding had previously been for pleasure—a morning at the local stable or an afternoon canter in the park. He said ruefully, "Well, you've got me there." He cast a quick look at the evening sky where storm clouds had appeared, and finished, "All right, I'll clean one, you follow my lead and fix the other. By the time we're done, you'll know how to butcher a duck. But we'd better hurry. It's getting dark and that looks like rain up there."

"How did you learn to do all this, Stormy?"

"Raw necessity, Miss Cooper . . . raw necessity." Now, he glanced up at the nearest cliff dwellings. "I think we'll evict a few pack rats, rattlesnakes, and scorpions and spend the night indoors tonight."

They skinned and cleaned the ducks. Sean dug a hole with his hunting knife and buried the entrails; then, handed the carcasses to Veracity. "You stay here with Spot while I go up there and see what the inside of one of those cubbyholes looks like." He picked his gun belt from the saddle horn and strapped it on over his still-damp underwear before he padded barefoot up and over rocks. Half-way, he got a thorn in his toe, and below by the pool, Veracity hid a smile as she watched him balance on one foot while he relieved the other of its problem.

Some western desperado, she thought, *standing there in his underwear and gun belt while he picks a sticker from his toe. Ruins his image!* It came to her that she was beginning to like Sean Evan "Stormy" Hood.

Careful, her instincts warned her. Sean Hood was merely a "subject." She was paid to deliver a message to him, and if possible, return him to New York City. Besides, he was only twenty-three. She had just turned twenty-five; she was an "older woman." Any thoughts other than of duty would never do. No, never.

Sean selected the left-end doorway beside a spacious open side-niche, hesitated to bend and peer into the darkness; then, disappeared inside. Almost immediately, two gunshots knocked a shudder of dust from the walls. Below, Veracity made a wild grab for Spot and succeeded in snagging a rein to keep the paint from bolting. She had the horse calmed by the time Hood stuck head and shoulders out the waist-high door and yelled down, "This'll do fine. Bring my clothes, the ducks, and Spot, and come on up."

"Really, I'm not your pack brute, Mister Hood! Come get your clothes and horse yourself!"

"Shit! All right, drape my stuff over the saddle, for Christ's sake, then just bring the birds. Night's comin' on fast, Miss Cooper. We've got to get set up while we still have some light!"

She sighed, flung Hood's shirt, pants, and chaps over Spot's saddle, put the hat on the horn, and was about to stuff Sean's boot tops through a stirrup when Hood yelled, "Hey, Spot! Come on up here, Spot!"

The pinto wheeled away from her and began to lunge up the steep incline toward the cliff dwellings, leaving Veracity standing alone by the lake with Hood's boots in one hand, the waterfowl in the other, and her mouth open.

Sean called, "You coming?"

Saying some quite unladylike things to herself (yes, she had *definitely* spent too much time with sailors and mule skinners!), Veracity followed the horse.

The inside of the cubicle was dark, lighted only by what little fading sun could enter through the low doorway. The walls and ceiling were still blackened with the soot of ancient fires. The room was only some ten or twelve feet long by perhaps eight feet wide, the door offset in the outside wall and a small smoke hole near the overhanging natural sandstone ceiling the only openings. Directly before the door, a rock-lined fire pit dented the floor. To the left, an abandoned *metate* minus its *mano* still sat near the front wall—a headless rattlesnake coiled in its grinding groove.

Just as Sean went out to tether Spot under the broad sheltering shelf at the left of the cubicle, lightning gushed not too far away and a blast of thunder trembled the cliff.

"Gonna rain, boy," he murmured to the horse, "but I think you'll be as dry here as we'll be in there." He removed saddle, bridle, bedrolls and carry-sacks, and toted them into the dwelling to find the ducks keeping clean atop the rattlesnake carcass while Veracity swept the floor with a leafy branch broken from a nearby bush. "What are you doing, setting up housekeeping?"

She smiled at him. "Why not? No sense in living in . . . um . . . squalor . . . if one can do otherwise. Would you *please* put some clothes on! What will the neighbors think!"

He laughed (he was beginning to like this Veracity Louise Cooper, Pinkerton Agent), dumped the saddle and bedrolls in a cleaned corner and felt the cloth over a thigh. "I think I'm about done. I'll dress for dinner. White tie and tails?"

"Not until after the squab is cooked." She jumped when the dwelling interior was lighted by another brilliant flash of lightning. When the thunder had died down, she whisked debris out the door and turned back to ask, "Stormy, is there any possibility of us staying here a couple of days? I don't know about you, but I have been traveling for months, and I'm tired. Besides, while *you* are clean, I, on the other hand . . ." She picked at her split skirt distastefully. "I had a good bath in Prescott, but I had to put my same old dirty clothes back on, and I'd like to wash them and take another bath before we go . . . unless you're in a real rush?"

He had removed his gun belt and was slipping into his pants. "Why didn't you change clothes in town?"

"I don't have any others and no . . ." She turned to look outside. "Uh . . . I'll get fuel for the fire before it starts to rain."

He paused, shirt in hand. "And no money to buy more? But Veracity, you carried my thousand dollars."

"But it was *your* money! I couldn't use it!"

She bent and vanished out the door, leaving him standing with his mouth open.

She'd had a thousand dollars in her possession for two or three weeks, yet had gone without simply because the money wasn't hers? Well! Once, in a long-ago lifetime, he wouldn't have given it a second thought; these days, to discover a scrupulously honest person was an amazement. Hastily, he donned his shirt, tucked in the tail, let his chaps lay and slapped his gun belt around his hips. He buckled the belt, tied down the holster, slipped into his socks and boots and was dressed by the time Veracity returned. Her arms were loaded with branches and deadwood.

It behooved him to be as considerate of her as she'd been of him. "Yes."

She lifted brows at him as she dropped the wood. "Yes . . . what?"

"Yes, we can stay here a couple of days. We can rest, you can launder your clothes, and . . ." He shrugged. "We have food, water, shelter thanks to the ancient Indians . . . I don't see why not."

"Thank you, Stormy. I need it."

Outside, the thick clouds rushed the darkness. He started the fire, then broiled the ducks while she watched him, and tonight, he was *aware* that she watched him. They ate in dry comfort with lightning flaring across the sky, thunder booming, and rain pouring in solid sheets from off the cliff overhang outside the door. When she spread

171

his bedroll at one end of the cubicle, hers at the other, though he didn't object to the arrangement, *tonight,* he found he was still human after all.

Damn it, he thought long after they had each bedded down separately, he with his pistol and Sharps handy, she with her derringer and Avenging Angel within instant reach, why couldn't that woman sleeping over there have been a ready-and-willing calico queen instead of a proper Philadelphia Pinkerton agent? Tonight, he needed some feminine companionship . . . *oh, Lord,* how he needed!

But he didn't do anything about it except watch lightning strike beyond the door and again wonder why all this had happened to him. The storm was over before he got to sleep.

The morning dawned clear, the storm clouds long-gone on their way south or east or to whatever their ultimate destiny. Early sun streamed into the tiny, ancient dwelling to light it with a wake-up glow. Outside, everything appeared washed clean, the greens greener, the broken cliff faces edging the sandstone sink more purely amber or white, the surface of the well unruffled blue, but Sean awoke with heart hammering and hands reaching for his side-arm and buffalo gun, because a shot shattered the last of his sleep. His eyes flashed open to see Veracity standing by the door. He froze half-lifted onto one arm when he focused on the weapon still pointed at him.

"Don't move, Stormy!" Scowling, Veracity took a step or two closer to him.

What the hell? Was she trying to take him prisoner or something? But then, he shifted his eyes from her to the floor beside his hip.

She said, "I nearly suffered a seizure when I saw that rattlesnake coiled there beside you. I had to startle it enough to get it to lift its head so I could shoot it, not you. Are you all right?"

He gasped, *"Huh!"* before he lunged upright and staggered back against the wall. "Yes! Jesus, I didn't even know the damned thing was there!"

"That's three times, now." She tucked Angel under her belt and smiled at him.

He looked from the snake to her. "Three . . . what?"

"Times that I've rescued you. Ummm . . . I heard from Mister Axt that rattlesnakes are really quite good eating. We have cold left-over duck for breakfast, or if you'll start a fire, we can roast the snakes. We have two of them . . . one each."

He pulled himself together. "Yeah. Whatever you want. Anything is fine with me." Watching the girl as she stepped to the door and looked out, he sat down beside the snake, shook out his boots and put them on.

"Oh, it's a *beautiful* day out there!"

Hood saw her bend, noted the well-rounded behind the skirt material outlined when fabric stretched over her backside, and a grim line appeared beside his mouth. Yes, he had been too damn long without a woman, hadn't he.

He dragged his eyes away, rose, joined her out on the walkway beyond the door, and it was as she had said . . . a fine, clear day.

She stretched arms against the sky before she sighed deeply and fluffed her hair, an unconscious but profoundly feminine gesture.

He abruptly turned away and went to check Spot.

They breakfasted on left-over duck—saved the snakes for later—then, she asked, "Do you have an old shirt I can borrow?"

"Why?"

"You wouldn't want me to run around stark naked while I'm washing my clothes, would you?"

Yes, his mind said to him before he could stop it. But he only nodded, rose, and went to his saddle bags. He fished out a new blue shirt—and for the first time, recalled that he'd left clothes behind in the Prescott bathhouse and laundry—and handed it to her. Asked, "Want britches, too?"

She shook the shirt out and held it up to herself. She was a small woman; the hem came almost to her knees. "No, this'll do fine. Do you have anything you want washed while I'm at it?"

"No, thank you."

He watched her drape the shirt over her arm,

smile at him; then, turn and start down the steep decline toward the water. When she reached the edge, she continued on past floating water plants until she found a barely-sunken ledge. She vanished behind a bush. Presently, she reappeared barefoot and wearing his shirt, her own clothing bunched in her arms.

He hunkered down in the shade and hoped she wouldn't notice him watching her. Somehow, seeing her small form down there crouched ankle-deep in clear water, her figure outlined by cliffs and the deep blue lake, the sun sparkling in her fair hair made him forget she was a Pinkerton agent paid to pursue him. She became merely a pretty young woman washing clothes in a primitive setting, and he knew that if this kept up, he would either have to try to talk her into lying down with him or abandon her for her own safety.

She had her shirt and split skirt washed now, and had draped them over nearby bushes to sun-dry. She started on her white under-things. Even as Sean watched, one garment escaped her and began to float out toward the center of the well. On hands and knees, she leaned forward to make a grab for it, her hand slipped and she did an ungraceful nosedive off the ledge.

Hood grinned. That would make both Veracity *and* her clothes clean. Even if she hadn't intended to take a bath, she was getting one.

But then, he saw her surface once and flail arms at the water. Her fingers clawed toward the sandstone shelf she couldn't quite reach before she sank again. He bounded to his feet as his brain warned him: *That damn girl doesn't know how to swim!*

He scrambled down the slope, bolted around the edge of the pool until he reached Veracity's clothes hanging from the bush, dropped his gun belt, ripped off his boots, flung his hat aside, and waded out onto the shelf to search the water for some sign of her.

It was deep here—he had no idea how far down the sink went, but when he, himself, had gone after the ducks yesterday, he'd felt the gentle tug of lower currents as if this well filled and emptied through hidden subterranean channels. If those currents were strong here . . .

There! He glimpsed a hand flash like the side of a rainbow trout about six feet away and some three feet under the surface. Unmindful of hidden stones or up-jutting tree stumps, he flung himself toward it, grabbed blindly for her wrist, and caught her hair instead.

She came into the air gasping, choking, wide-eyed and terrified, and sank him when she wrapped arms and legs around him. In her desperation to stay above the surface, she nearly drowned him, but he made it back to the ledge, dragged her up onto it; then, with her still clinging to him, turned to sit in the six-inch-deep water over the stone shelf.

Her arms were hard around him while she coughed water from her lungs. He returned the embrace, instinctively rubbed her back, and whispered, "It's all right. I've got you. You're all right, now."

She choked in his ear, "Th-thank you . . . thank you . . ." She didn't unwrap her arms from around his neck. He didn't try to untangle himself. But then, she pushed back slightly to frown at him when he said, "That's twice *I've* rescued *you,* now. And if you don't let go, you're gonna need rescuing again, this time from *me.*"

"T-Twice? No, that's o-once." She made a valiant effort to compose herself.

He chuckled. "No, that's twice. Who do you think walloped those soldiers who were after you in Prescott while you were on your way from the Palace to the hotel?"

"You? That was y-you?"

"Um-hmmm." His arms tightened around her.

"Thank you! Oh, Stormy, I can't swim, and I was s-so scared. . . ." She again pressed her cheek to his.

He continued to hold her. He held her for a long time, but now it was only to comfort, because despite what he'd said, the emergency had overshadowed all else.

• • •

Oscar Pratt and his gaggle of hardcases had come upon a stroke of luck. As they passed the ramshackle falling-down stockade that was Fort Whipple just two miles down the road from Prescott, they were nearly run over by a troop of cavalrymen cantering briskly out the gates and off in an easterly direction. While Pratt and crew hurriedly reined aside to let the soldiers pass, the bounty hunter noted a guard at post.

He nudged his black gelding in the boy's direction and inquired, "Where dey off to in such a hurry? Injun trouble out dere?"

"No," the private responded, "they're headed for rotation at Fort Verde."

"Ya don' say." Pratt rubbed chin-stubble. "Dey got any objections to company?"

The private shook his head. "I s'pose you could tag along, you keep up and don't get in their way. You goin' to Verde?"

"We is!" Oscar wheeled his mount, flapped an arm at his men, and pursued the cavalry. So it was that he and his hired killers got what amounted to an army escort all the way to their destination.

CHAPTER NINE

While he was still wet, Hood swam out to retrieve Veracity's bloomers from where they floated on the sinkhole lake surface; then, sat nearby, still only in his underwear, while both he and his clothes dried. He needed to be close at hand should his rescue services again be needed.

Veracity finished her washing before she perched on the rock beside him for a long while. At first, they merely sat in silence, each with their own thoughts, staring at the water, wordless but oddly *together.* Finally, he asked, "How did you plan to return east? Stagecoach? Railroad?"

"I hadn't thought that far ahead. I had no idea where I would be when I found you . . . *if* I found you."

"I think I recall you saying you came from the west. How'd you get there?"

"By ship." She told him of her journey across the Isthmus of Panama, and in the telling, it became funny high adventure instead of a trial.

They laughed together. Once, she reached over to take his hand, held it in both of hers until she looked up to see his dark eyes watching her steadily. And he wore the oddest expression . . .

She hurriedly dropped his hand; blurted, "What?"

He looked away quickly. "Nothing. Nothing. I was just thinking of . . . Elaine. Wondering if she hates me or waits for me. Trying to picture her here instead of you . . . having arrived as you did, and . . ."

"I'm sorry I'm not Elaine, Sean. I see you love her deeply."

He made a small bitter sound. "No, you don't understand. *Once,* I was . . . taken with her, yes. But now it seems I see her in a different light.

"She is . . . was . . . prettier than you, perhaps. Dark brown hair. Blue eyes. About your height, maybe. Possibly a little plumper. But . . . I don't know . . . *frivolous.* Everything was a joke to her. Constantly going to parties and teas and . . . laughing. No, *giggling.* Perpetual laughter can be as . . . irritating, long-term, I suppose, as constant gloom. I can't imagine her coming west by ship or coach or by any other means, much less *alone.* No, when I look at you, Veracity Louise, Elaine . . . suffers greatly by comparison."

Veracity studied him for almost as long a moment as he had looked at her before she murmured seriously, "Thank you, Stormy. That was a fine compliment. And may I say, Charles Poindexter Brandenberg can't hold a candle to you, either, even though he's about ten years older than you. When is your birthday?"

His brows rose. "Don't you know? Wasn't that in your records on me?"

"If it was, I've forgotten."

"December tenth. Born eighteen fifty-one, in the midst of the worst early snowstorm the region had seen in decades. And you?"

She lowered her eyes and smiled, "Now, Stormy, one never asks a woman her age. Bad form."

At that, he grinned. "An older woman, eh?"

"Certainly not!" Bright color bloomed in her cheeks. "My birthday is May twenty-fifth."

"What year?"

"Sean, I'm not going to tell you that!"

He reached to grab at her. His grin broadened further as he began to tickle ribs. "What year?"

"Stormy! Sean! Quit that!" Also laughing, she tried to squirm away.

"What year?"

"All right, darn it! Eighteen fifty-one! I *am* an older woman . . . *from May to December older!*" That was a lie, but she wouldn't confess it was a year and seven months.

He stopped tickling, but still held her, and when she met his eyes, her woman's instincts saw what hid there—not lust, but a need for human contact, for someone to love, for a soft hand to heal a mortally wounded soul. Instead of pulling away, she slipped her own arms around him and buried her face in his shoulder. "Oh, Sean, I'm so sorry all this has happened to you. You deserve far better. It's to your credit that you've survived as well as you have—it would have destroyed some men.

"Come on . . ." she gave him a motherly peck on the cheek and became brisk, ". . . we're dry now. Let's get dressed and go exploring. I want to see what is in those caves over there."

He held her a few seconds longer before he breathed a deep, shaking sigh, released her, and asked, "You all right?"

"Yes. I'm fine now. Thank you." She leaped up, grabbed her clothes from over the bushes and vanished behind a thicker clump to dress.

He said, "Oooo-kay," and also dressed.

They meandered around the sink perimeter, on the lookout for rattlesnakes, and instead, found flint arrowheads and an exquisite pinkish seashell long-ago carved into a bird-shape and garnished with many small rectangular pieces of turquoise, but without a thong. Hood smiled to himself as he held the artifact in his palm. "This looks like a gift to a lady. Hmph." He tucked it in his shirt pocket before they passed onward.

More caverns pierced the sandstone down fairly close to the waterline, and inside in the darkness, they could see that the ancients had also constructed dwellings among the nooks and crannies. Veracity started to enter, but Sean grabbed her arm to hold her back.

"Don't go in there, Veracity. There's something wrong with that cave."

She frowned up at him. "What makes you think so?" Then, she leaned away to smile, "What . . . are you afraid of old curses or the ghosts of witch doctors?"

"No, but look over there." He nodded to where a contorted, desiccated carcass lay on the floor of the cave by the far wall.

Veracity bent to peer into the dimness. "What is it?"

"I think it was once a bobcat, but who knows? And look . . . there's what might be a squirrel. Another over there. There is a coyote. All of them long dead but not decayed, and *uneaten* . . . as though no other animals dared go in there. I know it's arid around here, but they dried up without rotting. . . ."

"As though there is no air there. Or the air that *is* there is poisonous. Uh . . . I hear that coal miners take little caged birds down into the mines with them to check for bad air because the bird dies before they do if there is something wrong that men can't see or smell. Do you suppose . . . ?"

"Whatever, I think we'd better not chance it. There are a lot of other things to see, and, if you're up to it this afternoon, I can teach you to swim down there."

She backed out of the cave. "No! No, thank you! I've had enough water for the time being!"

That afternoon, storm clouds again built into

the sky, for the desert rainy season pounded the high plains as well as the lowlands. While Veracity leaned against the side of the old stone-and-mud wall beneath the overhanging ledge and watched lightning shatter against the land, Sean sat in the doorway to their cubicle and created a necklace from the turquoise-embellished pink shell bird and a saddle-tie thong. When he was done, he presented it to her. "The crown jewels, m'lady."

She blushed furiously when he tied the string around her neck, fingered the shell and smiled, "Thank you, Stormy. It's lovely. It makes me feel like I'm . . . *part* of this place, y'know? Like I belong here."

"Assembled by my own hands. You . . . do it proud."

She removed her red bandana to show the necklace off to better advantage, rolled the cloth and bound her hair back with it. "We have to go onward tomorrow, Stormy. Or tonight."

"Why?" He was beginning to like it here, just the two of them in this hidden haven.

She looked uncomfortable. "We . . . need to go on, that's all. We should move along tomorrow morning, at least."

Now, he understood. She was also getting to like it too much. He said, "Y'know that valley we rode through to get here? Lots of grass. There seems to be water enough. Doesn't appear that anyone owns it, even though it's a great place to run cattle. Maybe . . . when this is all over, I'll come back here and . . ." he flashed a grin at her, ". . . set up housekeeping. Relax, Miss Cooper. You're safe with me."

Still fingering the shell bird, she murmured, "I never thought I wasn't."

Like hell, he thought, chuckled, but didn't say anything else for a long while. He wouldn't have been heard in any case, for the storm thickened, thunder crashed, and an abrupt deluge drove them into their shelter.

It took the cavalry (and therefore, also Pratt and company) two full days of hard riding to arrive at Fort Verde. The bounty hunters stayed overnight in a camp they set up at the edge of the army compound, huddled soggily in the rain beneath makeshift, broken-branch lean-tos.

The next morning, they began their inquiries as to whether or not the soldiers or civilian personnel there had seen anyone resembling Sean Hood or Veracity Cooper. They heard a unanimous no, and eventually squatted by their horses to cogitate the situation.

Pratt said, "Dem dere miners we heard seen 'em, come from up north, din't dey. Okay, den maybe Hood an' dat petticoat is still north of us an' is headed down dis way. We got two choices; we can suck our thumbs here an' just wait fer 'em to show, or we can ride north an' try to find 'em somewheres up dere."

Wooster Stokes, one of his hirelings, said, "We wait an' let 'em git here, we cain't do our job with all them army boys lookin' on. They'd put the kibosh on us scraggin' 'em, fer sure. I say we git out in the free areas where there's no witnesses."

"Yeh know dis country?" Pratt asked.

"Some. The Verde River goes on north of here an' meets Wet Beaver Creek up yonder. Not much up there but rocks an' ol' Injun cliff dwellin's. Good ambush country. *Damn* good ambush country."

Oscar looked around at the others. "Anybody got any odder suggestions?"

They shook heads. One said, "Sounds good. I don't wantta do somebody, the army lookin' on, neither."

"Den, it's a go."

"Uh . . . gotta ask ya somethin', Pratt," Sam Peavy said. "Curiosity's killin' me. Whut's that gawdamn hatbox fer?"

Oscar chuckled nastily. "De gent by de name of *George* Hood who hired me t'do Stormy Hood wants proof de job's done. I mean, he ain't gonna jus' take me word fer it, y'know? So, I'm gonna take Hood's head back wit me, an' dat dere hatbox is jus' de right size to hold it."

Laughter exploded among the six men, but it was more from startlement than humor. They rolled eyes at each other—that was a bit much, even for them. Nevertheless, the promise of fifty dollars was a promised fifty dollars, and when Pratt cast a squint at the sky, said, " 'Bout ten o'clock. Day's young. Le's go," mounted up and rode out, this time northeast along the banks of the Verde, they again followed.

Sean and Veracity left their sanctuary early in the morning, riding double down the sandy banks beside the creek they'd located just beyond the sandstone sink. Water seemed to flow in the direction they wanted to go, the land around them became widened meadows peppered with sycamores and tall swaying cottonwood trees, and the traveling was easy.

After their two-day rest, neither felt any immediate need to hurry. They rode in silence for the most part, her arms around him, her cheek occasionally resting against his shoulder, each of them quiet . . . oddly *comfortable.* And Hood was profoundly glad nothing had happened between them to ruin this growing feeling of friendship. No, he thought, it was more than merely friend-ship—it was a *companionship* like that of two people who belonged together.

About mid-morning, he woah'ed Spot and turned to say softly over his shoulder, "Veracity, look up there."

They had gone some six or seven miles southward, merely following the creek's meander. High above in the rugged pale-beige and almost-white sandstone barrier that bordered one side of the creek, nearly a hundred feet up, a huge cavern pierced the cliffs. Spread from wall-to-cavern-wall, and built into the depression like a medieval castle blocking a fjord, stood an elegant, multi-faceted tan structure.

"Oh, my!" she gasped. "I've never seen anything like that! Look, there are ladders running up from level to level, but it's empty, isn't it? . . . like the place we stayed last night? Oh, Stormy, can we stop, please, and go inside?"

He nudged Spot onward, across the creek toward the ruins. "Curious lady, aren't you. You really like poking around in other people's houses."

"Maybe that's why I became a detective. Oh, Sean, once we leave here, I may never have an opportunity to see such a thing again. Please, can we go in?"

To go forward, to put the horrendous trip home behind him, to discover who it really was who had placed a price on his head, the need to live again as an un-hunted man nearly made him say: No, we have to press onward. But then, he thought: What can an hour hurt?

He nodded and halted the pinto. "All right. We'll leave Spot here by the creek and let him graze. There's good green grass, lots of water . . ."

Out of habit, he pulled his Sharps from its scabbard, moved a handful of shells from his saddlebags into his shirt pocket, threw a leg over, dismounted, and held a hand up to Veracity.

Her eyes still glued to the impressive cliff house, she also slid to the ground. "Isn't it beautiful! When I was in Sunday school, the minister declared that the world is only some four thousand years old . . . that by calculating the lengths of lives and number of generations in the Bible, it was proven that the Earth and Adam and Eve were created then, but . . ." she shook her head, ". . . I don't know, even that seems . . . older. Do you suppose different areas of the world came into being at separate times rather than all at once?"

His brows lifted. "I wouldn't know. For a woman, you think of odd things, don't you."

"What do you mean by that? Aren't women supposed to have imaginations?"

"I meant nothing! Nothing!" He lifted both hands as though she pointed a gun at him. "But most women I know . . . knew . . . only think about housekeeping and babies and . . ."

"Now, you sound like Charles!"

"Who?"

"Charles Poindexter Brandenberg, my ex-fiance."

"Oh, him." Stormy took his binoculars case out of a saddlebag and slung the strap over his shoulder beside the Sharps before he grinned at the girl. "Well, if Charles asked *you* to marry him, he must have exceptionally good judgment, so don't think I'll be insulted."

That totally disarmed Veracity. With nothing left to be huffy about, she again turned her attention to the cliff dwelling.

As they headed across river-bottom land that may in ages past have been the garden plots of the castle residents, she asked, "Aren't you going to tie Spot to something? Should he run off . . ."

Sean turned and ordered, "Spot . . . stay!"

The pinto lifted his head, looked in Hood's direction, and blew nostrils before he resumed cropping grass.

"I swear, that horse is as good as a dog," Veracity noted. "How did you ever train him to such obedience?"

"I didn't. He was that way when I traded my worn-out horse for him in Ehrenberg, but I'd give a hundred bucks to know who owned him before me. Here, I think we go this way."

They had reached the brush-guarded, jumbled-stone base of the cliff. To their right were several small cubicles whose doorways were reminiscent of the dwelling they had used at the well; upon investigation, they found the insides cramped, barren, and uninteresting. They had an easy climb up the rough horizontally-striated wall to where the first rickety ladder stood, and Sean observed, "This isn't ancient. Look, it's put together with metal nails. Someone has been here before us. Still, let me go first to see how safe it is."

Holding her breath (and once again wondering if there wasn't something rather obscene about a Pinkerton agent having such a good time while on a case), Veracity watched while he climbed the bending swaying ladder. He steadied the top until she made it up to the wide ledge there; then, with dark caverns at their elbows, they moved to their left toward the next ladder. This one was merely two long poles with round leather-lashed sticks separating them.

"I don't like the looks of that," Hood frowned. "That *is* old. It might collapse at the slightest touch."

"I'm smallest and lightest. Let me try." Before he could stop her, Veracity grasped the poles and started up. At the top, she looked down at him. "It's stronger than it seems. Come on!"

Swearing under his breath, and not liking this at all, he nevertheless followed. He could feel ancient tethers creak under his weight and expected something to give way at any second, but somehow the primitive ladder held until he stepped over onto the sandstone to join the girl.

They were now at the base of the constructed buildings, and Veracity had already started onward to find an entrance. Sean paused to look around. From this height, he had a commanding view of the valley—the creek almost became a river out there as it S-curved among cotton-woods, sycamores, ash trees, and shorter brushy mesquite, creosote, and other shrubs. Off on the horizon reared a ridge of dark hills.

"Look what I found! Do you have a lucifer?"

He did—he always carried a few matches in his binoculars case because the glasses were the last things he would allow to get wet if he could help it. Veracity had discovered a grass-wrapped stick, a modern torch someone had left leaning against the wall just inside a doorway.

This first room was small, but contained T-shaped openings to the rear and left, and a square hole in the ceiling that could be reached by a short sturdy pole-and-branch ladder. Above their heads, foot-thick sycamore logs and mud-sealed reeds formed what was the ceiling of this room and obviously, the floor of the next, above.

Sean didn't flame the torch in these outer rooms because enough light to see by streamed through rectangular windows, but as they delved deeper into the dwelling, darkness became an eerie weight, oppressive with age and a strange sickly-sweet odor. At the flare of his lucifer, something rustled overhead with the sound of silk crumpling, and Veracity gasped, "Oh!" for bats hung from the ceiling like twitching clusters of black grapes.

They moved onward through the arid dark-ness, mostly in silence, until Sean said, "Veracity, look here." His fingers traced a carving in one of the ceiling-support logs; torchlight picked out the words: *Pedro Garcia, 1541.* "Cortez . . . no, *Coronado!* Francisco Coronado's men came here over three hundred years ago! Three hundred and thirty-three years, to be exact!"

She breathed, "Isn't that something! To think we're walking where those early explorers did! I wonder if the Indians still lived here then?"

"I wouldn't know. I know *I* sure wouldn't want to live here full-time, especially not in these inside rooms. Look," he held the torch closer to the wall, "you can see the imprints of the builders' fingers there where they smoothed their mud-plaster, can't you. But look how smoke has blackened the walls. There's no ventilation hole. With no way to escape, smoke would fill up this place damn quickly, wouldn't it."

Veracity pointed at another large square hole in the ceiling. "Let's say your upstairs neighbors could become *smoked hams* if you weren't careful. It paid to be on good terms with those who lived below you." She mounted that ladder and disappeared into the darkness beyond. Presently, she bent to reach back for the torch.

Sean handed it up to her and climbed the ladder to join her. They counted seventeen rooms before they came out onto a sort of walled balcony whose thick railing was pierced with what might be called "windows."

"Well, what do you think of that!" Hood had snuffed the torch and was peering through the holes. "This is a defensive-fortress setup, Veracity. If you look through this window, you see the top of that ledge yonder. That one points down into the valley at the left, that one at the center, and so on." He moved onward. "This one targets those cliff tops to the right. Whoever lived here could keep eyes out for attackers and stay safe behind their thick walls while they shot arrows or threw spears at . . ." He lunged for her, seized her arm and dragged her down below the railing.

She began, *"Stormy, what . . . ?"*

"Hush! Sit still a minute." He let go of her and opened his binoculars case. Making use of an ancient Indian's brilliant architectural scheme, he focused the glasses through a slanted aperture. Presently, he breathed, "Pratt."

Veracity leaned close to also peer out the hole. Without glasses, all she could see were several riders approaching along the creek from the south. "Pratt? Are you sure?"

"Here, look for yourself." He handed her the glasses.

She adjusted them to her eyes. "Oh, darn, you're right! And he's got two . . . four . . . *six!* . . . six men with him! What do you suppose he is doing here? He should already be headed back to New York to earn the ten thousand dollars you ffered him to identify the man who hired him."

"I don't know what he's doing here, but you can bet he's up to no good." Hood grabbed the glasses back from Veracity and shifted to another viewpoint. "Shit! Spot is in plain sight down there. If we lose that horse, we're in deep trouble." He bit his lip for a moment before he handed the binoculars back to the girl, slipped out of the strap and set the case on the ancient adobe. As he picked the Sharps also off his shoulder, Veracity said, "*Darn!* I'm so *sorry, Stormy!* If I hadn't insisted on exploring this place, we . . ."

"We might have ridden right into them." He shoved the buffalo gun at her; picked shells from his shirt pocket. "Ever fire one of these?"

"A rifle—a Remington—yes. Occasionally, a shotgun. Never a Sharps. Why?"

"You stay here and cover me. Here . . ." Hurriedly, he dumped a small container out of the glasses case and unscrewed the top. There were twelve sulphur matches left. He took six, put six back into the cylinder and closed it. "You keep the torch. I'll light my way out with these. I'll go get Spot, leave your saddlebags and canteen . . . uh . . . over there at the base of that big cottonwood, see it? Then, Spot and I will vanish into the underbrush until Pratt and those other men are gone, all right?"

"No! Not all right! They're too close, Stormy!

By the time you make it out of here, they'll be right on top of you!"

"Veracity, if they see Spot and take him with them, we'll have to walk all the way to Fort Verde or back to Prescott, and the longer we argue, the closer they're getting. They don't know we're here. If I dump your belongings, even if they should waylay me, they won't know *you're* here. You are my ace in the hole, okay?" He grinned at her. "Just remember, that Sharps has a powerful kick." Before she could offer further objections, he turned on hands and knees, rose to a crouch and headed back into the ancient ruin.

"What'll I do if you don't come back?"

His muffled voice replied from the darkness, "Follow the creek to Fort Verde."

"Sean? *Sean?*" This time, there was no answer.

Hood used up five of his six lucifers before he found his way back down to the level where the highest outside ladder leaned against the rough stone and mud wall, and it was a ghostly, confusing passage lit only by a tiny flame. Grateful to again be outside, he eased carefully down the ladder, stepped gingerly on the frail rungs, and breathed a sigh of relief when he reached the lower shelf, because the final ladder was modern and more strongly built. Still, his major worry *was* that last ladder, for it passed over the face of the cliff and was well exposed to the eyes of anyone who happened to be looking in his direction.

Gritting teeth, he scrambled along the ledge to that ladder and hurriedly descended. Before him was the un-brushed broken riprap; then, the fringe of bushes. When he made it to the ground and over the rocks, he pushed through mesquite to the meadow, but crouched out of sight there before he called, "Spot! Hey, Spot! Come here, boy!"

The pinto lifted his head and looked in Hood's direction.

"Come here, Spot! Come to me, boy . . . come on!"

Reins dragging, the horse nickered and trotted his way. Sean waited until the pinto was fairly close before he rose and dashed out to meet him. He caught reins, vaulted into the saddle, and started to kick Spot northward when a distant voice yelled, "Hey, *hombre*, wait a minute!"

Hood turned his head to look behind him. Pratt and his six men were closing on him fast. At this point, they didn't know who he was, but obviously wanted to talk to him. He had two choices. If he stayed to face them, Pratt would shortly recognize him, and then he might have to try to best seven men in an open gunfight. His second choice was to run, try to get them to pursue, lead them away from Veracity who was essentially trapped up there in the ruins, then lose them, circle back, pick her up and head for Ft. Verde in earnest.

He lifted a hand to wave an acknowledgment to the approaching men as though merely saying hello, whirled Spot and urged him into a canter northward, back toward the great sandstone sink. But Pratt scowled, "Hey, I wantta talk to dat dere geezer." He grabbed his side-arm and fired as he shouted to his men, "Bring dat bastard down!"

High above, Veracity watched through Hood's binoculars. Her fingers whitened on the glasses when she saw Stormy duck a hail of bullets, but then fling arms up and plunge from Spot's back. Spooked by the gunfire, the riderless horse was driven into a panicked flight into the brush along the creek bed.

Heart pounding, she lowered the glasses and seized the Sharps. Now using its sight as a telescope, she watched the seven men ride up, dismount and converge on Stormy. She saw two bend and confiscate Hood's side-arm and hunting knife before they grabbed his arms and lifted him to his feet. She could tell by Sean's unsteadiness that he'd been hit, and her mind swirled under multiple questions—what should she do? . . . what should she *not* do now? . . . what . . .

But then, she saw Pratt raise his weapon and point it dead-on at Hood's forehead, and instinct took over. Without hesitation, she drew a careful bead on the bounty hunter. Above her, countless cave swallows were startled from their nests when she squeezed the trigger.

CHAPTER TEN

Sean was woozy and seeing double when he tried to shove himself up. He didn't make it. The bullet that had creased his jaw just below his right ear had knocked him out of the saddle, impact with the ground had driven breath from his lungs, and between the two assaults, his body wouldn't respond fast enough to get him to his feet before the oncoming riders reached him.

He tried to pull his side-arm to defend himself as horses circled him and men leaped from saddles, but it seemed to him that his hand was imbedded in cold molasses. The newcomers snagged his iron and knife before he could reach them; stood around him grinning down at him.

Blood hot on his neck became wet and sticky in his collar when hands seized his arms and shirt and hauled him upright. He strained to focus on the face wavering before him, but knew before he could really see that it was Pratt.

The New York longshoreman jammed the muzzle of his six-shooter against the bridge of Sean's nose and grated, "Gotcha! Two years, I been doggin' youse, and now I gotcha, yeh slippery bastard!" He laughed almost wildly, a harsh mixture of triumph and malice. "It's been one gawdamn long trail, but now youse is mine!

Finally mine!" He snapped to the others, "Hold 'im!" before he leaped back to his mount and yanked the hatbox from its saddle ties.

The inside of Sean's head swirled briefly before his thoughts sharpened and solidified. He could still feel the hard impression of warm steel against his skin as he blinked to focus on what Oscar now thrust at him—a large green-and-red-flowered cardboard hatbox.

Pratt held the box up beside Hood's face; turned it horizontally and vertically before he chortled, "It fits. It's big enough! By Gawd, it'll do!"

"Do what, Oscar?" Hood had re-gathered enough wit now to be able to talk coherently, though those few words pained his jaw.

Pratt whopped the box against the side of Stormy's skull. "Take yer head back east. I'm gonna leave d'rest of youse here fer d'vultures, but yer *head* goes to George Hood, yessir, it do, an' den I gets me reward!" He flung the box aside and again shoved his pistol barrel against Hood, this time over his heart. "Dere oughtta do it. Don' wantta mess up yer pretty face. Mister Hood's gotta be able to recognize yer phizog, now, don' he."

Sean's jaw stabbed him when he gritted teeth before he glanced at the others gathered around him. Two held his arms tightly. Two pointed battered side-arms at him. The other two merely stood by smirking. It was an untidy crew of strong arms and hired guns. He gasped, "Yeah, you finally caught me, Oscar, but you needed lots of help to do it, didn't you. How much are you paying these flunkies? They come cheap or do you have to share part of your five thousand dollars with them?" If he could just foment a little dissension in their ranks, maybe during the resulting argument, he could . . .

"Five thousan' dollars!" one of the hardcases scowled to Pratt. "You din't . . ." His words stuck in his throat and they all jumped when a bullet barely missed Oscar and blew a large hole through Deep-dirt Mo Smith.

Up on the ancient balcony, Veracity moaned. Legs splayed before her, she got back up onto her elbows before she choked to herself, "Get up . . . get up . . ." Stormy had warned her that the Sharps had a powerful kick, but she hadn't been prepared for its actual force—it felt like she, herself, had been shot.

The boom of the buffalo gun echoed and reechoed. "Where th' hell'd that come from?" Wooster Stokes croaked. He looked wildly at the cliffs, at bushes and trees. Sound bouncing around the valley from cliff faces and standing rocks made it all but impossible to locate the shootist until Bronco Barnes spotted blue smoke puffed against dark shadows of deep cavern recesses high above in the cliff dwelling.

He shouted, "Jeez . . . up there! This *hombre*'s got friends! Let's get the hell outta here!"

Up on the main balcony, now that she'd started this, Veracity got back to her knees, jammed another cartridge into the Sharps, sighted and fired again. That bullet sent Hiram Kuest to the ground with a fist-sized hole in his chest. The others jerked guns up and returned fire, peppering ancient walls with bullets. The deadly hail made Veracity hunker down behind the solid balcony for a moment.

In the brief following lull, Sean thought: *My God, that girl IS a dead shot!* Blood from the nick Pratt's bullet had cut at the edge of his jaw still ran down his neck and soaked his shirt, but his head had cleared now and he was less wounded than when the healed crease along his ribs had been fresh. He said urgently to Pratt's men, "Yes, I have friends here. Look, this wasn't your fight to begin with. Who are you . . . hired guns? Has Pratt already paid you? If so, you can just forget this whole . . ." Blood sprang from his nose when Pratt leaped forward and hit him.

Oscar's movement caused Veracity's next shot to breeze between him and Bronco Barnes, the first time she'd missed hitting someone. Billy Haig and Sam Peavy, who held Sean's arms, squawked alarm and crowded behind their prisoner to use him as a shield. Pratt, Stokes, and Barnes saw what they were doing and joined the others behind Hood, but Oscar jammed his side-arm barrel against the back of Stormy's head, looked up toward the run, and bellowed, "One more shot and dis bastard's vulture meat! Hold yer fire else he goes down! Whoever youse is, youse got dat?"

There was no verbal answer. Neither were more shots fired, but it had little to do with Pratt's threat. The enormity of what she had done crashed into Veracity. She huddled on the floor and leaned against the old adobe, the Sharps slanted between her drawn-up knees and her stomach, both hands pressed tightly over her mouth, wide eyes staring blindly at the back gape of the cavern above. She had just killed two men . . . tried to kill a third. She had never killed anyone before, *ever,* but now . . . The knowledge overwhelmed her. Weak and dizzy, she lowered her face to her knees and began to cry.

Down below, Sean continued to be used as a meager shield by the men retreating toward the brush by the creek. Two still held his arms tightly behind him while the others—their irons drawn and eyes flicking at any and every possible ambush site—snapped shots at the ancient pueblo dwelling, at nearby rocks, at a mesquite whose leaves were moved by a passing breeze. The buffalo gun didn't fire again. Dragging Hood backwards, they made it out of the clearing and into the brush along the creek where they crouched, panting and wary, to see what would happen next.

Nothing happened next except that Sean again said urgently to the gunnies, "Listen . . . listen . . . *this isn't your fight!* Pratt hired you to help him catch me, he's got me, and that's the end of it as far as you're concerned. If you let me go, I'll tell V . . . Cooper to let you ride out of here. Otherwise, you go down one-by-one. You've seen that he's a crack shot with that Sharps. The gun's got a scope and a three mile . . ."

This time, Pratt's knuckles hit Hood in the mouth. The bounty hunter snarled, "Cooper? Dat little Pinkerton skirt's d'one shootin' at us from up dere?" He squinted at the surrounding brush. "Well, if she fires blind at us in here, she's as like to hit youse as us. I figger she won' do dat. I mean, she wants t'take youse back east as much as I do, so . . ." he motioned to his men, ". . . wot we gotta do is keep Hood here outta her sight so's she won' know where he is while youse guys sneak up dere an' flush her out. Tie him up, den . . ."

"Hold it, Pratt!" Bronco Barnes grabbed at Hood's arm and yanked him away from Haig and Peavy. Abruptly unbalanced, Stormy stumbled and went to his knees at Barnes's feet. "This feller don't belong to *nobody* till we hear what's at stake here. Now, you're payin' us each fifty to do a job fer ya. That was to catch *him,* not kill off some woman. I draw the damn line at shootin' some li'l gal, I'll tell ya that! And if this *hombre*'s worth five thousan' . . ."

Gun still in his right, Oscar snared Sean's shirt with his left hand and tried to retrieve Hood. He began, "Youse hired on to . . ."

Barnes jerked Sean back. Pratt had lost his hold on Hood's shirt; seized it and again pulled hard. Stormy was recovered enough now to think clearly. Caught between the two men, each struggling to possess him for their own gain, when Pratt yanked at him, he shoved with his feet, wrenched his arm from Barnes's hold and rammed his shoulder into Oscar's chest. Pratt's gun went off as he was knocked backwards. The bullet hit the tip of Bronco's nose, plowed through his face and killed him instantly.

Haig, Peavy, and Stokes were startled into open-mouthed inactivity when Pratt and the prisoner hit the ground simultaneously with the corpse. Sean made a grab for the bounty hunter's iron—no way was he going to let Oscar carry his head back east! He got a good hold on the barrel and had just twisted the weapon out of Pratt's grip when the other men came alive.

Haig and Peavy leaned on Stormy from behind. Stokes grabbed his wrist in both hands and nearly tore his arm out of its shoulder socket when he yanked it back across his thighs. The weapon flew from Hood's abruptly weakened fingers;

Wooster's fist hit him twice, nearly knocked him out, and he collapsed onto his belly over Pratt's shins. Together, the men fell onto him to hold him down.

Yelling a string of curses that should have debarked nearby trees, Oscar got himself out from under Sean, pushed himself to his feet, yanked Hood's confiscated hunting knife from under his belt and lunged for Stormy, but Stokes leaned an elbow on Hood's shoulder and thumbed the hammer on his old six-shooter.

Scowling, Pratt stopped when Wooster snarled, "Huh-uh, friend. Now, ol' Bronco, he had a good idea. We knowed ol' Bronco a helluva lot longer than we knowed you . . . we don't take kindly to you doin' ol' Bronco in, but we could look on it as a *accident* should you cut us in fer part of the reward on this *hombre*'s haid. Billy . . . Sam . . . tie this feller up to keep him in one spot, then let's us all set an' dicker a while with Mister Pratt, here."

"Damn youse, Stokes," Pratt glowered, "Hood's mine! Youse . . ."

"Not now, he ain't." Stokes kept his weapon tight on Pratt while he rose and went to retrieve Oscar's iron from where it lay in the dirt a few feet away.

Stormy blinked sight back and again struggled cobwebs out of his head while Haig and Peavy used Billy's rolled bandana to bind his wrists in

208

front of him and then Peavy's belt to secure his ankles.

Wooster went on. "Right now, looks like we . . ." he waved the barrel of his iron in his left hand at his friends, ". . . own that *hombre*."

Oscar crouched, the knife up and ready. He yelled, *"No! No, I been chasin' Hood two years! OVER TWO YEARS! He's run me ragged . . . killed me partner . . . shot me in d'ass . . . he's mine, God dammit, and youse guys ain't gonna steal 'im from me!"*

"Back off, Pratt!" Wooster twitched the six-guns. "I never said nothin' about *stealin'*, now, did I? Cuttin' ourselfs in, yeah. Now, you set an' tell us all about this here feller."

Armed only with a knife, and faced with three men of uncertain morals, Oscar had little choice. He glared at Stokes for a moment before he nodded, shoved the knife back under his belt, and sank slowly to squat on his heel. Bound and surrounded, Hood lay where he was without speaking and listened carefully to Pratt's tale of being hired along with three others to run him down and bring him back to New York City, hoping for some clue that would tell him who the "George Hood" was who had put a price on his life, but heard nothing new.

Everyone looked at Sean when he blurted, "What did he look like? Tell me what the George Hood who hired you looked like, Oscar!"

Pratt shrugged. "Tall. Uh . . . blue peepers. Reddish hair. Nuttin' t'shout about."

Even before Oscar was done, Wooster Stokes shook his head. "Now, ain't that somethin'? Five thousan' dollars fer this here *hombre*, eh? Daid or alive, eh? George Hood in New York City, eh? I think that's 'bout all we need to know." He had holstered his own side-arm but still held Pratt's. He aimed the longshoreman's weapon and shot Oscar through the heart.

"No!" Sean shouted, but it was too late. In horror, he watched Pratt plunge backward and twitch on the dirt for a moment before lying still. He twisted to look up at Stokes, at Haig and Peavy; yelled, "You damn fools, now how'll you know who hired him? How will you get paid for bringing me in, you don't have him to guide you to the man who . . ."

Wooster kicked him in the stomach to shut him up. "Cain't be too many *George Hoods* in town. I mean, how big's that place, anyway? Two . . . three thousan' people, maybe? That shouldn't be no problem. Now, there's jus' three to split that money."

It was obvious to Sean that these men had never been to New York City, had no concept of its real size and population. He choked, "No, you don't understand! There are two or three *million* people there, and now that you've killed Pratt, *I'll* never know who sent him after me! I needed him alive to . . ."

"Your problem, not mine," Wooster said grimly. "We'll jus' keep haulin' you 'round to however many George Hoods there are, and when we find the right one, we'll have our money, now, won't we. *Our* first problem is gettin' past that calico you got stashed up in that there ruin. Haig . . . Peavy . . . come on. Bring that *hombre* and let's go git our hosses an' git ourselfs headed fer the east. That bounty's waitin' on us."

"You're crazy!" Sean cried when the two men grasped his arms, lifted him and started to drag him back toward the meadow. "You don't know what you're getting into!"

Wooster put a hand out to halt his friends. He said to Hood, "Well, it sure seems to me that if this George Hood knows you good 'nough to want you daid, you oughtta know him. Right? You're from New York, right? How many George Hoods can there be there, I ask ya?"

"Yes, I'm from New York . . . and I know of two George Hoods . . . my father and my brother . . . but now, without Pratt to identify the one who hired him, all they'll have to do is say: *It wasn't me,* and you're out of luck. You'll have gone to all this trouble for nothing!"

Wooster looked astonished. "Your pa or your own brother put a price on your haid? That don't

211

seem like no right thing for a family to do. Still, you can point 'em out to us. C'mon, boys, let's see what we can do 'bout gettin' that li'l female sharpshooter to give it up so's we can be on our way to gettin' our reward money."

Haig and Peavy nodded and again began to drag Hood toward the clearing. Through a break in the foliage around them, Sean could see the castle glowing with late afternoon sun and wondered what Veracity was doing at the moment. She was trapped there without water, without food . . . she would know from these men's horses grazing out in the meadow that they were still here, and by the fact that he hadn't reappeared, that he was still their prisoner.

He drew a deep breath and prepared himself to be hit again; tried, "Listen . . . listen to me. I want to go home to New York. If you want to go with me, or *take* me there, I'll go quietly. I swear I won't try to escape you. Then, when we get there, you can turn me over to whatever Hood will pay you, collect the bounty, go have your fun and what happens between him and me after you're gone is none of your concern. But leave the girl out of it. She . . ."

Wooster shoved his side-arm barrel against Stormy's throat. "Shut up. You give us any problems at all, sonny, an' I'll do what ol' Pratt was gonna do . . . take yer haid home in that there hatbox he brung an' leave the rest of ya here. You two, cover him close an' hard. Sam, gimmie your sweat-wiper."

Peavy's bandana had once been red but was now sun-bleached nearly to white. When he untied it from around his neck and handed it to Wooster, Stokes said again, "Cover Hood," before he broke a stick from one of the Desertwillows growing on the creek bank and tied the cloth to it like a flag. "Okay, bring him. Keep your side-arms tight on him an' follow me."

"We ain't goin' out there again, are we, Wooster?" Haig asked worriedly. "That there sharpshooter'll bring us down in nuthin' flat!"

Stokes shook his head. "Uh-uh. I don't think so . . . not if we make a big show of havin' Hood covered. Crack shot or not, if that there's a woman up in the ruin, ain't no woman I know gonna chance with her man's life. No, you keep him covered an' come on."

Hood had no choice but to move when Peavy and Haig pulled at his arms. His wrists and ankles were bound. Their weapons were pressed painfully hard against his temples, one from each side. His feet left a long cleared scrape in the leaf-littered dirt when they hauled him out of the brush and into the meadow.

Stokes led the way. Waving the pink flag as he went, he stepped aside so whoever was in the ruin would be able to see the prisoner when the others lowered Hood to his knees in the grass.

Wooster yelled, "Hey! Hey, you up there! Hey!"

Still high up on the balcony, Veracity had sat in shock for a long while before she'd recovered enough from knowledge of what she had done to wipe her eyes, run a shirt sleeve under her nose and sniff moistly. The sounds of occasional shots from beyond the fringe of brush across the meadow finally brought her out of her blue funk for they painted murder and mayhem into her mind and made her ease back to peer out the hole whose slant pinpointed the fields below.

At first, there was nothing but horseflesh out there. She had just started to stand up, when blurry figures emerged from the undergrowth. She blinked rapidly and looked again, but couldn't see well enough. She grabbed the binoculars and gasped, "Oh, no! Oh, Sean!"

The glasses showed his bound wrists. There was blood on his shirt and more on his face where it had leaked from his nose, a split in his lip, and a crease along his jaw line—those men had treated him badly! Then, she noticed the makeshift peace flag one waved, and presently a voice floated faintly up to her.

"Throw down that gun an' come on down here or yer partner's daid! You got one minute!"

Heart pounding, Veracity bit her lip while she scanned the area. She could still see Spot nipping at grass at the northern edge. There to her right, seven riderless horses continued to graze. All were too far away to be of any use.

She brought the glasses back to the group of men. Sean was battered and pale, but he looked all right otherwise, except that the glasses showed her his empty holster and knife scabbard. What should she do?

Down below, Stokes made her decision for her. The flag still in his left hand, he pulled his iron and also pressed it against Hood. "You can't possibly down us all afore we can blow Hood away! Put down yer gun an' come on out! You only got thirty seconds left!"

Veracity dropped the binoculars into their case, grabbed the Sharps, and holding it horizontally over her head in both hands, rose so the men could see her. "All right . . . all right! I'm coming down! But it will take me perhaps ten minutes to find my way out! Don't shoot him! I'm coming!"

Beside Hood, Haig gasped, "I'll be damned! It *is* a girl!"

Stokes yelled back, "*Five* minutes! You got five minutes before this *hombre* meets his maker!"

"I'll try! Don't shoot him! I'll do my best!" Veracity vanished again below the balcony railing.

Hurriedly, she grabbed the Avenging Angel from her belt and shoved its short barrel along her calf and into the inside top of her right boot beneath her skirt hem. She closed the binoculars case and passed the strap over her shoulder, stuck her head and an arm through the Sharps strap so the gun slanted across her back, grabbed the torch and matches and headed for the dark hole in the floor. Inside, she flamed the torch; those in the meadow below could follow her progress when light gleamed from this window or that. Once, they saw her backtrack—she'd taken a wrong turn, had met a cul-de-sac and had to find a different path—then Peavy gasped, "There she is—by Gawd, just a little calico. Just a little girl."

Veracity snuffed the torch and leaned the remains against the castle wall. She moved to the highest ladder and climbed gingerly down to the lower level, negotiated that ladder safely and headed for the meadow, but Stokes ordered, "Halt! Leave that there Big Fifty behind along with any other weapons ya got! I wantta see yer hands up an' empty, gal!"

Her voice high and tight, Veracity answered back, "My goodness, I'm not a soldier, sir! How many guns do you expect a *lady* to carry?"

Wooster grunted an, "Umph," before he yelled, "All right, git on out here *now,* dammit!"

Still on his knees with six-gun barrels pressed hard against his skull and spine, Hood watched Veracity, hands high, stride toward them. But when she got closer, her eyes widened, her expression shifted into horror, she cried, *"Oh, Sean, darling, look what they've done to you!"*

and flung herself at him to crouch on her left knee beside him. Grinning, the bounty hunters stepped back when she wrapped both arms around Hood's neck and pressed her cheek to his.

She whispered, "Angel's in my boot," before she babbled, "Oh, lover . . . sweetheart . . . oh, let me hold you!"

Under cover of her body and his, Sean found Angel's grip. He hissed, "Get away from me!"

As Veracity shoved hard with her feet to thrust herself aside, Hood yanked the sawed-off pistol from her boot top, also flung himself to the dirt, and began to roll over and over. His first bullet took out Sam Peavy. He had rolled against Haig's shins—even as his second bullet pierced Billy below the navel and exited between shoulder blades, Wooster Stokes fired at him. Stokes's shot plowed through his thigh, but almost simultaneously, a large round hole made a dark third eye between Wooster's brows. The man looked surprised, but his astonishment didn't last long—Veracity's derringer had given Hood the time he needed to fire again. Still on his back, he pulled the trigger, the Avenging Angel belched fire, the bullet took Stokes under the chin and blew out the back of his head.

Sean rolled over once more. Braced on elbows, his wrists still bound and Angel smoking in his hands, he surveyed the carnage through narrowed yes, watching for signs of life. There were none.

217

With a deep, regretful sigh, he let his head droop. *How he hated this! He wanted to go home, to stop running, to be able to relax in familiar places again, not to have to kill merely to live another few minutes!* He wanted this over and done with so badly that he was almost—but not quite—willing to die merely to see an end to it.

It finally came to him that somewhere behind him, a woman was weeping, and he shoved elbows to turn far enough to look over his shoulder. Veracity sat in the grass, the derringer in the dirt beside her, her face covered by both hands. Even as he looked, he saw tears leak between her fingers.

"Ahhh . . . my God," he whispered. He tried to get to his feet, but his bound ankles and the bullet hole in his thigh got his attention. Grimacing with pain, he let the Avenging Angel lay, bent, unbuckled the belt and freed his legs. He lurched upright and stumbled to where Veracity sat; collapsed beside her.

When he passed his linked arms around her to hold her to him, she grabbed at him and choked, "Oh, Stormy, I don't want to do this anymore! I don't want to be a Pinkerton detective anymore. I thought it would be interesting and exciting and worthwhile, and . . . and yes, for a while it *was* fun . . . but I never thought I'd have to *kill* people, Stormy! Oh, Stormy, I don't want to do this anymore! I just want to be somebody's wife and have lots of children and I don't want to *kill* people anymore!"

He held her more tightly; whispered, "It's all right. You had to do it; otherwise, they would have killed me."

She wailed, *"Yes, but to . . . to KILL people, Stormy . . ."* She sniffed sloppily, lifted her head to look at him, and he noticed that she looked terrible . . . her eyes were swollen, her nose red, her hair stringing and sweat-stuck to her face— and he abruptly thought she was about the most beautiful little woman he'd ever seen.

When she wiped her nose with the back of a hand and repeated, "I don't want to do this anymore, Stormy," before he knew what he was saying, he gasped, "Then, marry me, Veracity. I know that at this moment, I'm only a Remittance Man, but now that Father is dead, I s'pose I've been mentioned in his Will. I'm probably half, or at least part-owner of Hood Shipping, and if we can make it back to New York City, find out who put a price on my head and get that resolved, I think I can provide well for you. And then, you can resign from the Pinkerton Agency and just be my wife . . . raise our babies. . . ."

Her puffy eyes widened. She let go of him, scrubbed palms against her tear-spiked lashes, then still trapped in the circle of his arms, looked at him again. "But Sean, I'm an . . . older woman!"

"I don't give a damn about seven months." He lifted his arms from around her.

A year and seven months, her mind corrected, but she didn't say it.

Now that he'd gotten started with this, he was overwhelmingly glad his heart had better sense than his head. He prompted, "Veracity Hood only has five syllables. Even Charles Poindexter Whatever would think that's a proper name for a woman."

"Charles Poindexter *Brandenberg*." She began to laugh, and he noted it was a *real* laugh, full and rich and uninhibited, not Elaine's perpetual titter. When she again flung arms around him to hold him tight, he joined her laughter. Surrounded by corpses, they sat below the ancient ruin and laughed until she said yes and he silenced her with their first kiss. It had been a long time since he had kissed a woman like that—perhaps he'd never before kissed a woman like that—and it might have gone a lot farther there in the grassy meadow except that he was still bound and when she accidentally put her hand on the bullet hole in his thigh, she discovered for the first time that he was more wounded than what showed on his face.

After the bandana had been moved from his wrists to his leg to stop the bleeding, and after she said yes to his proposal again to reassure him she really meant it, they set about more serious chores.

CHAPTER ELEVEN

Veracity went to catch the horses so Sean wouldn't have to walk too much. Together, they gathered the bodies and tied them over saddles; but first, Hood went through the bounty hunters' pockets.

"Robbing the dead?" Veracity looked horrified.

"Nope." Hood had gotten to Oscar Pratt. He held up a wad of rumpled bills. "This is *my* money, remember? Oh, would you go get the Sharps, please? Though I hope we don't, we may need it again."

"Right." While she hurried back toward the cliff base where she'd propped the gun, he tied the funeral horses into a string. Back with the Sharps, Veracity asked, "Where's Spot?"

Sean looked around, saw the pinto at the far end of the meadow, whistled sharply and yelled, "Hey, Spot! Shootin's over! Come on, boy!"

As always, Spot lifted his head, nickered, and trotted toward them.

"Good as a dog," Veracity noted once again.

"Better. Can't ride a dog." Sean caught the pinto's bridle, slipped the bit back into place and tried to mount, but couldn't lift his left leg high enough to get a foot in the stirrup.

Again chuckling, Veracity gave him a boost before she swung up behind him, wrapped her arms around his middle, leaned her head against his shoulder and sighed comfortably. Leading the grisly string, they headed southward down the creek.

Presently, she asked, "Did you really mean that, or did you merely ask me to marry you because of your weakened condition?"

He thought about it for a long time before he answered, "I really mean it, Veracity. We work together too well for us to part now. Like Spot, here. I've had a lot of other horses, but Spot is special. Always will be. Not that I've had lots of other women . . . some, yes, I confess that, but . . . like Spot, you're very special."

She rested her chin on his shoulder. "I'm not sure I like being compared to a horse. And it sure took you long enough to answer. *And,* so far, I haven't heard one word about *love.*"

"Picky, picky! I didn't want to give you a snap response. Uh . . . how often did Charles Whoever-whatever tell you he loved you?"

"All the time! He was very profuse in his . . . Oh."

"Exactly. Wouldn't you rather be a cherished friend and companion than a possession brought out, shown off, then—as I believe you said—sent to your room like a child? I don't recall ever hearing or seeing my mother and father fuss over each other, yet I never knew two people more devoted to each other. Love should be profoundly shown, not lightly spoken." He leaned around her and looked back at the corpses draped over the line of horses. "Men, argue with me if I'm wrong." He grinned at Veracity; flexed brows. "They're not saying anything."

She unwrapped an arm long enough to pound a fist against his shoulder. "Stormy, that was disgusting!"

"Remittance Men are supposed to be disgusting, else they wouldn't be Remittance Men."

"You're incorrigible!" She re-wrapped her arms and snuggled against him again.

The expression in his eyes flashed from humor to grimness. He murmured, "I doubt I'd have lasted this long if I hadn't been."

She nodded. "Why didn't you just leave the bodies where they lay, Stormy? No one would have known who had killed them. Back east, perhaps there would have been an investigation, but out here . . . ?" She tipped her head. "Do you labor under a streak of innate decency?"

"No." He sighed heavily. "It's self-defense. They came from the south. Fort Verde's down there, and that's where we're headed. They were looking for us—who knows who they asked about us on the way? Anyone who sees those you shot will know they were taken out with a buffalo gun. I'm carrying a Sharps. I've been running from hired killers for over two years, Veracity, I don't want to have to start running from the law, too. We bring the bodies in, tell the authorities what happened, then we're the victims rather than the bushwhackers."

So it was that they created quite a stir at the army outpost when they rode in just at sunset and asked the nearest soldier where to find the commandant. The colonel came out to investigate the situation. Then, he called Sean and Veracity into his office to hear their story. He saw Veracity's Pinkerton credentials, which lent considerable weight to their word. He called the resident physician, who confirmed that Sean's condition had been created by gunshots and fists. While he was there, he cleaned and bandaged Hood's wounds. The upshot of the whole affair was that Stormy and Veracity were congratulated for successfully defending themselves from the ambush, were invited to dinner and to stay the night.

"Uhhh . . . what about the bodies, Colonel?" Hood asked.

"Not a problem. We have a boot hill here . . . I'll order a burial detail."

"And their mounts?"

The colonel shrugged. "They're yours to sell if you wish. If you don't want them, of course, I'll take them off your hands. The army can always use a few extra horses and mules."

Sean said, "I'd like to keep at least three—one for Miss Cooper, and two as backup mounts."

"Done," the colonel said.

"And speaking of Miss Cooper . . ." Hood reached to take her hand, ". . . do you have a chaplain here? I'd like to make her Missus Hood."

Veracity yanked her hand away. "Stormy! Sean! So soon?"

"Yeah! Why wait?"

She was flustered. Blushed hotly. Glanced from Hood to where the colonel smothered a smile.

Sean held up a hand, fingers spread. "Five syllables, Miss Cooper. A proper female name."

Her head rose. Still flushed and bright-eyed, she smiled, "Done, Stormy Hood! Why wait!"

They had dinner in the officers' mess, then were married at the colonel's house. The colonel's wife gave Veracity a lace curtain to use as a veil, made a wedding bouquet of dry wood roses from her table vase, and cried wetly throughout the ceremony. She temporarily lent Sean her own wedding ring for the service until he could buy one for Veracity. The chaplain filled out the marriage certificate he'd brought with him, Sean and Veracity signed, then the commandant called the few other officers and their wives to an impromptu party.

Sean and Veracity considered their wedding to be superb. The ensuing night was even better—

225

so what if he was a Remittance Man and she an Older Woman, they were now Mr. and Mrs. Sean Evan Hood!

Sean was up, dressed, and leaning against the wall beside the window to ease his wounded leg. He stared grimly at the cottonwood-shaded yard outside, his gut cramped by the deep-sunk feeling that he had made a cruel mistake. Because of his loneliness . . . in his need for human contact . . . in his yearning for some semblance of a normal life, and in the aftermath of the shock of being captured and beaten by hired gunnies and then after the deaths of seven men—some of whom he had personally slaughtered—he had asked Veracity Cooper to wed him. In her own need and trauma, she'd said yes. Then, events had swept forward, carrying them both along. Now, they were, in fact, married, but . . .

But now, Oscar Pratt was dead and he, himself, was still a Remittance Man with no future. Someone out there calling himself George Hood offered money for his head, but with Pratt permanently silenced, how would he now find out for sure who that was?

Now that the longshoreman-cum-manhunter was gone, would that so-called George Hood hire another to replace Oscar? And then another and another until the job was done? If yes, Veracity could be caught in the crossfire, and her injury or death would also weight his soul. True, she wasn't exactly an innocent bystander—as a Pinkerton agent, she had to take her chances with her surroundings because of the dangers that came along with the job . . .

Still . . .

He braced a hand against the wall and turned to look at his wife sleeping in the wide, rumpled bed. With her fair unbound hair spread around her face, the nightgown borrowed from the commandant's wife overly-large yet clinging to the soft roundness of her breasts, with her sunburned nose, and parted lips pink and moist, she looked painfully young and vulnerable, and his bleak expression deepened.

He knew he didn't love her. He felt warmth for her, yes, and the edge of responsibility now, but not what he thought of as love. Maybe he should just leave five or six hundred dollars on the bed stand for her and vanish before she awoke. Go his way. Cut her out of the loop. Let her return east, find a nice respectable, stable man and settle into a nice respectable, stable, *normal* life.

He shook his head slightly. But he'd discovered last night that he was her first man, that she'd never bedded with anyone before him. He didn't know how many times was required for a woman to conceive a child. Perhaps once or twice was enough, and that had been accomplished last night . . . *well* accomplished last night. His expression softened slightly and his small feeling of warmth deepened.

Last night. Sweet. Very sweet. Not at all like those hasty rough-and-tumble dalliances with some dirt-water calico cat invariably named Trixie or Rosie or Conchita that he was accustomed to. And if he put money on the stand and left, it would make her into a highly-paid whore rather than his wife, wouldn't it, and he couldn't do that to her.

He turned back to again stare out the window. No, he couldn't just abandon her. He'd wed her and bedded her; they were married and he was stuck with her now. He would "do the right thing" by her; otherwise, it would be as bad as his brother's treatment of poor little Melissa Hardesty. And perhaps, some day, if Veracity would persevere long enough, he could recapture enough of his lost humanity to learn to love her.

Unbidden, that inner cautionary voice whispered: *You don't really know her . . . is she merely using this method to ensure she can bring you back, her target successfully captured?*

He snorted a short, harsh, nearly silent laugh, and shook his head. For the first time, he told the voice to shut up and went back to watching cottonwood leaves dapple moving shadows across the morning.

• • •

Veracity awoke to the luxurious feeling of being totally satisfied with life only to find Sean dressed and staring sourly out the window. She sat up, the bed clothing clasped around her. "Good morning, Stormy." She could tell that his smile was forced when he turned his head to murmur, " 'Morning," because his dark eyes held a closed, guarded remoteness. He returned to the window.

Veracity studied him in silence for a long moment before she frowned. "Stormy? What's the matter? Are you having second thoughts?"

Again, he turned to look at her. His smile was no more real when he lied, "About you? About us? Never, Missus Hood. I was just thinking that now that Pratt's dead, I have no way to find out . . . to *really* discover whether the George Hood who hired him was my father or my brother." He shook his head. "I needed Pratt to identify the man. But now . . ."

She drew her legs up beneath the covers, wrapped arms around her shins and lowered her chin to her knees. "I know. But together, Stormy . . . working together, we can get to the truth. I'll help you, and . . ."

"What! You're going to rescue me again?" He spoke more sharply than he'd intended to.

She looked startled. "No! All I meant was that *together,* we . . ." She swallowed and lowered her eyes to contemplate the colorful lightweight hand-sewn quilt for a moment before she asked, "Uh . . . are we still headed east, back to New York now, or . . . ?"

"Yes, I think so. There are no hired gunnies chasing me at this moment that I know of . . ." he realized he'd snapped at her, again smiled faintly and tried for a joke, ". . . unless it's you."

His feeble jest fell flat. *"Sean!"* She frowned and flung back the covers, bounced out of bed, and the nightgown sagging about her, moved to him to slide arms around him. His own arms were slow to respond when she looked up at him with serious hazel eyes, but eventually enclosed her to hold her loosely. "Sean, you know I'm not. Do you think I married you just to keep an eye on you?" Before he could answer, she drew back slightly. "Is that why *you* married *me? So it would be easier for you to keep track of me?"*

"Good God, Veracity . . ."

She stepped completely back, and clutched at the nightgown. "It is, isn't it! You were rid of Pratt and his gang of ruffians and that left only me! What better way to keep tabs on a problem than to marry it!"

"Veracity, no. That's not . . ." He shook his head. "What I said about you being the only paid hunter still chasing me was meant to be humorous. It was a joke, Vera. I admit it was a bad joke because I'm out of practice at it, but . . ."

"Indeed you are! Many times, the truth is spoken disguised as a joke . . . AND DON'T CALL ME VERA!" She ripped off the nightgown, flung it onto the bed and leaped to where her old clothes lay over a chair.

Sean watched her dress. She had turned away from him, yet even the edge of anger couldn't dampen his appreciation of her strong, compact figure, the well-rounded hips, firm buttocks and thighs . . . or the warmth that rose in him.

When she'd donned her underclothing, shirt and split riding skirt, he stepped to her and tried to again take her in his arms, but she shoved at him.

"A false show of affection is not required, Mister Hood. I now understand you perfectly."

"No, you don't, dammit!" He jerked her around to face him. "*Yes,* I'll admit that I don't . . . *we* . . . *neither* of us . . . know each other well enough to have done what we did, but I didn't marry you just to keep an eye on you!"

"Then why, Mister Hood?" Her tone was cold. Icy.

He could have said: "Because I need you," or "Because I love you," the first not quite a lie, the second not quite the truth. Instead, he responded, "Because we'll be spending weeks together on our return back east, maybe months, and it's not proper for an unmarried man and woman to travel together over such a distance."

231

Her lip curled when she stiff-armed him aside and moved to a chair to slide into her boots. *"Oh, you needn't concern yourself about my reputation, Mister Hood, that's already well compromised!"* She jammed a foot into a boot, slid on the other stocking and yanked on that boot. She stood and started for the door, but Sean's Irish temper flared.

He snagged her wrist to stop her. "Wait a minute, Veracity. Why are you trying to make me out some kind of villain in this? Yes, it's true we don't know much about each other. Yes, it's true I may have asked you to marry me on the spur of the moment, but *you* are the one who said yes! *You* married *me! If I'm so suspect that I can't even make a joke, pity-poor though it was, why'd you go through with the damn ceremony, TELL ME THAT!"*

"Don't you dare raise your voice to me, Sean Hood! I'll not be spoken to in that tone!"

His tanned complexion, the bruises still dark from yesterday's beating by the miners and cowboys Pratt had hired, and his black morning stubble made his teeth seem very white when he bared them to a brief hard grin before he snapped back, "My mother, Kathleen, used to say: As ye holler in the woods, so shall ye be answered. Echo for echo, Missus Hood." He again seized her arm, dragged her to him and planted a long, fierce kiss on her lips. Still holding her frozen against him, he pulled back to note, "We've had our first wedded spat, Missus Hood. You want to go on fighting or call a truce now? We have a long way to go, and I'd rather travel with a friend and partner than with an enemy. It's your choice."

More quietly, she said, "I'm not your enemy, Stormy. I've never been your enemy, and I was paid to deliver a message to you, not to bring you in. Not to keep an eye on you. As for choices, if you go back east, it will be your choice, not mine." She glanced aside, her anger gone as quickly as it had flared. "I confess I don't care who hired Oscar Pratt to hunt you, but if you need to find out the truth, then I'll help you. After all, I'm a Pinkerton detective, y'know. Between the two of us, we should be able to sort things out . . . I've been trained to that and you're not stupid, so . . ."

He hugged her to him again, this time warmly; whispered, "I'm sorry I yelled at you. I apologize for what I said . . . it was really intended to be a joke but I can see now how it must have sounded to you."

"Maybe I'm just overly sensitive. I haven't had my morning coffee yet."

His brows rose. "Oh, one of those, eh?"

"One of those. Or haven't you noticed?"

"I hadn't." He worked hard to stifle his temper and to be pleasant; felt he owed it to her. He tipped a brow toward the door. "Shall we go see if we can weasel some of that coffee and a few scrambled eggs out of our hostess?"

She also tried for congeniality—after all, it was her first day as Mrs. Sean Evan Hood. "Race you to the coffee pot."

With Veracity riding Spot, and Stormy astride Oscar Pratt's black gelding and leading a rangy rawboned bay and a big black mule with four notches cut deep into its right ear as backup mounts and pack animals, Mr. and Mrs. Sean Hood said good-bye and thanks to the Ft. Verde commander and his wife and began the fifty-mile journey back through the mountains to Prescott. The army physician had looked at Sean's thigh, at the bullet crease along his jaw, and at his other bruises and scrapes before they left, had pronounced all un-fevered but had advised Veracity to keep her husband out of trouble for at least a week. He also ordered Sean to have a Prescott or Ft. Whipple doctor look at his leg when they arrived to make sure infection wasn't setting in.

Unlike Pratt and his men, Sean and Veracity had no escort for the journey, but in its own way, that was a blessing—it allowed them to take their time. And to talk. They had talked before, of course, but their conversations had always been semi-guarded. Now, he told her about his own childhood and how—because of his mother's frailty and his father's business involvements— he'd been raised more by the butler, Burkhart, than by his parents. He related how he and Burkhart used to eavesdrop at the speaker tubes running from various rooms in the mansion to the butler's quarters. So it was, that he garnered a business sense and an insight into the workings of Hood Shipping without being formally taught, and that the family retainer knew things a butler should never have been privy to.

Before they reached The Springs, mid-point in their fifty-mile trek, they were back to the semi-relaxed association they'd enjoyed at the sandstone sink up north, and though neither confessed a mad infatuation for the other, were developing what Stormy thought was a very comfortable relationship.

Still, there was a grimness about him that Veracity's wit and light banter couldn't penetrate. He knew she sensed it; tried valiantly to conquer the back-of-the-mind voice that whispered relentlessly: *How will you ever know whether it was Father or Georgie who sent hired killers after you? With Oscar dead, how will you ever know for sure that it wasn't your own father? If only Oscar was still alive . . .*

Considering how well-traveled the road between Forts Verde and Whipple was, it was a wonder that they had The Springs glade all to themselves that night. They arrived just at sunset . . . and for once, it wasn't raining. The Ft. Verde commander's wife had plied them with trail food. Veracity had had to be quite firm about not accepting the picnic basket the woman offered because she doubted she'd ever be able to return it. Nevertheless, what had been transferred from the basket to both her and Sean's saddlebags provided an ample lunch and adequate dinner for them.

Remembering their brief but heated squabble this morning, after dinner, in the fire-lighted darkness under fragrant pines, with the bubbling spring providing a soft moistness to the air around them, Hood set about actively wooing his new wife. He took it slow and easy, murmuring words of love he didn't think he felt, never stopping to wonder how it was they readily passed his lips without much guidance from his mind. It was obvious to him that Veracity didn't object to hearing them. One thing led naturally to another as though it had been much longer than merely twenty-four hours since the wedding ceremony. Sean finally fell asleep with Veracity's head on his shoulder, her palm resting over his heart, an unaccustomed feeling of well-being curving a smile to his lips, and the fleeting thought that perhaps, just perhaps, after his years of hardship and loneliness, things might finally be going his way.

● ● ●

They bypassed Fort Whipple and reentered Prescott late in the afternoon of the following day. Citizens and soldiers still clogged the streets, off-duty army personnel lounged on the boardwalks outside the bars of Whiskey Row, and soiled doves perched on their balcony above the Palace Bar's front entrance.

Veracity asked, "How's your leg, Stormy?"

"Sorer than hell, but not really getting any worse. Why?"

She nodded to the side. "Because there's a doctor's office. I wish you'd stop and let him take a look at it."

"I will later on. First things first—we need lodging for the night."

"Certainly not that horrible *Du Shane's* boarding house! I stepped inside once, and once was enough!"

He chuckled. "The only other place around is the hotel. After our midnight retreat out their back window, I'm not sure they'll let us in the door again."

She also laughed. "Why don't we merely walk in as though we owned the place, act as though nothing untoward ever happened, and see how things go?"

"We can try that, but . . . there! That's what *I* was looking for." He indicated a sign that said: *Jewelry, Assay, & Pawn.* "Come on, we're going to get you a proper wedding ring."

"In a *pawn* shop?"

"Why not?" He grinned at her. "What's that saying you brides follow . . . something old, something new . . ."

"Really, Sean!"

"Well, we'll see what we can come up with. Woah, horse."

Spot planted his feet and stopped, but Stormy wasn't riding the pinto. Pratt's black ambled on until Hood reined in, and shaking his head, turned the gelding around.

Veracity asked, "You want Spot back?"

"No, not yet." Hood dismounted stiffly and limped to tether the black to the nearest hitching ring imbedded into the stone before the boardwalk. "Come on, wife, let's get you a ring."

The inside of the shop was mostly pawn, secondly assay complete with scales and miniature forge and crucible, thirdly jewelry. Stormy cast an eye over what had been pawned for quick cash—side-arms, a few rifles, a Blackfoot Indian war bonnet that had somehow gotten to Prescott, and a couple of tomahawks; a few gold pocket watches and several skimpy rings—but saw nothing he liked until he spotted a dozen or so rough gold nuggets lying on a piece of dusty black velvet. "*Here* we go!"

The proprietor, a thin graying man nearly as dusty as his establishment, smiled a yellow-toothed grin. "See somethin' ya want, cowboy?"

"Yes." Sean pointed at the nuggets. "How long would it take you to make those into a wedding ring for my wife?"

The proprietor's brows rose. "Oh, meby a hour. A few minutes to melt them nuggets down . . ."

"No, I want them left as nuggets as far as possible, merely made into a band."

"Still a hour. Fusin' an' finishin', y'know. Cool-down, an' the like."

"Good. How much?"

The proprietor grabbed the cloth and dumped the nuggets onto his scales; frowned at the results. "Two an' a half ounces of pure gold at twenty dollars an' sixty-seven cents a ounce . . . that's . . . ummm . . . fifty-one sixty-seven, plus five bucks fer my work is fifty-six sixty-seven."

"Done." Stormy pulled bills from his pocket.

"Oh, well," the proprietor scowled at the paper money, "takes three hundred greenbacks to buy one hundred dollars in gold, y'know. That'd make yer wife's ring amount to . . . ummm . . . fifty-one sixty seven times three equals 'bout a hundred an' seventy dollars."

Veracity scowled, "Oh, no, Stormy, that's too much for a ring. No, I don't . . ."

"Hush up. I'm buying this, Missus Hood. We'll do it right or not at all." Sean nodded to the proprietor and peeled more bills off the wad.

"Your labor also charged at the variance? I figure a hundred and fifty-five dollars."

Again, the man's horse-teeth flashed. "Agreed." He held up a string. "Gimmie yer finger, Missus, so I can measure. You fixin' to put on meat?"

"Wh-What?" Veracity was startled by the question.

"Fat! You fixin' to get fat? If so, I'll make the ring with some room for expansion!"

"Oh! N-No! No, I don't . . . uh . . . no."

The proprietor had measured her ring finger; stood back with long grimy fingernails pinching the string at the proper spot. "All right, come back in about forty minutes an' you got yerself one fine weddin' ring."

Sean nodded and took Veracity's elbow. "We'll be back. Now, I'll go to the doctor and have him look at this leg."

But as they stepped back out onto the boardwalk, they found men gathered around their horses. One scowled at Hood; asked, "Ya claim this here string, *hombre*?"

Sean returned frown for frown. "If you're talking about the pinto, the black, the bay, and that mule, yes. Why?"

The spokesman for the group, a burly, rough-cut miner, jerked a thumb at the notch-eared mule. A breath of whiskey and onions accompanied his snarled, "How'd ya come by old Deep-dirt Mo Smith's beast, I ask ya! Last time I looked, ol' Deep-dirt Mo was right fond of his ol' mule, here. I cain't believe ol' Deep-dirt Mo'd ever *voluntary* part with him. How'd you come by him?"

Stormy's eyes flicked at the hard-faced group; there was solid menace if he ever saw it. He said, "I don't know anyone named Deep-dirt Mo Smith, but we've just come from over to Fort Verde way. My wife and I happened upon seven men laid out dead in a valley north of there. We took them and their mounts into the Fort and turned them over to the army. The army kept four of the animals and let us take these other three. You got a problem with that, you go discuss it with the cavalry at Fort Verde. Now, step aside."

"A likely tale," the spokesman growled. "I do believe we got ourselfs a hoss thief here, boys."

"Get a rope," one of the men suggested.

CHAPTER TWELVE

"Now, hold everything!" Sean began. "Do you have a sheriff here in town? Let's get him to . . ."

"We don't need no sheriff to help us handle a hoss thief!" A crowd of passers was gathering, men and women, some of them merely curious, many of them scowling ominously, only a few showing any signs of doubt. It was as though Hood was guilty until proven innocent.

"Tree handy over in the Plaza for a hangin'," a man noted. "Cain't let no hoss thief get off Scott free. Set a bad example fer others."

Stormy tried to shove Veracity behind him. He didn't want to draw-down on the lot. He was only one gun; there were at least ten or twelve men standing around, and half as many women and children. To start shooting now might injure a mother or child, and he couldn't do that. He said urgently, "Look, I'm not a horse thief. I came by those animals honestly . . . the black, the mule, and the bay as I said. Their owners are dead and the army gave them to me. I got the pinto at the livery stable in Ehrenberg down on the Colorado."

"Then, you must have yerself some bills of sale or the like," someone said.

"No, I . . ." Sean cast a quick look around. The

243

citizens formed a solid arc from boardwalk to boardwalk, cutting off all escape. He continued, "I didn't *buy* the pinto at Ehrenberg, I exchanged my other horse for him. I . . ."

"*Sure,* ya did," the spokesman leered. Grinning, he glanced around at the others. "Any of y'all know a stable man who just trades one hoss fer 'nother, even across the board?" He looked back at Hood. "Come on, man, you can do better than that! I say we caught us a hoss thief red-handed, and . . ."

"What seems to be the problem here?" a different voice asked, and Sean and Veracity turned to see a nattily-dressed man leaning against the side of a building a few feet down the boardwalk, his cheroot smoking in his left hand, his right hidden inside his jacket pocket. His smile was cool and polite, but the blue eyes hard and watchful.

The miner who had first asked Sean about the mule dipped his head in a deferential half-bow. "I think we got ourselfs a hoss thief here, Mistuh Reynolds. He give some cock-an'-bull story 'bout findin' the mule in the backlands near some daid bodies, but . . ."

"Ah. Really. Well, you can have him, boys, but take him over to Sheriff Mosher's office and let Jake deal with him. The woman, however, comes with me. We had an agreement, she and I, and no one welches on a deal with me."

"Now, wait just a goddamn minute!" Stormy began. Building desperation moved his hand toward the six-shooter at his hip, but his arm froze half-way, because the man called Reynolds pulled his own hand out of his pocket and Hood found himself menaced by a small but deadly derringer.

"I wouldn't try that, were I you," Reynolds smiled.

Sean raised his arms. He gasped, "Look, I didn't steal the mule . . . or those other horses, either. We . . ."

"I don't care whether you did or not," Reynolds cut in. "We'll just let Sheriff Moser get to the bottom of it." He nodded back at the crowd. "Take him to the jail, men, but no unsanctioned hanging here. Keep it civilized. After all, we're not barbarians. Prescott is going to be the capitol again one day and we have our reputation to consider. Do it right, y'hear? But, in the meantime, you, Miss Cooper, can come with me."

The miners leaped in, relieved Hood of his knife and firearm, grabbed his arms and the animals' reins and began moving on down the street, leaving Veracity staring after them with her mouth open. When the man in the dark suit replaced his derringer in his pocket and snagged her wrist, she tried to jerk away.

"Sir, I don't know you!"

"Oh, yes, you do. Bart Reynolds, at your

service, Miss Cooper. We had a hand-shake agreement for you to work for me, or don't you recall? You're my piano player." Chuckling, he escorted her off the boardwalk and toward the Palace Bar on the other side of the Plaza while— leading the horses and the mule, their hands hard on their prisoner—the crowd forced Sean toward the sheriff's office.

For his own safety, Hood didn't struggle, but he cursed steadily to himself as he was hustled onward. The irony of this was overwhelming; over two years of running, of successfully defending himself from hired gunslingers, and now to be hung as a horse thief? . . . by God, this was too much.

The sheriff's office was a sturdy, square single-story adobe-brick building holding a cluttered office in front and a row of four tiny cells at the back, one occupied by a recovering drunk. Sheriff Mosher eased his heels from among the wanted posters and dirty dishes atop his desk, hoisted his paunch off his thighs, sat straighter in his wooden swivel chair and scowled when four of the group gathering outside his office all but flung a fifth man through the front door, then led a big black mule in after them.

"What the hell!" he roared. "Git that gawdamn mule outta my jail! What the hell you think you're doing . . . this ain't no barn! An' put them goddamn irons away, my Gawd, you'd think this was the Wild West, for Gawd's sake!"

Stormy caught himself on the edge of the desk before he hit the floor. He spun around to see men holstering side-arms but solidly barring the only exit from the office. Panting, he half-crouched and waited to see what would happen next.

One of the miners retorted, "Brung ya a hoss thief . . . well, a *mule* thief . . . Sheriff. Caught this bastard red-handed with Deep-dirt Mo Smith's beast. *Would* have hanged him without botherin' ya none, but Mistuh Reynolds said we oughtta let you handle the job."

Hood began, "I tell you I didn't . . ." but abruptly, the single prisoner in the cell block began to laugh.

"Shut up back there, Neff," the sheriff snapped.

Still laughing, Neff fell off the cell bunk onto the floor. Seemingly caught in unstoppable hysterics, he lay with his feet up on the cot and choked, "That pore bastard steal Deep-dirt's mule? Hell, so what? That damn mule's been stoled so many times now it'd be a sin to sell 'im!"

"You're still drunk, Neff," Mosher growled. "Shut yer face an' let . . ."

"Wait a minute," Hood interrupted. "I want to hear what he has to say! After all, it's my neck that's on the line here."

Neff slid his legs off the bunk, turned over onto

his belly, and still giggling drunkenly, propped his chin in a palm and pointed a finger at the mule. "See them notches in his ear? That's ol' Lucky. He can smell water or gold a mile away. Ever'body wants 'im. Ol' Mo stoled 'im back from Missoura Green after Missoura'd stoled 'im from *him* after he'd stoled 'im from Darcy Levins . . ."

"You ain't makin' no sense a'tall, Neff! An' I told you to shut up!" Mosher turned back to frown at Sean.

Neff rolled over again, flung arms out and crossed shins back up on the bunk. "What I'm sayin', Sheriff, is that that damn mule's been stoled so many times he don't belong to *nobody* now. Best you can git *that* pore *hombre* on is receivin' stoled goods! I advise ya to keep ol' Lucky fer yerself, quit sheriffin', go prospectin', an' let Lucky find ya a pot other than the one yer wearin' unner yer belt. Them notches in his ear? . . . each one's a gold strike. Yer missin' a good bet, here, Sheriff, ya don' keep ol' Lucky fer yerself."

"Well, shit," Mosher snarled, "looks like you didn't catch yourselves no horse thief after all, men. Gowan. Git that mule outta my office and leave that man alone."

"Nobody wants the mule, I'll take 'im," Neff sang from his cell.

"No, gawdammit, I guess it's finders, keepers."

248

Mosher thrust his beefy chin at Sean. "You got 'im, you can keep 'im. Now, alla ya, out of my office. *You,* mister, take yer gawdamn mule with ya!" Mosher replaced his heels on his desk and shoved his hat down over his eyes to announce that the incident was closed as far as he was concerned.

Hood glared at the crowd. "Give me my weapons back."

The miners scowled, but handed over his six-shooter and hunting knife before, muttering among themselves, they began to shuffle toward the street.

"And my animals, dammit!" Hood snapped. He wasn't particular about the mule, but it was a matter of principle. He slammed his iron back into its holster, shoved the knife into its scabbard, seized the mule's halter and started outside to retrieve Spot and the other two horses. The prisoner's laughter and the sheriff's, "Cut it out, Neff!" stopped him.

He turned back to ask through the jail's open door, "Is he in for anything besides being drunk, Sheriff?"

Without removing his feet from the desk, shoving up his hat, or even unfolding his hands from across his ample belly, Mosher answered, "Just a li'l brawl."

"Any bail set?"

"Seven bucks gits 'im out."

Sean fished in his pocket, brought out seven dollars and still leading the mule, limped back into the office. He plunked the money onto the desk top. "Here's his bail. You want to let him go?"

"Keys are over there on the wall." Mosher didn't move. "An' git that damn mule outta my office!"

Hood nodded. He went to pick the key ring from its hook, unlocked Neff's cell, replaced the keys and led the mule back out onto the boardwalk. "Have a nice evening, Sheriff."

This time, Mosher didn't respond.

Neff had grabbed his hat from the end of the bunk. He was still fifty-percent drunk, but caught up with Sean in the street. "Thanks fer the bail, friend. Good of ya."

"Thank *you* for speaking up in there. Fortunate for me you could identify this mule and knew his history, else I might have been swinging from a rafter about now."

Neff laughed uproariously and slapped a hand against Hood's shoulder. "Hell, I never seen that there mule before in my life. It was a purty damn good story, though, wasn't it! Us mis-cre-*ants* gotta help each other out as we can, don't we. See ya, friend." He turned away and lurched toward *Du Shane's*, leaving Hood standing with his mouth open and *I'll be damned!* again running through his mind.

He hesitated behind the dispersing crowd to look around at what he could see of the town. He figured it was now pushing five o'clock in the evening, or later. Leading his animals, he hurried back toward the *Jewelry, Assay, & Pawn* shop to get Veracity's ring before the store closed.

First, the ring, then find Veracity, then a place to stay. Then . . . ?

He found the jeweler just putting the finishing touches on a truly magnificent ring—the man had fused nuggets into a circle then had polished the inside of the band and left the outside as rough and as true to the native shapes as possible to create a unique wedding ring. He gave the band a final swipe with the cloth as he lifted eyebrows at Hood. "Well, fer a while there, I thought I was goin' to get to keep the money *and* this here work of art. How'd you get away from that lynch mob?"

"By the skin of my teeth. Who was that man who kept me from being hanged on the spot and who ran off with my wife?"

"That there was Mister Bart Reynolds. He owns the Palace Saloon over on t'other side of the Plaza. You reckon he's gonna give ya yer missus back?"

Stormy accepted the ring, scrutinized it, nodded, and buttoned it into his shirt pocket along with the folded wedding certificate. "He'd better. My gratitude for his help only goes so far."

"You be careful of him, cowboy. Mister Reynolds all but runs Prescott. He's head cheese of the Granite Creek Gold Mining Association, 's got a finger in the pie in some others, owns the Palace and a big ranch out in Skull Valley, and is lookin' to be the next guv'nor of either the Ar'zona Territory or State. His motto is: *Ar'zona fer Ar'zonans.* He don't take kindly to strangers raisin' dust in his town . . . 'cept to spend their money here, y'know." He shook his head. "They say he's even got his own private trigger-man. If he sics Malcom Harms on ya, yer in big trouble."

Stormy cocked his head. "A man runs off with another man's wife, he's got to expect some dust to be raised. You did a good job on the ring. Thank you . . . and thanks for the information."

The jeweler grinned his long-toothed smile. "You never heard nothin' from me, cowboy. Good luck."

Outside, Hood cast a quick look across the Plaza toward the Palace, half-inclined to go to the bar first before he collected his animals and headed for the hotel. No, get a room—and the clerk in there had better not give him any lip because he was in no mood for more trouble. After he had the horses off the street and settled, he would go have dinner at the Palace and in the process, see if he could locate Veracity.

A lump rose into his throat. What would he do if he couldn't find her? Suppose Reynolds had her

252

tucked away somewhere with his other women—for what purpose, he couldn't imagine—but suppose . . .

Like the catch in his throat, the knowledge: *I love her!* sprang without warning into his mind, and he was totally astonished by it. What he'd thought of as a necessary association, or perhaps a marriage of convenience (or even as one of propriety) had evolved quite without him noticing it into . . . one hell of a lot more!

No, he couldn't lose her now. By God, he *wouldn't* lose her now! If Reynolds had Veracity hidden somewhere for *whatever* reason, he'd tear the damn place apart until he found her. If Reynolds had persuaded her to work for him, he would buy her back or steal her back, or . . . Prescott wasn't that big a place; still, the thought that he might not be able to locate Veracity again raised such a fear into his heart that—leading his string, and despite his game leg—he almost ran toward the hotel.

Veracity had been stunned into inaction by the turn of events. It was all too much—the carnage at the Indian ruin, her and Stormy's impromptu wedding, and now her new husband hauled off to jail as a horse thief. . . . When Bart Reynolds hustled her toward the Palace, her mind blurred into a fog of shock. She didn't even think about resisting, for the moment forgot about the

Avenging Angel in her reticule and the derringer in her boot. She saw the crowd—not yet quite a mob—close around Sean before moving the horses, the mule, and their prisoner rapidly on down the street, and did gather herself enough to cry, *"Stormy!"*

Reynolds urged her onward in the opposite direction. "No, no, Miss Cooper, you don't want to get mixed up in that. You won't do anyone any good by putting yourself in jeopardy. Come with me now, Miss Cooper."

"Missus Hood!" Veracity roused herself. "I'm not Miss Cooper . . . I'm Missus Hood, and my husband . . ."

"He'll be all right. Sheriff Mosher cleaves to loafing, and pursues a policy of *laissez-faire*."

She looked up at him. She didn't understand. "A policy of what?"

"*Laissez-faire* . . . a deliberate avoidance of action. He doesn't like violence . . . likes a nice quiet town. Though Prescott isn't a hanging town, you should still wait this out in my office. Come on. Come on, now, Miss . . . Missus Hood." He guided her over Plaza grass, past the gazebo, across Montezuma Street and to the Palace doors.

There, Veracity wrenched her arm from Reynolds's hold. Her expression screwed into concern, she whirled and headed back toward where she could see the crowd nearing a building marked by a faded sign announcing: *Sheriff's*

Office over there at the southern edge of the park.

Again, the Palace owner caught her and held her back. "Missus Hood, I'm not trying to do you harm. Your husband has enough to worry about without having to concern himself with your safety as well. *Please,* come with me. We can wait this out in my office."

Veracity turned to face him. Eyes blazing, she cried, "Unhand me, sir! I am a Pinkerton agent who can vouch for Stormy's innocence, and my credentials will surely convince your sheriff of my veracity! But they do no good if the man never sees them!"

Reynolds grinned. "Proof of Veracity's veracity?" He took her elbow a third time. "And you a Pinkerton agent? Oh, come now, Missus Hood!"

"I am! I most certainly am!" Veracity still didn't move. She looked pained at Reynolds making a pun of her name, but dug in her reticule and snapped, "Let me show you something, Mister Reynolds."

He had evidently expected her to produce the credentials in question; he wasn't prepared to defend himself when, instead of papers, she pulled her Avenging Angel from her bag and shoved the sawed-off muzzle against his stomach.

He let go of her arm, took a step back, and lifted both hands shoulder-high. His smile broadened as his eyes sparkled to humor. "You're not going to shoot me out here on the street, Missus Hood. I'm not a villain. Didn't I help your husband over there by calming the crowd? I kept Mister Hood from being lynched as a horse thief, Veracity. I have no malice at heart, I assure you. In fact, quite the opposite." He reached to cover her gun hand with his own, and his palm was as soft as if he'd never done a day's physical work in his life. His smile stayed. His eyebrows lifted encouragingly.

Veracity licked her lips and glanced back toward the sheriff's office. The crowd had massed on the boardwalk outside the front door now. All seemed fairly quiet. Still looking in that direction, she opened her mouth to continue her protest, but Reynolds said smoothly, "See? The worst that is happening to . . . Stormy? . . . you called him Stormy? . . . is that he's in a jail cell. After the citizens go about their business, we'll go over and get him out. But you might do him more harm than good if you interfere there now." He let go of the Avenging Angel and again offered her his arm.

His logic finally got through to her. Besides, she'd tried to rescue Stormy before . . . *had* rescued him before, but in the process, had botched things up as far as he was concerned. Maybe this time it was better to do as Mr. Reynolds suggested. Grimly, she nodded, replaced Angel into her bag, cinched the top, ignored Reynolds's arm, and stalked onward into the Palace.

Grinning, he followed.

His office was on the ground floor at the rear of the Palace behind the gambling area and to the right of the wide stairs leading to the brothel above. Veracity didn't know what she expected to see, but the room was a far cry from what a saloon and whorehouse owner's private quarters might have been.

The floor was softened by a thick dark carpet discreetly-patterned beneath heavy leather-upholstered wingback chairs arranged around a huge mahogany desk. The wall behind the desk held shelves containing law books and fine literature; the walls, themselves, were well-sanded and oiled wooden slats decorated here and there by framed daguerreotypes of beautiful horses and an even more lovely countryside.

A carved whiskey cabinet sat against another wall. Its open doors presented bottles of expensive liquor and elegant crystal decanters surrounded by etched glass stemware. A large bay window at the right of the bookcase hosted a small round table attended by two chairs whose needlepoint cushions were done in maroon and beige. Beyond the window lay a tiny well-fenced private garden. All very masculine. Exceedingly high-class.

"Please be seated, Missus Hood. Would you

care for a little brandy to settle your nerves?"

"I don't drink," Veracity snapped. Her detective training made her look at what papers she could see cluttering the desk top. Bills. Business transactions. Horse breeding and bloodline records.

"Of course not. Medicinal purposes, only." Despite her refusal, Reynolds moved to the liquor cabinet, filled a glass for her, a larger one for himself, and again indicated a chair. He handed her the glass as he nodded to the seat. "Relax, Missus Hood, I'm not going to bite you. To the contrary, haven't I tried to help? Please sit and tell me about yourself and . . . Stormy. You say you're a Pinkerton agent? I didn't know Pinkerton agents brought their spouses with them when they . . . But wait! Barely a week ago, you introduced yourself to me as *Miss Cooper*. Or was that merely an alias?" He eased into the chair behind his desk, leaned back and sipped at his glass, his blue eyes studying her curiously.

She also sipped. The brandy was golden, smooth, and warmed her throat without burning. "No, then I *was* Miss Cooper. Sean and I have only been married two days . . . two and a half days."

"Sean? I expect *Sean* and *Stormy* are the same person? I hadn't been aware you knew people in this locality or had come west to wed. I got the impression you were new here and alone in Prescott."

"I was. I don't. I . . . didn't." *What was happening to Stormy? How could she just sit here and talk over brandy to this man when perhaps Sean needed her. . . .*

"Oh? Then, you just met Mister Hood?"

"Well, yes. Uh . . . no . . . uh . . ." *. . . to rescue him again? Maybe this time, he REALLY needed rescuing! Suppose, in spite of Mister Reynolds's assurances, they DID hang Stormy, then what would she do?*

Reynolds tipped his head. "Are you saying you married someone you've only known a few days, Miss . . . Missus Hood?"

"No, I . . . well, yes. It was a spur-of-the-moment thing, I'll admit that, but . . ." *But I love him!*

That revelation took her aback for a moment. Abruptly, she found herself relating the whole case to Reynolds. She knew in her heart that she was talking too much and was being defensive about it, but kept on—somehow, she didn't want Reynolds to think her a flighty girl who wed the first man who asked her, or even one who jumped from man-to-man merely to ensure a male presence in a strange land. She told him about her home in Philadelphia, and he chuckled at her reasons for breaking her engagement to Charles. He listened with fascination to her travel tales and guffawed over her and Hood's flight from the hotel. At one point, he interrupted her long enough to order dinner brought in and set up at the window table. While they ate an excellently-prepared meal served on fine china, he heard of the events at the ancient cliff dwelling and then about the wedding at Ft. Verde.

"So you see, Mister Reynolds," Veracity dabbed her lips with a damask napkin and crumpled cloth beside the *flàn* dish, "I have known Stormy Hood longer than a few days . . . by case records, if not in person. And he is *not* a horse thief!"

"Nor even a philanderer, it seems. That was a fascinating story, Missus Hood." Reynolds threw down his own napkin. "Now, if you're feeling better and are done eating, let's go see if we can extricate Sean from his present predicament."

"Yes!" She rose immediately and headed for the door, but then hesitated. "Oh. H-How much do I owe you for the meal, Mister Reynolds?"

"Bart," he smiled. He reached around her to open the panel for her, and Veracity flinched from the noise and smoke that blasted through at them from the bar and gambling area in front. "Please call me Bart. Ummm . . . perhaps you could play the piano for me a while this evening—that will be ample payment for dinner." He took her elbow to escort her toward the street doors.

They met Hood just coming in as they were going out.

"Stormy!" Veracity cried. She broke away from Reynolds, rushed to meet Sean and flung arms around him to hug tightly to him. "Are you all right? Did they hurt you? Is everything all right? What happened!"

Overwhelmingly glad to see her, Sean returned the embrace. He whispered into her hair, "Fine . . . fine, now that I've found you again. At least they didn't hang me. Are you . . . ?"

"Okay!" She pushed back to search his face anxiously to discover whether he was lying or not. There was nothing there but the fading bruises and healing cuts caused by Oscar Pratt's hired hardcases' fists—nothing new except a softness in his eyes that made her gasp. With her own eyes lingering on him, she took his hand and turned to where the Palace owner stood waiting with a half-smile on his lips. "Stormy, I'd like you to meet Mister Bart Reynolds. Mister Reynolds, my husband, Sean Hood."

Left arm still around Veracity, Stormy nodded to Reynolds but didn't offer to shake his hand. "We've met. The last time, he was pointing a derringer at me."

Reynolds chuckled. "I wanted to make sure you didn't do anything so foolish you would get yourself killed. It . . . seemed the best course of action at the time."

"Why!" Hood frowned. "Why do you care what happens to me? What am I to you?"

Again, Reynolds laughed. Instead of answering, he asked, "Have you had dinner yet?"

"No," Stormy answered cautiously. The ingrained instinct that had kept him alive throughout his run across the continent grabbed at his gut. Arm still around Veracity, he took a step back toward the door. He said, tensely, "Thank you for caring for my wife during that incident out there. I'm grateful, but we have to be going now." He took another step back. His right hand hovered near his gun butt.

If Reynolds noticed the nearness of Stormy's fingers to the weapon, he didn't mention it. Instead, he nodded toward an empty table. "Missus Hood has promised to play the piano a while for me tonight. She calls it payment for her dinner. . . ."

"*I* can pay for her dinner," Sean snapped.

". . . but *I* call it a pleasurable interlude in an otherwise boring day."

"*My* day has not been boring." Sean's arm tightened around Veracity. "I've rented a room at the hotel. . . ."

"The food there is not what I call eatable," Reynolds noted. "I'll even throw in *your* meal as an incentive. What can an hour hurt, Mister Hood? And it would give me an opportunity to get to know you better . . . if I may join you while Veracity entertains us?"

What does this hombre *have up his sleeve?* Sean wondered. *WHY is he being so "nice"? And the last time I thought there would be no harm in delaying an hour or so was at the Indian ruins . . . look what happened there!* He glanced down at Veracity.

She read his puzzlement and wariness; said quickly, "I *did* promise to play tonight, Stormy."

Sean hesitated a breath longer, but then nodded. "All right. She can play for her dinner and as my thanks to you for keepin' me from gettin' my neck stretched out there, but I'll pay for my own meal. It's the least I can do. *One hour,* and then we go home."

He released Veracity, moved to the table and loosened his side-arm in its holster. He sat with his back to the wall so he could keep an eye on the door, the room, and Veracity where she would be seated at the piano, but most especially on the man named Bart Reynolds, because something odd was going on here, something he couldn't yet fathom, and it made him nervous as hell!

CHAPTER THIRTEEN

Reynolds waited until his guest had ordered dinner—steak rare, fried potatoes, greens, apple pie and coffee—and Veracity had ousted Mike at the piano to begin with: *Oh, My Darling Clementine*, before he asked, "You intend to stay the night in Prescott?"

"Yes." Hood's response was curt and to the point. That he didn't trust Reynolds was more than obvious.

"Planning on leaving tomorrow?"

"Yes."

"Headed back to New York City?"

"Veracity told you that's where I'm from?"

"Yes, I persuaded her to tell me about you."

"Why? Why do you care about me?"

"Stormy . . ."

"Only my wife or my friends call me that, Mister Reynolds."

Bart tipped his head in acknowledgment. "All right, *Mister Hood,* it would please me a great deal if you could see your way clear to stay in Prescott a couple of days."

Stormy again scowled; again asked, "Why?"

"Oh, I thought perhaps you would like to see some of the countryside around here. It's quite nice, you know."

"I've seen some of the countryside around here. It *is* nice, but so what? Lots of countryside is nice." Eyes still on Reynolds, Hood attacked the meal Mike had delivered.

Bart took a sharp breath. Let it out. "Ummm . . . I have a ranch in what's called Skull Valley just to the west of town . . . sorry for the dramatic name, but I had no part in choosing it. I understand you and Veracity have had quite a trial recently. Perhaps you could stay a few days with me at my place. Rest up. Enjoy life for a change."

Sean's eyes narrowed another notch. He finished his steak, lay down his knife and fork, picked up his coffee mug and as he had before, asked, "Why?"

Reynolds reached to catch the wrist of one of his passing saloon girls. "Elba, bring Mister Hood, here, a glass of my special private stock. Whiskey, Mister Hood?"

"Don't mind if I do, thank you. Why, Mister Reynolds? No one . . . or few, I should say . . . ever does something for nothing. What's behind all this?"

Reynolds's smile deepened. "As I understand it, *you* did a great deal essentially for nothing . . . taking the blame for your brother's indiscretion, and all." When Stormy stiffened, he nodded. "Oh, yes, your wife told me all about you. Your action was commendable, perhaps, but as far as I'm concerned, stupid."

266

"My wife talks too much."

"Then, perhaps you should find yourself one more close-mouthed. In all fairness, let me tell *you* about *myself,* Mister Hood. I've owned the Palace for about six years. While there is a brothel upstairs, I do not run that . . . I rent space to Madame Aletha and her girls." He grinned wryly. "Their presence doesn't hurt my business at all.

"I have a very nice ranch outside of town. I'm educated in law and government, and I have my eye on becoming either the next territorial governor *or* first governor of the *State* of Arizona."

"I'd heard that," Stormy said shortly.

Reynolds nodded. "Now, I know you haven't spent much time here as yet, Mister Hood, but if you'd had an opportunity to look around, you would have noted three kinds of females in this area. There are the officers' wives out at Fort Whipple. Women accustomed to military protocol. Excellent hostesses. Generally well-bred ladies . . . but *taken,* yes?

"There are the town women or those from outlying ranches . . . strong, reliable, prolific . . . the pioneer type . . . but for the most part . . . unsophisticated. I'm looking for a woman qualified to become First Lady of Arizona, and certain attributes are required for that position, none of which any of the decent local women possess.

"*And* then, of course, there are the prostitutes, certainly none of whom could ever be considered. In short, Mister Hood, I *had* resigned myself to looking outside the territory for a suitable consort . . . until Miss Cooper appeared. *Ah-ah-ah!* Let me finish!"

Stormy had sat bolt upright in his chair, wide-eyed and half-laughing with disbelief. He gasped, "You're telling me you want . . . you want Veracity to . . ."

The girl, Elba, had returned with a half-glass of dark whiskey. She set it in front of Sean and lingered until Reynolds waved a hand at her to shoo her away. Without taking his eyes off Hood, he continued, "As I understand it, you originate from a wealthy eastern family, Mister Hood. True, *there,* you may be a man of means . . . *or you may not be!* Your father may have cut you entirely from his Will. Your brother may have employed lawyers to overturn any inheritance you might have received . . . after all, you haven't been there to defend your interests. At this moment, you are a next-to-destitute drifter, your fortunes dependent on regular remittances sent—*or not sent*—from back east for your support. Failing to receive money to fund food and a roof over your head, you must obtain work as a temporary ranch hand, trail driver, or perhaps hired gun, when and where you can find the job. The hunters you just defeated may, *or may not,* be the only ones after you. What kind of a life is that for a woman of Miss Cooper's obvious breeding and quality?

"I, on the other hand, Mister Hood, am a man of property and have a career of prominence and perhaps fame in my future. If you have any feelings for Veracity at all, can you deny that an alliance with me is much more beneficial to her long-term welfare than marriage to you?"

Sean was so astounded that he could hardly speak. He sat in ice-cold shock for a long moment before he gasped, "You slimy, conniving son of a bitch, you expect me to give up my wife merely because . . ."

"Think of *Veracity,* Mister Hood, not of yourself."

"I am. She's my wife! Our marriage has been consummated! She's not a . . ."

"That whiskey you're about to drink, Mister Hood," Reynolds interrupted. "Try it . . . you'll find it excellent. Drink it and then tell me . . . can you truthfully say it is less invigorating merely because the bottle had previously been . . . opened? No, that Miss Cooper is no longer completely virginal is of no consequence. Besides, we men must take care of the ladies in this world . . . few know what's best for them, and . . ."

"That one does! By God, you can't ask me to . . ." Sean's voice choked when he realized that slightly less than two days ago, in the commandant's borrowed bedroom at Ft. Verde, he'd struggled with the same thoughts Reynolds now put into words. He had almost left money on the bed table and vanished into the wilderness then, but had talked himself out of it. Since that moment, though, he had come to realize he loved Veracity.

But so what? He didn't know whether she loved him or had merely been as caught up by the moment as he'd been and now "lived with" her decision. Certainly, Reynolds was right; life as the wife of the governor of Arizona would be much more stable and rewarding for Veracity in the long run than life as the wife of a Remittance Man.

He reached for the whiskey. It was indeed smooth—he didn't even shudder as it went down—and the bitter aftertaste it left was probably from his own acceptance of Reynolds's argument. Across the room, Veracity was playing a lively rendition of *Little Brown Jug*. Yes, she deserved better than what he could give her. He opened his mouth to agree—and at that moment, Reynolds would have won had he kept his own mouth shut.

Bart asked, "Do you have a good horse, Mister Hood?"

"What?"

"A good horse. Tell you what, Mister Hood. I'm a sporting man. Since we both know that women are sometimes illogical in matters of the heart, or are perhaps overly-swayed by some misbegotten feelings of . . . um . . . loyalty? . . . we'll keep this just between ourselves. I have a good horse. You have a good horse? We'll hold a race tomorrow, let's say the length of Montezuma Street. You win, you and Veracity go your way, and that will be that. I win, *you* go your way for her benefit. I can have Judge Welforth make sure she's properly divorced before you leave. A sporting deal, Mister Hood. What do you say?"

Stormy's astonishment solidified into cold humor . . . the situation was becoming so bizarre that it settled his mind back into its usual cool assessment. He stifled the urge to leap up and blow Reynolds's head off; instead, he said, "You're making Veracity into a mere pawn in your political advancement scheme, aren't you. I wonder how she would like that? Do you honestly believe she would accept the role as your *consort* when her hand was won as a result of a horse race?"

"It's for her ultimate benefit, Mister Hood. Besides, she won't know. I'm not going to tell her."

"You'd better believe *I* am, you bastard. Women are *people,* not merely chattel! . . . and *she* is . . ."

"She's merely a female, Mister Hood. Her

function is to be a charming hostess, produce heirs, and otherwise . . ."

"Be sent off to bed like a child. That's why she broke her engagement with Charles Whoever-whatever back in Philadelphia, or didn't she tell you that?" Sean licked his lips. They seemed numb and dry. He noted that his fingers tingled, but didn't have time to focus on that because Reynolds nodded.

"Oh, yes. But then, I believe her circumstances were some different."

Sean finished off the whiskey, set the glass softly onto the table top, and pushed back his chair. "No thank you, Reynolds. Believe it or not, I find that I happen to love my wife. And I respect her as a human being. She's not someone to be a stake in a horse race. Secondly, I believe her hour of giving you a piano recital is about to be cut short."

"Too bad, Mister Hood. I had hoped we could be civilized about this and could work out a gentleman's agreement. I see I made a serious mistake, both here *and* earlier when I kept the crowd from lynching you.

"Mister Hood, this is my town. I can see to it that you never reach the city limits, that the charges originally brought against you are reinstated, and then I'm sure that Veracity, as your *widow,* would be amenable to my approach. After all, a woman alone in the frontier—even a licensed Pinkerton agent—needs the protection of a successful man's strong arm, doesn't she?"

Stormy started to stand, but abruptly found that his legs wouldn't work. Again, he licked his lips; began, "You're threatening to h-have me . . . have me killed . . ." A sudden knowledge pierced the mist rising in his brain. "Why, you b-bastard, you sl-slipped me a drugged drink, didn't . . ." Somehow, he couldn't finish the accusation.

"Race me for Veracity, walk out of here on your own and never come back, or hang as a horse thief, Mister Hood," Bart grinned, watching him closely. "It's all up to you, now." He reached to move Sean's plate aside when Hood again tried to stand but instead collapsed unconscious over the table; finished to no one in particular, "And a night in jail will keep you from talking too much to my woman." He raised a hand to beckon to his bouncers.

At the piano, Veracity played *Beautiful Dreamer* while the regular pianist, Mike, sang. Her back was to the room. She didn't see Ike and Grant carry Stormy out, and the disposal of a falling-down drunk was such a normal occurrence in the saloon, none of the other patrons took much, if any, notice.

After the men had taken Hood away, Reynolds called Elba back to his table and spoke to her at length. She seemed reluctant at first, but when he handed her a twenty-dollar gold piece, she smiled, flounced her beribboned rear, and hurried up the stairs to see if she could round up what he'd ordered.

Unaware of what had gone on behind her, Veracity played the piano for another half-hour or forty-five minutes. The slip of paper Bart gave her when she finished said succinctly: *V. I have something I have to do. See you tomorrow. S.*

The only sample of Stormy's handwriting she had ever seen was his signature on their marriage certificate; she didn't know that Reynolds had penned the note himself. She frowned from the paper to Bart. "This is all? He didn't tell you where he was going or why?"

Reynolds shook his head. "He merely said he had business to attend to, and that he would be back tomorrow morning. Your playing was delightful, Vera. Perhaps . . ."

"Veracity," she snapped. "Veracity! *Not Vera!*"

"Of course. Sorry. *But,* you can consider yourself paid in full here, my dear. Uh . . . I believe I heard Mister Hood say he'd rented a room at the hotel . . . may I escort you there?" He extended his arm.

Perplexed by Stormy's absence, but without any real reason to protest, Veracity slipped her hand through Bart's elbow and allowed him to walk her around the Plaza. In eastern cities, the men walked near the street to shield their ladies from water or debris thrown up by passing buggy wheels. Here, Reynolds walked on the inside to protect Veracity from drunks either voluntarily exiting or forcibly evicted from the saloons. It was a leisurely stroll punctuated by hats tipped to them by what men they met and a running commentary on the town from Reynolds, himself. Clearly, he considered Prescott his, Prescott knew it was his, he made sure Veracity understood this, and none of it was lost on her.

He bid her good night at the foot of the hotel stairs before he said sternly to the desk clerks, "Take good care of Missus Hood . . . she's my very good friend, gentlemen," and left with a "See you tomorrow," to Veracity.

She almost yelled after him, "I'm *not* your *very good friend!*" but then thought that might make matters worse, and merely hurried on up the stairs. Despite the pitcher of lemonade and the potted plant brought immediately to her room, she spent an uneasy night wondering where Stormy had gone, and why.

Sean came to an hour later with a queasy stomach, a raging headache, and to find himself behind bars in the same cell the drunk, Neff, had once occupied. He sat on the bunk, his head in his hands until the effects of the drug really wore off, and listened to Sheriff Mosher snore in his chair out front.

Finally, he yelled until he woke Mosher, and

demanded to be let out. The sheriff ignored him. He tried to get a piece of paper and a pencil to send a message to Veracity. Mosher told him no. He asked the sheriff to at least get someone to carry a verbal message to her so she would know where he was. Mosher again began to snore. He rattled bars and maligned Mosher, Prescott, Arizona, and everything else he could think of, with no results. At last, resigned to a night in jail, he returned to his bunk, sat, drew up a knee and spent a while thinking.

Reynolds had stated clearly that he'd pegged Veracity as his preferred future wife . . . *consort,* he'd called her. He had also clearly demonstrated that in this town, he had the power to easily overcome by force any kind of objection he, Sean, might raise. Still, instead of merely having him taken out into the greasewood and shot, the man had opted for a contest, which said he might not be a total bastard.

All right, then, he would get his contest. But the stakes had to be higher. As it stood, if Reynolds won, he gained a wife—supposedly (Sean couldn't by any stretch of his imagination, believe that Veracity would go along with this!)— while if *he* won, he got to keep her. He already had her, and since his unexpected realization that he loved her, by God, he wasn't going to lose her.

But merely keeping his marriage intact wasn't enough. There had to be an excuse for running the race tomorrow, some stake other than Veracity's hand, because despite what he'd said to Reynolds, he preferred that she didn't know what the contest was really about. He could envision her being as outraged at him as she would be at Reynolds, and that was as good a way to lose his wife as not winning the race.

What did Reynolds have that would do? The saloon? No, he couldn't picture himself running a western bar or brothel, no matter how . . . ah!

His glower became a grim smile. Yes, that was it. He shifted on the bunk, lay back, propped his hat over his eyes and tried to sleep, but worry over Veracity alone out there with Bart Reynolds, worry about which horse to use tomorrow—Pratt's black, the big rangy bay, *sure* not that damn mule, or Spot—and a residual headache behind his eyes kept him awake.

Spot. Spot was strong, willing, and incredibly well-trained, but was he fast enough? He wasn't a particularly big horse, and if Reynolds brought out some long-legged thoroughbred . . .

Still, Spot. It had to be Spot, didn't it.

"Did you get any breakfast?"

Sean looked coldly at Bart Reynolds. It was about nine fifteen in the morning. He had been escorted by three hefty toughs from the jail to the saloon owner's office at the rear of the Palace and stood in front of the desk. Reynolds sat in his

277

chair, elbows on its arms, a pen held horizontally before his teeth and what looked suspiciously like a contract laid out on the desk top before him.

"I tried some of that bilge water the sheriff passes off for coffee and decided that if it was an indication of the rest of the meal, I could live without it."

Reynolds laughed. "Yes. *Du Shane's* services the jail." He nodded to the chair. "Sit and read this, then sign it."

Sean glanced at the bouncers standing behind and beside him. No one had returned his weapons—they had vanished somewhere last night—and his "escort" was unanimously armed with heavy muscles, broad backs, and evil dispositions. He sat.

Reynolds pushed the paper toward him. "I take it you can read?"

"Yep." Hood took the paper and scanned it. It said that if he lost the horse race, he agreed to depart Prescott carrying none of his possessions (including his wife) along, with the exception of one horse, one saddle and bridle, his bedroll and weapons, and was never to return to the area. If he won, he could keep everything, but still agreed to leave Arizona.

"No," he said.

Reynolds's brows rose. "No?" He indicated his men. "I don't believe you're in any position to say no, Mister Hood. I prefer to do things legally and . . . amicably . . . but this is . . . dangerous country. Indians, you know. A variety of other hazards? Men have a habit of turning up *accidentally dead* here. I suggest you rethink your refusal."

"I had a whole night in jail to think about this." Stormy tossed the paper back to Reynolds. "I agree on the horse race, yes. I agree that if I lose, I'll go peacefully and . . . alone. But if I win, as this contract stands, I'll have nothing to show for my victory except what I've got now. That's not good enough, Reynolds. You win, you gain a wife and my absence. *I* win, I keep Veracity, *and* you sign that ranch out in Skull Valley you been talkin' about over to me. And I want it in writing. Make out a new contract."

"You're out of your mind! That ranch is worth far more than . . ."

"Hey!" Stormy cut him off. He spread his hands and grinned, "I'm not the one who wants to be a big fish around here. You're the one who insists on this whole thing." He leaned back and crossed one ankle over the other knee. "Sure, you can have these varmits kill me. But just remember that Veracity may look like a pretty, sometimes kind of frazzled little woman, but she's a trained Pinkerton agent. People—male *or* female—don't become detectives unless they have a naturally nosy nature. You do me in, I never show up again. Given that she knows we were headed east together as man and wife, she'll decide something strange happened to me. She'll start asking questions. *Investigating,* Reynolds, as she's been trained to investigate. One day, she'll come up with the answer, and as we saw last night, she sometimes talks too much. Then, think of the damage she could do to your political career!

"You want her, you've got to pay for her. You'll have to take the chance I'll lose the race and you'll not only gain a woman but get to keep your land. But I win, well, that's your gamble. After all, you said you were a *sporting man.*"

Bart tipped his head and tapped the pen against bared teeth for a long moment. His bouncers seemed poised to do mayhem upon their charge. They looked disappointed when Reynolds nodded, swept up the contract, crumpled it, produced another paper and wrote rapidly. He blew on the ink to dry it before he presented the new deal to Sean. "Try that, Mister Hood."

Again, Stormy took the paper and read it carefully. This time when he was finished, he reached for the pen, also signed, and sailed the sheet back to Reynolds. "Where's my wife?"

"I assume still getting her beauty sleep at the hotel. I invited her to breakfast with me, but she hasn't appeared, so . . ." Bart folded the contract and put it into the inside breast pocket of his jacket. "I also assume you have a horse you want to ride? Where is it?"

"In the hotel stable."

"All right. Ike, Grant, and Tardy will accompany you while you check him out and to assure that you appear on time for the race."

"And when will that be?"

"Ummm . . . ten o'clock. My head wrangler is even now bringing my horse in from Skull Valley . . . he'll be here by that time. That gives you about fifteen minutes to ready your mount. You will be back here in front of the Palace at ten, sharp."

He shifted his attention to his bouncers. "Men, he can go to the hotel stable to check his horse, but stand guard over him. I *will* have him here at ten, mounted and ready to ride, understand?" His expression hardened. "And he is not to talk to anyone . . . *no one at all before the race, do you understand that!*"

They nodded and grasped Hood to lift him out of the chair. Stormy stood and jerked his arms free. "I know the way to the stable." He stalked out with the hardcases close on his heels.

CHAPTER FOURTEEN

Veracity had seriously overslept. She hadn't awakened until a knock at her door brought her bleary-eyed and headachy from a night of tossing, turning, and worrying about Stormy. She struggled out of bed in her camisole and bloomers, stumbled to the door and asked, "Who is it?"

"Tom, your bellhop, Missus Hood. I got a package for you."

A package? More awake now, she realized she had no robe available to cover herself. "Uh . . . just set it down outside the door, please. I'll get it later, Tom. Thank you."

"As you wish, Ma'm."

When she was sure he'd gone, Veracity unlocked the door, cracked it and peered into the hall. A large cardboard box rested on the rug. She stuck her head out and looked both ways to make sure no one would see her in her under-things, found the corridor empty, hastily grabbed the box and retreated into the safety of the room.

Frowning, she carried the box to the bed, untied the string and lifted the top. Inside, beneath a single folded sheet of paper, was a crisp white blouse, a long cotton waist-slip, and a tailored skirt and jacket—a suit in dark ruby red. *A red outfit!*

"Oh, Sean! Oh, Stormy!" So *that's* where he'd gone last night—out to find a red dress for her! But why hadn't he brought it himself?

She picked up the note—saw it was written by the same hand as his note telling her he "had something to do"—and quickly read it. It said: *Sorry the clothing is second-hand, but it was the best I could do on such short notice. Hope it fits. We'll have another made just for you as soon as possible. Please wear it and come have breakfast at the Palace.* And it was signed . . .

"Bart? *Bart Reynolds?*" She flung the note back onto the blouse. Mister Reynolds had presented her with a gift . . . *of clothing?* How presumptuous of him! How forward! No lady accepted gifts from strange men, much less something as personal as *clothing! How dare* . . .

Her eyes widened as her heart squeezed. She grabbed the note from where it had fallen and dashed around the end of the bed to her reticule sitting atop the lamp table, opened it, and searched within it for that *other* note, the one Stormy had left her last evening. There! There it was!

Fingers trembling to a somehow frightening suspicion, she compared the two. Yes, she was right. The writing *was* the same. Then, if Bart Reynolds had sent *today's* missive, he'd also

284

written the note yesterday evening. Which meant that Sean hadn't written it. Which meant that wherever Sean had gone, he may not have done so voluntarily. Which meant that . . .

Whispering, "Oh, Stormy! Oh, Sean . . . oh, my, Stormy!" she leaped back to the box, dropped the note inside, slammed on the lid and hurried to dress in her old clothing. She brushed out her hair and jammed her hat over it. Fury and fear clutching at her throat, she slid Angel beneath her belt, seized the box, and with it under her arm, dashed out into the hall. She rushed down the stairs, across the lobby, and out the front door just too late to see Reynolds's bullyboys escort Sean around to the rear of the building on their way to the hotel stable.

Female citizens going about their business on the streets stepped aside and whispered behind their hands, wondering who the obviously outraged young woman in the odd floppy straw hat, man's shirt, and split riding skirt was, whose boot heels rang on the boardwalk as she strode toward Whiskey Row. Some stopped to watch her progress; then, their mouths fell open when the girl shoved unhesitatingly on the Palace doors and vanished inside. A calico cat, they decided. Not a lady, because no respectable woman ever went into a place like that unless it was to retrieve a wayward husband, and at this time of the morning? Well!

But then, they began to drift toward the Palace, because a ranch hand trotted up Gurley Street leading a saddled quarter horse, obviously one of Mr. Reynolds's by the gleaming chestnut coat and expensive outfitting, and then several men burst from the bar to begin shouting through the doors of the other establishments along Montezuma Street.

The women drew others with them. A crowd began to form. People up and down Gurley and from Cortez across the Plaza noted the occurrence and hurried to join in. Presently, Mr. Reynolds, himself, stepped out onto the boardwalk in front of the Palace. He was accompanied by the girl in the strange straw hat—she was without the box, but still flushed and seemingly furious. They all appeared to be waiting for something to happen or for someone else to arrive.

"Stormy," Veracity breathed with relief.

Flanked by three burly men, he led Spot at a walk down Gurley from the vicinity of the hotel stable. He was still dressed in what he'd worn yesterday. His hat hung down his back by the chin string to let black hair blow in the wind. His movements were calm, yet Veracity thought she'd never seen him look so grim. The crowd parted to let him and his guards through to where she and Reynolds stood; Sean met her eyes, but merely nodded to her. He didn't speak or smile.

It was Reynolds who said, "This is my head wrangler, Jack Dwiggins, Mister Hood."

Sean turned as the cowboy dismounted the lead horse. The man was at least four inches shorter than he, red-haired and rawhide-thin—must have weighed twenty pounds less. He tipped a finger to Dwiggins, hoping Jack wasn't going to be Reynolds's jockey, because the weight variance, alone, would put Spot at a disadvantage.

"And *this* . . ." Reynolds stepped to the quarter horse to stroke the animal's neck, ". . . is Flame." He raised brows to Hood as though asking: *Still want to go through with this?*

"Good lookin' horse," Sean acknowledged. He had to admit that beside the sleek quarter horse, Spot was a scrub.

Again, he glanced over at Veracity. Frowning, she mouthed a silent, "What's going on?"

He gritted his teeth, checked Spot's saddle cinch, and swung astride. Beside him, Dwiggins handed his lead horse over to a bystander before he also tightened Flame's cinch and mounted.

Reynolds lifted his voice to what was now a considerable crowd. "We're going to hold a race here, folks, from this point . . ." He stepped off the boardwalk and began to draw a line in the dirt across Montezuma Street with the edge of his boot sole, ". . . to South Pine, *around* the tree and back to this line." He smiled at the town folks. "Mister Hood, here, thinks his

287

cayuse can best my Flame." While citizens chuckled and muttered among themselves and moved back to clear the starting line, Reynolds indicated the pinto. "Your pony have a name, Hood?"

"Spot."

"Spot! That's a dog's name!"

"Yes, well, so be it. I take it *South Pine* is that tree you've left standing in the middle of the road down yonder?"

"Yes. Any other questions before we start?"

"Yes. Don't you think you should tell these good people what the stakes are in this race, *Mister Reynolds?*"

Bart made a gesture of dismissal. "Oh, that's not relevant. We're merely seeing who has the best horse here."

"No, we're not, Reynolds." Hood reached back, snagged his hat, settled it over his hair and tightened the string under his chin. "The stakes are real damn high, and I think *they* . . ." his eyebrow indicated the crowd, though he was really talking to Veracity, ". . . would be interested. Did you bring the deed to your ranch with you in case I win?"

"Deed to your ranch?" Dwiggins looked astonished. "You mean if I lose this race, I'll be workin' fer *him,* Mister Reynolds?"

Beside Bart, Veracity's own eyes widened, not only at the revelation of the stakes, but because she'd just noticed that while Stormy wore his holster and knife sheath, both were empty.

Sean answered for Reynolds, loudly, so he knew everyone could hear him. "You got it, Dwiggins. I win, the deed is mine and you're *my* head wrangler. You have the deed, *Mister Reynolds?*"

"It's in my office," Bart said. "Are you ready, gentlemen?" He pulled his derringer.

Veracity's eyes narrowed. She stifled an, "Ah!" before she smoothed her expression and said suddenly, "Mister Reynolds, why don't you use this instead?" She drew the Avenging Angel from her belt and offered it to him. "It's louder than your little pocket gun. Then, no one can say they didn't hear the starting pistol."

"All right." Bert tucked the derringer back into his jacket and accepted Angel.

Her eyes met Stormy's. He grinned appreciation at her and nodded acknowledgment. He understood perfectly. She smiled back. Both of them watched Reynolds walk up beside Spot and raise the sawed-off six-shooter into the air.

"Step back a little, Reynolds. I wouldn't want to run over you," Hood advised.

Bart shrugged and moved back a couple of paces.

Sean pulled down his hat brim, set his teeth, and took a firm hold on the saddle horn with his left hand when Reynolds shouted, "Ready! . . . set! . . ." He squeezed the trigger.

Spot exploded as though he'd been shot out of a cannon. The Avenging Angel going off so close beside him galvanized him into a leap that—even though Hood was ready for it—nearly unseated his rider. Sean recovered, and leaning low over the pinto's back, urged him onward up Whiskey Row toward what was called South Pine. Beside and behind them, townsfolk shouted encouragement. Some of the men also fired weapons into the air. Driven forward in a panicked flight from the noise, and unchecked by his rider, the gun-shy pinto initially outdistanced the other horse.

But Flame was a quarter horse capable of great bursts of speed over short distances. As they neared South Pine and left the gunfire behind, Spot began to calm down. From the corner of his eye, Hood saw Dwiggins spurring Flame to greater effort. Carrying less weight than the pinto, and with his strength, the quarter horse was catching up. Had caught up. Was a nose ahead.

Sean yelled at Spot, *"Come on! We lose, and we lose Veracity! Come on, boy!"* He didn't like to do it, but was forced to whip his mount with the reins.

They reached the tree. When Sean saw that Dwiggins had to fight Flame into a wide turn to head back, he involuntarily yelled, *"Ha!"*

It seemed that Spot understood his rider's outburst to be "Haw!" . . . turn left. He reared on hind legs and wheeled like a cutting horse (and almost tossed Hood in the process, because Sean hadn't expected such a reaction to his shout), and pounded back toward the crowd. They again had a lead, but only temporarily.

Once more, the quarter horse caught up with Spot and surged ahead. Nearly lying along the pinto's neck, Sean thought: *Spot hates guns and Indians!* He gave a wild Apache war whoop before he yelled, *"Bang! Pow! BangBang!"* He felt muscles bunch beneath him; then, a surge of speed.

Spot laid his ears back, stretched his neck, and foam flying from his open mouth, lengthened his stride, closed the gap, and now he and Flame were in a dead heat.

"BANG!" Hood put everything he had behind his shout. They pulled ahead by a nostril. Sean yelled, whooped, yodeled, and ki-yiied. Now, they were ahead by a neck.

In the end, Reynolds actually beat himself. He had picked a race track just a little too long. As they neared the finish line, the quarter horse began to lag. Tough little working horse that he was, Spot had more stamina in the long haul— he carried his rider across the line drawn in the dirt at the Palace Bar neck-and-shoulders ahead of Flame.

Afraid that if he "woah'ed" Spot verbally, the pinto would plant his feet and he would take an embarrassing dive over Spot's head and end up in the dirt, Sean braced his legs, leaned back against the cantle, and calmed the horse with gentle tugs at the reins. They were half-way down the next block before he tried a tentative, "Haw?"

Spot wheeled. They returned to the crowd at a slow canter, and *then,* Hood "woah'ed" Spot in front of where Reynolds stood looking as though he was about to kill somebody and Veracity danced from foot-to-foot with a less than dignified grin on her face.

Sean leaped from the saddle and at her. Arms outstretched as though she hadn't seen him in a month, she lunged to meet him. In full view of the citizens of Prescott, he kissed her soundly, crushed her in his arms and panted, "I love you! We did it! We won the race and I love you, dammit, Missus Hood, I should have said it before, but . . . here! Here!" He moved back and his fingers were so clumsy with urgency that he tore the button off his shirt pocket before he could get the ring out. He grabbed her left hand and slid the nugget band into place; gasped, "With *this* ring, I thee wed, Missus Hood, we're so good together you and that Avenging Angel, that was a damn sneaky move on your part do *you* love *me?*"

"I do! I do!" She flung arms around his neck

and covered his lips with hers before she asked, "We won! . . . yes, we won! . . . but *what* did we win?"

"Ah-*hah!*" Arm still around his wife, Sean stepped aside and nodded to the Palace owner. "I'll have my deed now, Mister Reynolds."

Red-faced and glowering, Reynolds began hotly, "It was a trick! Some kind of a trick! *No way* could crow-bait like that pinto best my blooded quarter horse!"

"Mister Reynolds," Sean waved a hand at the now-quietly listening crowd, "everyone witnessed the race. They heard the stakes before we started it. They saw the beginning, the middle, and the end. No tricks on my part, Mister Reynolds. Ol' Spot, here, just plain outlasted your quarter horse. You bet your Skull Valley ranch and you lost it. Now, pay up."

Still, Reynolds hesitated. He looked from Sean to Veracity; back to Sean when Hood asked softly so only the three of them could hear, "You want me to tell them what you would have taken from *me* had I lost? I think these good folks'd be quite interested in what you forced me to ante. And keep in mind your possible future in politics, Reynolds."

Bart sighed heavily. Presently, he nodded; said, "I'll be right back," and disappeared into the Palace.

Veracity frowned up at Sean. "What is it you

293

have that he *forced* you to put up as your side of the bet, Stormy? We only have a few dollars and three horses and a mule to our name!"

"Be patient. I'll tell you all about it tonight. First, we're going to go look at our new ranch and see to it ol' Spot, here, has a good, peaceful, *quiet* home as his reward for a job well done. And *then,* Missus Hood, we're going east to get this Remittance Man thing straightened out once and for all."

Reynolds was back. He had evidently composed himself with a swig of brandy while in his office because a breath of liquor floated away with the breeze when he handed the deed over to Stormy. He put on a rueful smile and said, "That's the land and buildings only. The stock is still mine. I'll have them off your ranch as soon as I can locate a suitable area." He nodded to where Dwiggins, beside Flame, stood looking like he'd lost his last friend. "You're fired. You can show them where the ranch is and tell the rest of the hands that they still work for me, but *you are fired!*"

Sean took the deed and tucked it into his back pocket before he turned to Dwiggins. "How much was Reynolds paying you?"

Jack told him.

Hood's brows rose. "Paid good! You want to work for me, I'll up your salary a dollar a month. You'll have nothing to do for a while but protect my property and take care of one horse. You think you'll get lonesome, pick yourself one other man to spell you. Deal?"

Dwiggins glanced from Hood to Reynolds and back to Sean. He grinned shyly and nodded. "It's a deal . . . Boss."

Sean patted his pocket. He asked of Reynolds, "I have to formally register this land transfer?"

Bart shrugged. "Some day, probably. I signed it. The townsfolk witnessed it. It should do you. Ummm . . . no hard feelings, Stormy?"

Sean looked slantwise at him. "I'll . . . think about it."

"Well, come election time, I'd appreciate your vote."

"I'll think about that, too."

Reynolds sighed. He looked at Veracity, seemed about to say something, but then merely bowed slightly and murmured, "Missus Hood, if you ever feel so inclined, the Palace piano is always at your disposal." He turned on his heel and reentered the saloon.

"Stormy Hood," Veracity breathed, "if you don't tell me what went on last night, we will shortly have our *second* wedded spat!"

He laughed, and leading Spot and followed by his new employee, headed through cheers and congratulations back toward the hotel stable to get a mount for Veracity.

Just to be on the safe side, Sean located the land office and registered the deed in his name,

295

before Dwiggins, leading Flame back to what was now only a temporary home, guided them out to Skull Valley. Stormy and Veracity found their ranch to be beautiful, the house sturdy and completely furnished, with a double dirt-filled roof for coolness and as protection against Indian arrows.

They checked out of the hotel and stayed three days at their new home, during which time Veracity heard what had happened to Hood at Reynolds's hands. That brought incensed ranting from her about that "overbearing-as-bad-as-Charles-clod . . . what did Bart Reynolds think she was that she would *ever* accept his hand. . . ." And on. *And* on.

Sean spent a good deal of the time calming her—not that he really minded, because he discovered that his wife now considered him to be a Knight in Shining Armor who had defended her at some risk and in open contest. He found he liked being a hero.

When Reynolds sent men to remove the furniture and other personal items from the ranch, the Hoods reluctantly decided it was also time for them to move on, perhaps into what would be the last phase of their lives before they could return to settle down in peace. Sean bit the bullet and bought two tickets on the stage to Phoenix.

CHAPTER FIFTEEN

Very early in the morning, and accompanied by Jack Dwiggins, Stormy and Veracity rode from the ranch back into Prescott to catch the Arizona Stage Company coach down into the low desert. Sean had asked Veracity whether or not she wanted to buy new clothing for the trip; she said no, why ruin something new when her old split skirt, checked shirt, and Panama hat were still serviceable? So it was that they began their journey looking much like they had prior to becoming successful land owners.

In Prescott, Sean turned Spot and the black gelding Veracity had ridden over to his foreman and grinned, "I guess I lied when I said all you would have to care for while we were gone was the ranch and one horse, Jack. It's three horses and a mule. Is that a problem for you?"

"Hell, no, Boss! No problem at all. Uh . . . when do you and the missus figger to be back?"

As if he could see New York from the Arizona Territory, Sean turned to look eastward for a moment before he shook his head sharply. "I don't know, Jack. Hopefully, before winter sets in, but . . ." He shrugged and was silent for a space before he finished, "It depends on a . . . lot of things."

"Uh . . . not to bring evil down on you by talkin' about it, but . . . what should I do if you *never* . . . ? I mean, it's one damn long trip from here to where yore goin', an' . . . I mean, the trail is full of Injuns an' road agents, an' who knows what else 'tween here an' . . . Uh . . . how long should I wait before I take it you ain't comin' back at all?"

"A year," Hood decided grimly. "If we're not back at the ranch by this time next year, the place is yours, Jack. We . . ."

"All 'board that's goin'!" the stage driver shouted. *"We're headed fer Dewey, Humboldt, Mayer, Cordes, Bumble Bee, Rock Springs, AND Phee-NIX! Git on, folks!"*

Stormy thrust a hand out to Dwiggins. When Jack clasped it, he shook the man's hand strongly and said, "I'm trustin' you to look after my interests here while Missus Hood and I are gone, Jack. See to it that Bart Reynolds doesn't come back and . . . um . . . confiscate anything that used to be his and is now mine, okay? And take good care of ol' Spot, here . . . he has earned a rest in a nice quiet pasture."

"Will do, Mister Hood. You can count on me!" Dwiggins stood back with the horses to watch while Sean handed Veracity up into the stage. He waved energetically while the door closed, the driver climbed up top, released the brake and slapped reins.

The stage didn't go down the same hill Sean had used or that the freight wagons Veracity had ridden with had toiled up. Instead, it cut east a ways, then south at the tiny town of Dewey onto what was called either the Woolsey Trail or the Black Canyon Road—once again, Veracity wished locals in this area would settle on a name and then stick to it! This trail was longer but less steep until they hit Antelope Hill, its narrow winding switchback ruts the last descent down off the escarpment before they reached the low desert.

The down-grade entailed a lot of cursing, *"Woah!"* and *"Hold up, thar!"* from the driver, and the grind from outside the coach of the wooden brake against metal wheel rims. More than once, the stage tipped dangerously as though it was going to go completely over. Somehow, amazingly it seemed, it didn't; nevertheless, after the fourth or fifth time of resettling his wife into her seat beside him when she was tossed against him by a particularly violent jolt, Sean growled, "Maybe we should have ridden our horses down to Phoenix. This is . . ."

Now, he bumped Veracity.

Instead of being aggravated, she grinned, passed arms around his neck, hugged to him, and despite raised brows from the middle-aged matron occupying the seat across from them, breathed, "Mmmm . . . nice to *meet* you, sir!"

He chuckled. "Seems we've met and met and *met* before, and our trip has just started. If this keeps up, we'll be black and blue by the time we reach New York."

"Oh, well, I find this rather exciting, don't you?"

"If we live through it," he laughed, and kept holding her.

The trip from Prescott to Phoenix took a day-and-a-half, during which the landscape gradually changed from fragrant Ponderosa and Jack pine to stubby mesquite, greasewood, and stands of cholla and barrel cactus. They spent the night at a ramshackle waystation at Rock Springs just south of the *Agua Fria*, a river that actually contained water. The beds were only mattress-less shelves under an open-air ocotillo-thatched roof where little lizards rustled and hunted, but at least the food was ample and well-cooked. They continued their journey just before dawn the next day, but without their traveling companion. The middle-aged woman—who had not spoken once from Prescott to Rock Springs—had evidently reached her destination.

Unlike yesterday's plunge off the escarpment, today's descent from Rock Springs to Phoenix entailed only about a thousand feet; more gradual, if hotter and dustier. The driver whipped the team into a breakneck pace across the desert to keep on schedule and reach Phoenix in time to catch the east-bound Butterfield Overland Stage. They made it with twelve minutes to spare, just enough time for Stormy to purchase tickets, for them to relieve themselves at the station outhouse, and then clamber aboard.

The driver of this new coach introduced himself as Gus Flowers. He informed them that their shotgun guard was Eb Churchill, and that the two of them would be with them all the way to Socorro in the New Mexico Territory. He tossed Veracity's carpetbag—her and Sean's only luggage besides his Sharps—up top the stage, tied the rifle to the luggage rail, saw his passengers seated, and himself climbed aboard beside the already-perched shotgun guard. He released the brake and had just started to slap reins when a voice yelled, "Hold on! You got another passenger!"

Sean looked out the coach window. He didn't like the looks of what he saw headed their way at a swift walk, and asked in a low voice, "What'd you do with our money? Is it in your reticule?"

"No. I'm wearing it inside my camisole next to my skin," Veracity answered. "Why?"

He shifted slightly to bring his side-arm into easier reach just as the coach door was yanked open and a tall, slim man dressed in dusty black climbed aboard. The man slammed the door behind him and eased down onto the seat opposite the one the Hoods occupied just as the driver yelled, did in fact slap reins, and the coach lurched into motion.

The man lifted brows to Sean, touched a finger to his hat brim to Veracity, and grinned mildly. "Well, I just barely made it, didn't I."

"Looks like," Stormy agreed. Something about this man raised his hackles. When the passenger unbuttoned the front of his black jacket, Hood noted the pearl handles of ornate six-guns residing in a gleaming black-leather double-holster. The buckle that secured the belt was a turquoise-centered carved-silver circle half the size of a tea saucer. The black boots were dusty from recent use, but when the man pushed back his hat and crossed one ankle over the other knee to relax, Stormy saw the boot top was polished black inlaid with white scrolling.

"Where you folks headed?"

"To the nearest railroad tracks," Sean answered carefully. "And you?"

"Ummm . . ." It seemed to take the man a moment to decide on a destination. Finally, he said, "Denver. Or possibly . . . Provo up in Utah."

Stormy's eyes narrowed. "To the nearest railroad tracks?"

"Yeah." The man grinned abruptly. His teeth were white and even below his sweeping dark-brown handlebar moustache. Somehow, it seemed to Stormy that the smile didn't warm the pale blue eyes. "You could say that. Uh . . . since it appears that we might be travelin' together for quite a spell, my name's Malcom Harms. M-A-L-C-O-M, no *E*. And you are . . . ?"

Veracity slid a look sideways at Stormy. She was pressed against him on the narrow seat and felt him stiffen before he answered, "Mister and Missus John Evans." Something was clearly bothering Sean, but she didn't say anything to him about it; she would have to wait until they had at least a little privacy.

Hood studied the man across from them, pondering where he'd heard that name before. He searched his memory. St. Louis? . . . no. Santa Fe? . . . no. Ehrenberg? . . . no. Any of the towns in between? . . . not that he could recall. Prescott? Yes, Prescott. But where and who . . . ?

Harms was asking, "You folks from around here, Missus Evans?"

Veracity took her cue from Stormy; answered vaguely, "Up north."

"And where are you from, Mister Harms?" Sean asked suddenly.

"Oh . . ." Harms shifted on the seat again, and now Hood could see the hilt of a big knife also partially hidden under his coat. ". . . here and there. I go where my job takes me."

"And what's your line of work?"

"I'm a . . . um . . . problem-solver."

Stormy's eyes narrowed another notch. "Whose problems do you solve?"

Again, Harms grinned. "Whoever has a need at the moment."

"Hired gun?" Veracity murmured her question.

Harms shrugged. "Some might call me that. I prefer to think of it as performin' a necessary service for my employer."

"And just who is your employer at the moment, Mister Harms?"

"That's nuthin' you should concern yourself about, Ma'm." Harms reached up, removed his hat with one hand, brushed the palm of the other across his thick dark-brown hair to ruffle it and let in what breeze there was before he ran fingers through it to comb it. That done, he settled himself into the corner, braced his back against the stage wall, a foot against the other on the far side and propped his hat over his eyes. He laced fingers across his belly and seemed to be prepared to go to sleep in spite of the stage's rocking jolts.

Sean and Veracity both stared at Harms for a long silent moment before they again glanced at each other. Though it could have been mere shadow cast by the flowing moustache, it appeared to both of them that Mr. Harms wore a slight smile on his lips while he snoozed.

Well behind them, another traveler rode a dark bay quarter horse and led a saddled backup mount. He followed at a discreet distance, but kept pace while the stage rattled along.

• • •

The Butterfield Overland coach had departed Phoenix late in the day. Only four hours later, Gus Flowers pulled the team into a waystation backed by the stark red-brown treeless upjuts of a rugged miniature mountain range rearing unexpectedly from the desert floor. A multitude of dogs in various sizes from adult to barely ambulatory puppies dashed out to surround the stage when Flowers climbed down and opened the coach door.

Gus said, "Gonna stay here t'night, folks. *Señora* Escalante's got vittles an' beds waitin' on ya." He hesitated to kick around at the dogs. "*Git,* yew mangy curs, shit All Mighty!" To his passengers, he further informed, "We'll take out at dawn t'morry, so git yer rest. Enybody want enything from up top the coach?"

"Yes, please." Veracity rose stiffly, and with her reticule strings over her arm, let Sean hand her out of the stage. "Our carpetbag."

Harms had beaten Sean to the ground. He grinned, "Allow me, Missus Evans," and started to lift hands to the shotgun guard, Eb Churchill, who leaned back to snag the bag from beside the mail trunk.

Veracity said, "My husband is perfectly capable, thank you, Mister Harms. And, for that matter, so am I."

Sean's sheathed Sharps was tied on to the rail

next to Veracity's carpetbag. Harms noted it and asked who it belonged to.

"It's mine," Stormy snapped. He stepped out to stand beside Veracity.

Her brows rose before they lowered to a frown when Harms and Stormy eyed each other. The man in black—automatically, it seemed—shoved both sides of his jacket back to expose his side-arms. His and Sean's eyes locked for a long moment until, still watching Harms out of the corner of his eye, Stormy picked the carpetbag from Veracity's hands, took her elbow, and accompanied by now-silent dogs, escorted her into the waystation.

She whispered, "What was that all about, Sean? You two looked like you were about to fight a duel! What . . . ?"

"I don't know. There's somethin' . . . I know I've heard that *hombre*'s name somewhere before, I just can't recall when or where . . . *yet*. But I'm workin' on it. Here, let me get that for you." He reached around her to shove the partially ajar station door farther open.

This waystation was a solid adobe building roofed by *viga*-supported ocotillo and mesquite thatches mud-sealed against infrequent rains. The inside was cool and dim, the dirt floor swept clean, the air redolent with braising meat, beans cooked with Mexican seasoning then mashed and again fried, and freshly-baked *tortillas*.

Surrounded by almost as many stair-step children as there were dogs outside, sturdy and buxom *Señora* Escalante beamed, waved a hand at the plank table, and yelled, "Sit! Sit! *La comida está* ready! *La comida está servida*! Eat, before it git cold!"

A platter bearing many *tortillas* rolled around meat and beans had already been set on the table beside a large cracked earthenware pitcher of makeshift *sangria*—red wine and apple cider thinned with an ample dose of water.

Malcom Harms beat Sean to Veracity's chair and held it for her. He seized the platter before Hood could do it and offered it to Veracity while she took two *burritos*. He grabbed the moisture-beaded *sangria* pitcher and asked, "A drink Missus Evans?" before Stormy could reach it. At her nod, he poured; then, expression almost a smirk, met Sean's eyes and asked, "You, Mister . . . Evans?"

Stormy felt anger creeping red up his neck even as he nodded, "Yes, thank you." He watched Harms's grin broaden while the man poured; thought: *It's almost like he's trying to goad me into . . . something. Why?* He was again pondering where he'd heard the name Malcom Harms when a teen-aged girl dashed in to ask, "*Dónde Raimundo, Mamá?*"

Señora Escalante answered, "*Raimón matar un perro por desayuna por la mañana.*"

"*Gracias, Mamá.*"

Sean was momentarily distracted from Malcom Harms. He had acquired some of the language during his years in the southwest, but understood more than he spoke. He slid a look at his wife eating her dinner with gusto, and asked, "Uh . . . Veracity, I don't know if you speak any Spanish or not."

She looked surprised. Chewed and swallowed before she shook her head. "No. None. Why?"

"Oh, just . . . curious." He wasn't going to tell her that whoever Ramón was, the man was out killing a dog for tomorrow's breakfast.

Harms chuckled. He'd obviously understood the exchange. He held up a *burrito*. "*Señora*, this is excellent, but . . . what kind of meat is in it?"

"*Harms!*" Sean growled.

He was too late. The *señora* answered, "*Perro.* Uh . . . dog. Puppy. Nice an' tender, no?"

Veracity's eyes widened. She dropped her half-eaten second burrito back into her plate, hastily grabbed her glass and used *sangria* to wash down what remained in her mouth. Harms leaped up to hold her chair when she rose hastily and gasped, "D-Dog? We've been eating *d-dog* meat?"

Malcom took her elbow with his left hand; his right hovered near one pearl-handled six-gun grip. He said smoothly, "Why, yes. Since your husband knew it all along, I assumed you did, also, Veracity."

She speared Sean with horrified eyes. *"You knew, but you let me . . ."*

"No! No, I didn't know until that girl . . ."

"But you *still* didn't tell me?"

"By that time, it was too late! You'd already . . ."

"Ohhhh!" She yanked away from Malcom, grabbed her reticule and carpetbag, and spine stiff, strode out of the station.

Sean watched her go before he looked back at Malcom. The man met his eyes silently. A broad grin spread his moustache. He didn't move other than to once again slowly push back the sides of his jacket to expose weapons. It was an open challenge.

Stormy breathed, "What is it with you, Harms? What are you trying to do?"

"Me? Am I trying to do something, Mister . . . Evans?"

"Yes, you are. You want me to draw-down on you, is that it?"

"Now, why would I want that, Mister . . . Evans? After all, we've just met."

"I don't know. But you don't back off from my wife, I *will* meet you outside."

"Any time, Mister . . . Evans, *any* time." Chuckling, Malcom sidled past Sean and out the door.

Stormy watched him go. He gritted teeth for a moment before he said to the cook, *"La comida muy sabrosa, Señora."*

She smiled, "*Gracias, Señor. No hay nada coma la comida casera, no?*"

Sean understood that to be: There's nothing like home cooking, is there? "*Es verdad. Buenos noches.*" He fished in his watch pocket, brought out a dollar and dropped it on the table before he strode out into the yard in search of Veracity and to keep an eye on Harms.

Malcom Harms. Where *had* he heard that name before?

The man who followed them didn't approach the station. He halted about a mile west and also bedded down for the night.

CHAPTER SIXTEEN

Gus Flowers and Eb Churchill entered the station to eat just as Hood left. Pursued by a cheerful mix of Spanish and English, Sean squinted around the chicken-, children-, and dog-cluttered yard for a moment before he headed for the bunkhouse. He located Veracity sitting on the edge of one of the beds there. She looked decidedly pale and not a little unhappy.

Instead of being merely a roofed lean-to like last night's stopover, these sleeping quarters were a windowless adobe square with a door at either end. The room contained two poster-beds along one wall and four single-wide cots crowding the other, with an open path down the middle of the room from door-to-door. Each cot sported a blanket clearly marked *U.S. Army* folded on its foot and a thin case-less pillow at the head. The beds held a double number of each, but no sheets over the stained mattress ticking.

Wherever Malcom Harms was, he wasn't in sight when Sean moved across the room. Leather webbing creaked and the straw-filled mattress crackled when Stormy sat down beside Veracity and put an arm around her. "You all right?"

She slid a wan, miffed look his way. "No. Though I guess I shouldn't be so . . . so squeamish. I confess that we ate monkey meat when crossing the Isthmus, and . . . and then you and I had rattlesnake at the lake, remember? But d-dog? Puppy? I mean, dogs are *pets,* and . . ."

"That's why I didn't tell you. You had already eaten a lot of it before I heard what it was. If Harms had kept his mouth shut, you'd never have known the difference. Are you going to be sick?"

She took a deep breath. Let it out. "No, I guess not. Who *is* that man, anyway?"

"Harms?"

"Yes. I don't like him, Stormy. He's too . . . too . . . uh . . . unctuous, you know? Slimy. He gives me the shudders. And it's almost like he's trying to . . . oh, I don't know . . . cause some kind of a problem between you and me. You be careful of him, y'hear? *Nothing* he does or says is worth getting yourself killed over!"

"You care? *Uh!*"

She had poked him in the ribs; said tartly, "Well, I s'pose I have to. I'm married to you, aren't I?"

He chuckled and rose. "Come on. Let's go find an outhouse and then turn in. It has been a long day, and I expect that tomorrow won't be any easier. By the way, how is our money doing?"

She patted her stomach. "It itches, but under my camisole and with my belt holding it, it's not going anyplace."

They returned to the bunkhouse to find Malcom Harms still fully armed and lying on one of the cots, his fingers laced across his belly and hat propped over his eyes. They didn't disturb him. Veracity shook a scorpion out of the blanket, took off her boots, set them by the foot of the bed and loosened the top of her reticule for easy access to Angel before she crawled across to lie down next to the wall. Sean likewise shucked off his boots and set them beside hers. He seriously considered sleeping in his gun belt, but finally shook his head, removed and buckled the belt into a circle, and hung it over the bed post to be within easy reach.

While Veracity sighed once and was asleep, Sean was kept awake for a while pondering Harms. He *knew* he'd heard the name before! But where?

"C'mon, folks! Up an' at 'em. *Señora* Escalante's got breakfast on!"

Malcom Harms, and the shotgun guard Eb Churchill, were all up and gone from the bunkhouse by the time Sean and Veracity were jolted awake by Gus Flowers's shout. Stormy swung his feet over the edge of the bed—he felt stuffy and bleary-eyed even though he'd slept solidly all night—as he bent to pick up his boots . . . but hesitated. He could have sworn he'd left them sitting side-by-side next to Veracity's, yet now, one had tipped over onto its side with the other boot's heel partially stuffed in the top. Scowling at the boots, he flung out an arm to halt Veracity who was crawling off the bed behind him.

She asked, "What?"

"Just a minute, love." Without getting up, he bent, seized one boot and moved it away from the other. Nothing happened.

Again, Veracity asked, "What is it, Stormy?"

"Probably nothing. Maybe one of the dogs got after my boots during the night, but . . ." He picked the other boot up, knocked the heel against the dirt, turned it upside down and shook it. Two small brown scorpions, tails erect and a globe of poison sparkling at the tip of one's sting, fell to the floor. *"Shit!"*

"Oh, my!"

"Yeah." He repeated the process with both boots to ensure that no more scorpions or maybe a small rattler still hid within them before he slid feet into them. "Better check yours before you put them on." He stood and ground the scorpions dead with his boot sole before he picked his gun belt from the bed post, opened the buckle and fastened the belt over his hips.

Veracity's boots were untenanted. Sean carried the carpetbag while they hurried out into a pale blue dawn coolly-fresh at the moment but already hinting at the hot day ahead, went to the outhouse, then to the primer pump to wash and comb hair.

She asked, "Are you going to shave?"

He ran fingers over his two-day stubble. "Guess not. I think I'll let my beard grow until we hit New York. Simpler that way. Come on, let's go eat. Uh . . . Veracity . . . The meat . . ."

She grimaced. "I know. But since I ate it yesterday and am still alive and healthy this morning . . ."

They found the others already wolfing down twice-fried beans mixed with dog meat, hot biscuits, gravy, and coffee. Gus and Eb nodded to them, but Malcom rose to offer a chair, smiled expansively, and greeted, "Good morning, Veracity! Did you sleep well?"

Sean watched the man closely, but bit back a smile when Veracity murmured, "Very, Mister Harms . . . and you are being entirely too presumptuous. It's *Missus Evans*. Please remember that."

Harms chuckled. "I stand corrected . . . Missus Evans." He ignored Sean as though Hood didn't exist, sat and finished his breakfast.

Both Veracity and Stormy ate everything on their plates.

Abruptly, Gus finished his coffee, pulled out a pocket watch, flipped it open and consulted the time. He belched before he snapped the watch cover shut and rose. "Five thutty, folks. Gotta move out. We'll be headin' east fer a while, then some north up into the mountains. The team's hitched an' rarin' to go, so climb on." He nodded to Veracity. "Lemme putcher bag back aboard, Missus."

Eb also rose and followed Flowers out. The passengers rushed to finish breakfast and likewise followed. Harms strode ahead to hold the door for Veracity; offered her his hand to step up into the stage. She ignored it, climbed in on her own and sank onto the rear seat.

Stormy nodded to Harms, pushed past him, grinned, "Thanks," and sat down next to his wife, leaving Malcom to follow and close the panel. When Harms lowered himself to the seat opposite them, Hood raised brows at him. "I didn't know Butterfield hired doormen and porters for their coaches. How much they payin' you, Harms?"

Malcom's expression hardened. He stiffened on the seat just as Gus slapped reins, shouted the team into motion, and the coach lurched forward. Either the stage's or his own movement toppled Harms into Stormy's lap. It seemed that Malcom tried to catch himself, and in doing so, his stiffened fingers rammed into Hood's belly.

Eyes wide, Veracity tensed. She yanked open her reticule and grabbed at the Avenging Angel there, but didn't pull it because Sean seized

Malcom's arms and held hard for a moment while he got his breath back.

The two men stared at each other in silence until Stormy shoved Malcom away and smiled coldly. "Gotta watch yourself on these rough roads, Mister Harms, else you could get hurt."

Malcom performed what seemed to Sean to be an almost automatic response. He reseated himself, pushed back his jacket tails, drew one of his pearl-handled six-guns, stared back at Hood and spun the cylinder while he murmured, "Oh, I doubt that . . ." He shifted his gaze to Veracity, ". . . don't you, Missus . . . Evans?"

Veracity said nothing. She slid a look aside at Sean and hesitated a long moment before she pulled an empty hand from her reticule, cinched the top, and turned her face to stare out the window.

That lone rider had eaten a quick, cold breakfast, saddled his mounts, and vacated his camp. He again stayed well behind the stagecoach, but as yesterday, still followed.

The heat increased as the day aged, but after that initial incident in the interior of the stage, the morning was uneventful. They reached another waystation shortly before noon, where they ate, relieved themselves, stretched legs while the team was being changed for fresh horses; then, thundered onward. Behind them, the lone rider also rested himself and his horses before he followed up into forested mountains.

The road—such as it was—became progressively steeper, narrower, and more winding. About two in the afternoon, Gus reined the team over into one of the few wide spots and yelled down to his passengers, "Gonna set here a few minutes, folks. I see the west-bound comin' on up yonder. Downgrade coach always has the right-of-way, so yew kin git out an' stretch yer laigs till it passes. Keep outta its way, though. If ol' Sam Getty's drivin', he don't stop fer nothin'. Like as not, he'd run ya over without battin' a eye!"

Sean leaned immediately to open the coach door. He stepped out and turned to hand Veracity down. For once, Harms let him.

They were now relatively high in the mountains, with Ponderosa pines smelling of vanilla on either side of the road, needles soughing softly to a slight breeze high above and layered into slippery shingles underfoot. A steep cliff plunged almost a hundred feet down beside the turn-out to where a narrow but vibrant stream frothed white water around up-jutting boulders. Its roar almost drowned-out the rattle of coach wheels, the squeal of the wooden brake, and steel-shod hooves pounding dirt and gravel from the fast-approaching stage, but not Veracity's scream when Malcom stepped out of their coach. His foot slipped on pine needles, he fell into Sean, and Hood was knocked to the cliff edge.

Sean had one boot in the air. Arms flailing and expression taut with horror, he teetered backwards. When Veracity leaped toward him, he instinctively clutched at anything available to keep from plunging to the rocks below. He snared her wrist, and never thinking that he might be pulling her to destruction, hung on hard.

His weight yanked her flat as he fell, but now she had her other hand on his shirt sleeve and likewise hung on. She was sliding over the edge when Gus yelled, *"Shit All Mighty!"* He and Eb leaped to the ground to help.

Harms was still on one knee. He cast a quick look at the driver and guard, thrust himself upright and lunged to grab Veracity's ankles. He kept her from sliding farther, but didn't try to rescue Sean.

Gus and Eb made it to the scene. Both bellied down one on each side of Veracity, seized Sean's forearms and hoisted him back up onto level ground. With Veracity sitting beside him, Hood lay white and shaking for a minute before he flushed to abrupt rage. Just as the westbound stage clattered past, he snarled, *"Why you . . ."* leaped upright and at Malcom.

Harms scrambled to his feet and flung both hands skyward. He stepped back and yelled, "I'm *sorry!* It was an accident! I slipped when I got out . . . I tell you, it was an accident! . . . nothin' but an *accident!*"

Sean caught himself. He cast a quick look at the Butterfield employees just getting up from where they sat on the dirt. He looked back at Harms. The man still held up hands. His expression was more than apologetic; in fact, he appeared about to burst into tears. If he attacked Malcom now, *he* would be the one in the wrong. And if Harms drew one of those pearl-handled six-shooters and killed him, it would look like an act of self-defense.

He turned away abruptly and nodded to Gus and Eb. "Thanks. If you hadn't been here, both my wife and I would probably be dead by now." He bent to help Veracity up from where she still sat fanning herself with her hat. "Are you all right? Are you hurt?"

"No." She jammed the hat back over her hair. "But you, Stormy? You . . ."

"I'm fine. Let's get back on the stage, else more . . ." he shot a glower at Harms, ". . . *accidents* happen."

This time, their traveling companion stood well back when Sean handed Veracity into the coach. Nor did he fall into Hood's lap when Gus urged the team onward.

Barely a half-mile down the trail, the lone rider had held his horses aside while the westbound also passed him. Like the stage ahead, he now nudged his mounts on up the trail.

Silence held for the most part onboard the eastbound. Harms tried again to apologize, but Stormy cut him off with a curt, "Forget it." Veracity recalled how it felt to fall over a cliff and told Sean the story of her and Oscar Pratt's altercation on the way to Prescott. By the time she finished describing the accidental "carom shot" at Pratt, and Leroy Axt's assertion that she'd just made a name for herself all over the Arizona Territory, Sean had stopped shaking and was grinning.

An hour on, they came up and over a pass summit and were negotiating the eastern downgrade when Malcom suddenly turned to look up toward the front of the coach. He scowled, "What the hell . . . ? Something's wrong up there!"

Hood also frowned. He said, "I don't hear anything."

"I do!" Malcom yanked off his hat, stood, bent past Sean to open the coach door and leaned outside. Presently, he reached up, caught the guard rail restraining roof-stored luggage, planted a foot on the window sill and heaved himself atop the coach. Just as Stormy also started to see what was going on, Eb Churchill plunged past the door—his startled yell cut off abruptly when he met the dirt. There as a burst of profanity from the outside and several clunks against coach walls before Gus Flowers also sailed off the coach and vanished.

The stage had been being braked on the down-grade. Now, it picked up speed. Stormy snapped to Veracity, "I think we've got a run-away! Stay here!" Like Harms, he seized the edge of the door, braced a foot on the seat, eased outside and reached for the luggage rail with his left hand. He didn't know what he expected to see, but it wasn't Malcom Harms holding the reins. Still clinging with his left, he reached down with his right, unclipped the trigger guard, pulled his six-shooter, boosted himself up to get an elbow hooked over the rail, and yelled, *"Harms, stop the stage . . . NOW!"*

Malcom looked back over his shoulder at Stormy. He grinned nastily, and still holding the ends of the multiple reins, stood and stepped up onto the roof. Sean didn't wait for the man to draw one of his fancy side-arms. He pressed the trigger twice, once to rotate the cylinder past his habitual empty chamber, once to fire.

Nothing happened. The hammer clicked, but no bullet stopped Harms. Thinking it was a misfire, Stormy squeezed the trigger again. Still nothing happened except that the steel-reinforced toe of Malcom's polished boot met his temple, and like Eb and Gus, he plunged from the top of the stage to lie unmoving beneath the slowly-settling dust raised by coach wheels.

CHAPTER SEVENTEEN

Veracity saw Sean lose his grip and fall. The moment Harms got the stage halted, she lunged out of the coach and began to dash back up the trail toward where Stormy lay sprawled, but Malcom leaped to the ground, ran her down, snagged her shirt and held her back.

She immediately launched a roundhouse uppercut at him. She connected solidly, but though she staggered him, she didn't knock him out or loosen his grip on her.

He gritted, *"Veracity! MISSUS EVANS, STOP IT! LISTEN TO ME!"*

She almost got away from him when her boot toe met his kneecap, but he held on. She yelled, *"Stormy! Let go, I've got to go to . . ."*

"Listen, dammit!" He shook her. "Stop! I'll go see if your husband is . . ."

She had left Angel in her reticule inside the coach, but still carried her derringer in her boot. Just as she bent to pull it, two shots rang out and Malcom Harms fell away from her to lie twitching at her feet. Her mouth open, and expecting to see Sean up with a smoking weapon in his hand, she whirled to look behind her.

Stormy still lay where he had fallen. A man in ordinary range clothes, and riding a dark bay quarter horse and leading a saddled chestnut, had reined-in beside Sean. Even as Veracity stood momentarily frozen, she saw the newcomer leather his side-arm, step down, kneel on one knee beside Stormy and press fingers to Hood's throat. Presently, he shook his head.

"No . . ." Veracity whispered.

The man slid a hand inside Stormy's shirt to feel for a heartbeat. Again, he shook his head.

"No!" Veracity unfroze. She cried, *"No, Sean . . . NO . . ."* as she started toward him.

The stranger rose and hurried toward her. He met her half-way, intercepted her and held her hard even as he said, "He's dead, Veracity. I'm sorry. Veracity . . . *Vera, listen to me!* There's *nothing* you can do for him now. *Vera, stop struggling!*"

Veracity did stop fighting, for the newcomer was Bart Reynolds. Even in her shock and under building grief, her mouth automatically whispered, "Don't . . . don't call me Vera! Don't you *dare* call . . . what are *you* doing here?"

Still holding her to him, Reynolds said, "I'm on my way to Santa Fe to confer with the New Mexico Territorial Governor there. I hate stagecoach travel . . . much prefer riding alone . . . and after all, if I become Arizona's governor, it behooves me to get to know my country first-hand. You can't see much from a coach, so . . . *Veracity!*"

She had again tried to shove away from him. She strained to look back toward Sean's motionless figure and gasped, "Let me go, Mister Reynolds!"

He held her; said, "Bart. Call me Bart, dear. Veracity, there is nothing you can do for him now. You go sit in the coach. I'll bury him, or make a cairn for him." He cast a quick look back at Hood; he seemed to have some urgent need to get Veracity out of here and Sean interred, however he planned to do it. "Go! Go! *I'll* take care of his body for you!"

"No, I want to HOLD him! I want to at LEAST kiss him good-bye! Let me . . ."

Reynolds looked as startled as Harms had when yet another gunshot shattered the air. His hands slid down Veracity's arms as he went to his knees; when she sprang away from him, her mouth and eyes wide in total shock, he fell on his face in the road and she saw a dark blot of blood spreading a widening stain over his spine.

Movement caught the corner of her eye. She jerked around to see Malcom Harms trying to steady his shaking hand enough to fire again. He lay on his belly, both his head and the hand that held his weapon wavering enough that—in fear that he would shoot her—Veracity dashed toward him, bent, and had no trouble at all wresting the ornate six-shooter from his fingers.

Harms looked blearily up at her. He croaked, "Sonabitch d-double-crossed me."

"What?" Holding the weapon well away so there was no chance he could grab it, Veracity bent closer. *"What?"*

"R-Reynolds. He h-hired me t'kill your h-husband. S-Said Stormy cheated h-him outta ranch."

"No!" Veracity shook her head violently. "No, Sean won it from him fair and . . ."

Harms went on as though she wasn't talking. "R-Reynolds said . . . make it look like . . . acci-dent, then you . . . come back to him."

"*Back* to him?" Now, she knelt beside Malcom. "I never was *his* in the first place, how could I come *back* to . . ."

"Tried to m-make accident," Malcom gasped. "Scorpions . . . din't work. Cliff din't w-work. H-Hood wouldn' c-call me out s-so I could gun him . . . Finally got j-job done . . . earned my f-five hundred . . . then Reynolds comes along an' double-crosses me. Sh-shoots me."

"Plays the hero," Veracity snapped. "Makes it look like he is *rescuing* me so I'll be *grateful* to him and let him take care of me back on *his ranch* while he played the Arizona governor and . . . Mister Harms? *Malcom?*"

Harms's head had fallen to the dirt. Veracity reached slowly to touch him. "Mister Harms?" There was no answer. He was done talking.

She stood up, and surrounded by bodies, looked around. She was overwhelmed into immobility by the silence of the wilderness forest and its dead for a long moment before she pulled herself out of it and walked slowly to where Sean lay. She sank to sit beside him, gathered him onto her lap and held his cheek to her breast. She noticed the blackly-swollen bruise over his temple and pressed lips softly to it before she began to cry. She rocked him and wept over him for a long time before he opened his eyes and said, "Veracity, you're d-drippin' all over me, love."

"Yeow!" She lurched back from him and dropped him onto the road. Hands braced behind her, knees drawn up and mouth open, she stared in shock when Stormy winced, got himself propped on an elbow and lifted a hand to his head. He grimaced in pain for a moment before he wiped his face with a sleeve and asked, "Why are you crying all over me? I may be a little . . ."

Abruptly, she lunged at him and wrapped arms around him again. "You're *not* dead!" Hugging him to her, she babbled, "You're not dead! Bart said you were dead and I took his word for it I should have *known* he was a liar *you're not dead! . . . oh, Stormy, I thought I'd lost you but you're not . . . mmmfff!"*

He slid a hand under her hair at the back of her neck to pull her into a kiss and shut her up. When he moved to press his cheek to hers, they merely clung for a minute before he asked, "Who said I was dead?"

"Bart. Bart Reynolds."

Now, he leaned away from her and frowned. "Bart? No, Veracity, we left him in Prescott thoroughly riled-up over loss of his ranch *and* you, but . . . *that's* where I heard Malcom Harms's name! The jeweler in Prescott where we bought your wedding ring told me that Harms was Reynolds's private gun! *Now,* I remember!"

"But love, Reynolds is still in Prescott! How could he have . . ."

"No, no. Huh-uh. Look over there." She nodded to where Bart lay.

Sean shifted to stare at Reynolds's body, then at Harms's corpse. He pressed a palm to his temple and squinted hard for a moment as though his eyes didn't work quite right yet before he gasped, "My God, it is him! What the hell happened here, Veracity?"

They continued to sit in the middle of the road while she told him about the shootings and what she'd heard from Malcom before he died; ended, ". . . and though Bart said to me that he was on his way to Santa Fe to see the New Mexico governor there, I think that was just a cover-up. I think he trailed us all the way from Prescott . . . or at least from Phoenix . . . just waiting for Harms to do you in and then he would be in the right place at the right time to become my hero. Look, he was so sure of himself that he even brought an extra mount along for me to ride."

"And then," Sean put in grimly, "naturally, he expected that alone, you would have no use for a big ranch and would probably be happy to either give it back to him or sell it back cheap. . . ."

"Or," she cut in, "maybe he thought he could just marry his way back onto it after I became a widow. Kill two birds with one stone, as it were."

Sean shook his head. "But you said he checked on me. He *had* to know I wasn't . . ." His expression took on a deeper horror. "What was he going to do if I came around before he got me buried? . . . actually kill me when you weren't looking? *And if I didn't, was he just goin' to bury me alive?*"

She shuddered. "I don't know. I really don't . . . want to think about that! Stormy, are you really all right? How . . . how do you feel? Can you stand up?"

"I feel rotten." He again pressed fingers gingerly to the bruise over his temple. "But I don't think anything is broken. I think I went out when Harms kicked me in the head . . . I don't even remember hitting the ground."

"Here, let me help you." Veracity scrambled to her feet to pull Sean upright. He was slow about it; she still had an arm around his waist to steady him when a voice asked, "Shit All Mighty, whut happened here?"

Gus Flowers came limping up the road. The driver held his left arm tightly with his right hand. There was blood on his face and he walked as though an ankle or knee was badly sprained, but he halted when he saw the bodies.

Once again, Veracity explained before Hood asked, "Where's your guard, Gus?"

Flowers shook his head glumly. "Back there on the trail. He musta landed on his haid an' broke his neck when thet bastard flung him off the coach. Sonovabitch . . . he din't have to do that! Ol' Eb's got a wife an' seven kids!" He sighed heavily. "I tried to pack him on up here, but I sprung my shoulder-bone when I lit, an' my laig . . ." He again shook his head. "Couldn' do it. I don' wantta jes leave him lay, but . . ."

"I'll go get him," Hood offered.

Veracity frowned, "Stormy, are you sure you're up to it? I mean . . ."

"I'll take Reynolds's horses. You wait here with Gus, Veracity . . . but in the meantime, would you please see if you can find my side-arm somewhere along here? I think I dropped it when I fell, but I want to look at it. There seems to be something wrong with it."

While Sean stiffly mounted Reynolds's bay and led the chestnut that he recognized as Flame, the quarter horse he and Spot had bested in the Prescott race, back up the trail in search of Eb Churchill's body, and Gus sat resting on the lowered coach doorstep, Veracity searched road edges for Stormy's six-gun. She finally found it nearly hidden under a bush and had it in hand by the time Sean returned with the corpse draped over Flame's saddle.

Together, the Hoods put Eb on a seat in the coach. They picked up Reynolds and Harms and propped them side-by-side on the other seat. Sean tied Flame and the bay to the rear of the stage before he retrieved his side-arm from Veracity, aimed at the trees, and pulled the trigger. The hammer clicked uselessly against the cartridge. He tried it again and again with the same results.

"Shit All Mighty," Gus observed, "looks like yew got a full load of duds there, young feller."

"Yeah, well, they didn't start out that way." Sean broke open the cylinder and extracted a bullet. He turned it over and over in his fingers.

"Look at the scratches on the bullet," Veracity noted.

"Um-hmm." Hood clenched lead between his teeth and worked it loose from the brass casing. The bullet came apart too easily. He tapped the open end of the casing against his palm. Nothing came out. "Somebody emptied all the powder, didn't they. It must have happened last night when we were asleep."

"I'll bet it was Malcom Harms," Veracity breathed. "If he could have goaded you into a gunfight today, it would have been a safe sure thing for him, wouldn't it! Are all the others the same?"

"I don't doubt it." Sean emptied the cylinder, discarded the charge-less bullets, and reloaded with potent ones. He again aimed at the forest. This time, lead scattered needles from a pine. "All right. Mister Flowers, are you up to driving?"

Gus grimaced. "Waall, I'll do my best." But when Flowers tried to climb back up to the seat, he winced, clutched his left arm, and leaned weakly against the coach side. "Shit All Mighty . . ."

"Tell you what," Sean offered, "I've never driven a team-of-six before, but if you'll show me how and be the guide, I'll drive. I'm not too swift myself, but at least my arms work. Do you want to ride inside?"

"Hell, no! I ain't gonna set the trip with three daid bodies! If yew'll he'p me, here . . ."

With Sean lifting from the driver's seat, and Veracity pushing from below, they got Gus up onto the coach roof and bolstered against the carpet bag and mail box back rest.

Stormy said to Veracity, "You should ride inside, not . . ."

She mimicked Gus, and Flowers cackled a laugh when she said, "No, no! I ain't gonna set the trip with three daid bodies!" She climbed up onto the driver's seat, leaned over the back beside the driver, untied strings and slid Sean's

Sharps from its sheath. "In fact, I'll ride shotgun. Yew got eny problems with thet, love?"

Before Sean could answer, Gus chortled, "Yew better not, young feller, not whilst she's holdin' thet thar Big Fifty! I'll wager she kin use it, too!"

"You have no idea how well, Mister Flowers," Hood grinned. He seated himself and picked up the reins. "All right, what do I do here?"

"Ain't nuthin' to it, young feller. Left three reins goes in the left hand, right three in the right. Separate them reins each with a finger. Keep 'em tight 'nuf that them steeds knows they're bein' directed but not so tight it worries their mouths. Jes' slap 'em an' tell 'em to git along."

Sean slapped and yelled, "Get along!" The team had rested while the humans lived or died; they lurched into an instant gallop that—because of the down-slope—alarmed not only Hood but lifted the hair on Flowers's head. Sean's boot heel jammed against the brake and repeated tugs on the reins slowed the team to a more reasonable gait, and by a half-hour on, Stormy had the hang of it.

Beside him on the seat, with the stage rocking beneath her and the buffalo gun across her knees, Veracity murmured, "Now that we're still both alive, I have to confess something, Stormy. Uh . . . I've often thought it was . . . um . . . not quite right for a Pinkerton agent to . . .

shall we say . . . have so much . . . I guess I shouldn't call it *fun,* let's call it *excitement* . . . while at work. *If* you can say I'm still *at work.*" She took a deep breath to appreciate the late afternoon high-mountain air; glanced around at the passing forest green below higher red-rock bluffs and gray-granite cliffs rearing against an unclouded deep-blue sky, and shook her head in wonder.

As a buck and two does dashed across the road ahead of them, she continued. "I've never felt so . . . so *western* . . . as I do at this moment! . . . like I'm living some sort of . . . um . . . dime novel! How about you?"

He slid a half-amused, half-somber look at her. "If we live through this, maybe I'll feel the same. But I can't really relax and have as good a time as you seem to be having until I get New York behind me." They were coming to an upgrade. He yelled, "*Yah!* there! *Yah!* . . . *YAH!*" and slapped reins.

They were very late reaching their next way-station. Since Gus was even more stiff and sore the next morning and was even less able to function than the day before, Sean continued as driver under Flowers's guidance, with Veracity and the Sharps beside him.

They disposed of Reynolds's and Harms's bodies at the waystation. As he and the station manager carted Bart to a shed for storage before burial, Sean noted, "Y'know, this *hombre* was hopin' to be the next Arizona governor. I think the citizens here have no idea how close they came to having a first-class skunk run the Territory."

"But high class, Stormy." Veracity lay Reynolds's hat over his face. "He may have been a murderer and a conniver, but at least he had flair." But then, Hood stifled a grin when she cast a sour look at the corpse and added, "His *consort,* indeed! *Clod!*"

They carried Eb onward to Fort Apache where Gus knew the guard had family, and left Churchill in the hands of caring relatives. When they reached Socorro, New Mexico, the end of Flowers's run, they got a new driver and guard, and the Hoods retreated to the relative comfort of the stage interior. Gus saw them off with assurances to Sean that if Hood ever needed a job, he would provide references.

Thence, their stage took them up to Albuquerque and Santa Fe, through Raton Pass to Trinidad in Colorado, and on to Denver where Veracity telegraphed the Pinkerton Agency to let her boss know she had located Sean Hood and had delivered Liam Hardesty's message of forgiveness.

They collected remittance dollars from several towns en route so Sean could pay his own way, but used Veracity's travel voucher for her fare.

Near Provo, Utah, they boarded an east-bound Union Pacific train. It was a long, hard journey across country, and was mid-September by the time they reached New York City.

CHAPTER EIGHTEEN

The clerk at the register desk in the posh New York hotel lobby cast a false professional grimace not quite a smile at the young couple approaching across the thick rug. He didn't need a practiced eye to tell that they were obviously unsophisticated rustics—their clothing clearly announced that. Not to mention his unkempt hair and many days' growth of stubble that was not quite a beard, the man wore a long-slept-in blue shirt, grimy black britches beneath leather leggings, crude boots, *and,* of all things, on his hip a side-arm exposed to public view. A heavy rifle was slung over his shoulder beside worn saddlebags. The woman who accompanied him was dressed no better.

When the man (certainly not a gentleman) stepped up to the desk and inquired about accommodations, he was naturally prompted to advise, "Perhaps another hotel would be more to your . . . means, sir."

Sean lifted a brow and looked around the elegant wood-and-velvet-rich lobby. "No, this one should be adequate. Do you have a room available?"

The clerk's nose pinched (Stormy noted that there was that expression again; once more thought there had to be classes for it!). "Our least expensive accommodations are three dollars a day, sir."

"What's next up?"

The clerk squinted past Hood to again study the woman silently holding a carpetbag in both hands. His eyes noted the wide wedding band— why, the ring appeared to be merely raw nuggets of pure gold roughly-beaten and fused into jewelry. *Very* impressive. He said, "Our rooms run three, four, and five dollars a day. Suites are ten and twenty dollars, and of course, the Presidential Suite is . . ."

"The ten-dollar suite will be fine, thank you."

"That is payment in advance, sir."

Veracity stifled a smile when Sean looked back at her briefly; she could see anger flashing red lights into his black eyes. When he drawled, "Y'all thank we can 'ford such highfalutin prices, Ma?" she answered in kind, "Ah reckon so, Pa."

Sean snapped back at the clerk, "We are not all savages and bumpkins in the Territories, man." He pulled bills from his pocket, handed over fifty dollars, seized the pen from the inkwell and signed the register: *Mr. and Mrs. John Evans, Skull Valley, Arizona Terr.* before he continued coldly, "We may be staying five days, perhaps longer. We'll see our suite now. Also, please ask the concierge to send a tailor and a dressmaker up to our suite as soon as possible. We have come a

338

long way, we're tired, we want baths, and dinner served in our quarters. You *can* handle that, can you not?"

By the patron's diction and tone, *and* at the sight of ample funds, the clerk knew he had made a serious error in judgment. His own voice shifted to imperious briskness when he called the bellboy to carry Mr. and Mrs. Evans's minimal luggage and to escort them up the wide carpeted stairs and down the third-floor corridor to Suite 301.

Inside, as Sean tipped the boy, he asked, "How do I arrange to have a message sent across town?"

"I can see to that for you, sir. The name's Danny. When you wants to send your correspondence, just ask for me and I'll see to it a runner takes it toot-sweet, sir."

"What's today's date?"

"September nineteenth, sir."

"What day of the week?"

"Tuesday. sir."

"Thank you. I'll call you, Danny, when the note is ready."

The boy touched a finger to his cap and left. Sean turned to find that Veracity had flung her hat onto the bed beside the bags and was now looking out the window at the busy street below.

"Y'know," she murmured when he joined her, "I thought I missed all this . . . the hustle and bustle . . . the people . . . the big-city atmosphere . . .

But—I don't know—for some reason, it seems . . . too crowded. Too noisy. Too . . . *dirty*. Did you notice how bad the air smells here, Stormy? Coal smoke and garbage. People waste! I wonder how I ever stood it before?"

He slid arms around her waist and held her to him; murmured into her hair, "I know what you mean. I think the West spoiled us. Have you looked at the bathroom yet? How about a long hot bath, then dinner, and then?" He flexed brows.

She sensed something forced in his good humor and turned around to face him and cup his chin in both palms. "We have it all planned, Stormy. We've spent weeks planning exactly what we're going to do and how to do it. There has always been this . . . this *deep well* of anger and hurt inside you, but I could tell that the closer we got to New York, the nearer to the surface it crept. Take it slow and easy, my love. Don't let your temper ruin everything now."

He shook his head sharply, and his black eyes grew somehow darker. "You don't understand, Veracity. It's not all anger . . . or hurt. I'm . . . *afraid,* y'know?" He laughed without humor. "You have no idea how damn scared I was in those first days out. There I was doing something I'd never wanted to do . . . something I'd never *dreamed* of *ever* doing—barely twenty years old and running for my life in the middle of a winter's night . . . taking the blame for a thing I hadn't done to preserve my brother's reputation . . . for his family's sake . . . *God,* I was so terrified!

"But now, I'm almost more afraid, because it comes to me that in all this, it's my own brother I hate, not Liam Hardesty. I *understand* Hardesty . . . his only daughter violated . . . pregnant . . . ruined . . . dead. But for Georgie to persuade Father to ask . . . no, to *beg* me to take responsibility, not only to shatter my life but also Father's by making the Old Man die knowing what he'd been party to . . ." Again, he shook his head. "I hate Georgie for Mother's and Father's sakes more than for my own, but . . ."

He sighed heavily. "And then, to have him maybe put a price on me. To hire men to hunt me down and kill me. . . . I know it wasn't Father who did that, it was Georgie. It had to be Georgie. I'm terrified that the moment I lay eyes on him now, I will kill him. Kill my own brother. That's what scares me."

"You won't. I know you won't. We have your father's last letter to you which proves to everyone in sight that it was George who was the culprit, not you. Since Mister Hardesty has forgiven *you,* even though he thinks you were the one who dallied with his daughter's affections, surely he can forgive George when he learns the truth. You and Georgie can make your peace, and then it'll be all over and we can get on with *our* lives." She kissed him softly; murmured against his lips, "I'm dying to show you off to my mother and sisters. I'll be the envy of all Philadelphia. Come on, let's go take that bath."

They bathed. The tailor appeared, presented suit fabrics, measured Sean, and for an extra ten dollars, promised to have three suits ready for him, including shirts and cravats, by this time tomorrow.

Veracity fell by accident into a bonanza. When the dressmaker came to the suite and discovered the client's measurements, she grew round-eyed and inquired whether the lady would find it repugnant to wear a dead girl's clothing—it seemed that a certain Miss Penelope White of the James White family, had ordered her trousseau, it had been finished, but before Miss White could receive the clothing, she'd been run down by a horse-trolley. The seamstress said she would let the outfits go cheap.

Veracity allowed that she held no reservations about wearing the dresses and agreed to look at them. The seamstress bustled out, returned in a half-hour with two package-laden aides, and shortly—*and* for a mere forty dollars—Veracity had bought the prettiest wardrobe she'd ever owned, complete with matching gloves, bonnets, purses, lacy under-things, peignoirs and parasols. Sean—who had never seen his wife in anything but her makeshift western outfit or her skin—was more than impressed.

They sent their old clothes to the hotel laundry, their boots to be shined, heard that all would be returned by eight thirty the next morning, and then ordered room service to bring their dinner. They indeed sat around dressed in nothing but towels, drank fine wine and watched the traffic go by below their darkened window. That night, they slept in each others' arms, clinging as though it might be their last night together.

Early Wednesday morning, while Hood dictated, Veracity wrote two notes on hotel stationery. The first one was to Liam Hardesty:

> Dear Sir:
> Under your contract, the Allen Pinkerton National Detective Agency has located Mr. Sean Evan Hood and has delivered to him your message of forgiveness. If I may join you at your home at 1:00 P.M. today, I will be happy to guide you to personally meet with Mr. Hood, should you so desire. Please advise by return message.
>
> Sincerely,
V. L. Cooper, Agent
Rm. 301

"Now, to Georgie," Hood said.
Veracity took a fresh piece of paper and again dipped the pen.

Dear Mr. Hood:

I have important news of your brother, Sean. Will you be at home and receiving visitors today at 1:30 P.M.? Please advise by return message.

Urgently,
V. L. Cooper, Pinkerton Agent
Rm. 301

"And enclose your business card in each note," Sean concluded.

Veracity dug her card holder from her old reticule, selected the least dog-eared, folded the papers and inserted the cards and notes into their respective envelopes.

At 8:00 A.M., Sean called the bellboy, Danny, and sent the messages on their way with instructions that the delivery boy was to wait for an answer at each location.

At 8:30 A.M., a discreet knock on the door brought their clothes—fully laundered and pressed—and their boots shined to as high a gloss as battered leather would accept. Veracity had already dressed in a forest-green travel out-fit complete with a jaunty veil-less hat, tan kid gloves and purse to match, but Hood's city clothing had not yet arrived. Out of necessity, he wore his faded blue shirt and black britches.

When he slid his legs into the shotgun chaps and strapped on his side-arm, Veracity frowned.

"Stormy, you're going to stick out like a sore thumb in that. Why are you wearing your chaps and weapons?"

He paused in pulling on his boots. "I don't know. But why did I just see you transferring Angel from your old bag to that one?" He nodded at the neat beige purse.

She blushed and raised brows at him. "You caught me. My derringer and knife are in my boot top, too. I guess I . . . well, I just feel . . . *naked* without them now, y'know?"

He patted his six-gun. "I know. You have everything you need to take with you?"

"Yes. And you?"

"Yep." He stood abruptly—it was a tense, jerky movement—and her brows lowered to a frown.

She said, "Stormy . . . Sean . . ." She moved to take his hands in hers and held them over her heart, ". . . it'll be all right! You've lived through too much for it to all fall apart now. Let's go to breakfast, and hopefully, we'll have some kind of responses by the time we get back."

At 9:30 A.M., they ate a late breakfast in the hotel dining room. It was nearly 10:30 and they were about to rise to return to their room, when a messenger panted into the lobby and was asked to wait while a bellboy stood at the dining room door and said loudly, *"Call for V. L. Cooper . . . call for V. L. Cooper . . ."*

Veracity flashed a look at Sean and raised her hand. "Here!"

The bellhop hurried two envelopes across the room. Sean tipped him; handed him a dollar and said, "Give this to the messenger for his fast service," then bent his head to look at the notes.

Veracity's fingers trembled when she opened the one addressed to Hardesty. Penned at the bottom of the paper was: *Mr. Cooper . . . I will see you at one o'clock at my residence. Liam Hardesty.*

"So far, so good," Sean murmured.

The response from Georgie was: *I will be available at 2:00 today. Please come to my home then. George P. Hood.*

Stormy whipped a rumpled paper from his shirt pocket, spread the two notes on the table and held the third near them to compare handwriting. Presently, he and Veracity stared round-eyed at each other.

She gasped, "Would you believe that! Neither Hardesty nor Georgie wrote that note. Who sent five hundred dollars to so many places and kept telling you to come home?"

Grimly, he shook his head. "I don't know, but this gets thicker and thicker." He handed the invitations back to her, folded the paper saying: *Come home. George Patrick Hood,* and returned it to his pocket, then said, "Okay. It's now near eleven. It takes an hour, give or take a few minutes either way, to get from here to Liam Hardesty's home. He lives only a few doors down from my home—we'll take a hansom together, you let me off at my place, then continue on to Hardesty's." He smiled almost nastily. "I think it's time to make an unexpected call on Georgie."

She indicated his clothing. "Are you going to go like that? . . . the beard and all?"

"Uh-huh. Might be good for my brother's soul to see me in what has become my . . . natural state."

"Oh, my," Veracity breathed as she looked through ornate wrought-iron gates piercing the high red-brick wall facing the street. "I didn't know you lived in such splendor!"

They had killed an hour in their room while biding their time until it was appropriate to call a hansom, and she had watched Sean's nerves growing tighter with each passing minute. By now, he was about to snap; she saw him glance at the elegant residence at the apex of the wide curving paved driveway, at the flowered gardens and wrought-iron lampposts, and saw the grim lines framing his mouth deepened.

He said, "Yes. Well, remember that I don't live here anymore." He kissed her quickly. "Good luck with Hardesty. I'll see you here at one-thirty."

"Stormy . . . Stormy, don't do anything foolish. Remember that I love you, Stormy, and . . . be calm."

He nodded, climbed out of the cab and motioned the driver to move onward up the street before he turned to face the gates.

Abruptly, he felt awkward and unsure dressed like this, as though he was an actor in some stage play rather than a valid person. But then, he squared his shoulders and took a deep breath. No, if anyone should be hesitant about this, it should be Georgie, not him. Georgie was the miscreant here; he, Sean, the innocent party.

He stepped to the gate and pushed against the iron, found it closed but not locked. No matter what his rationalization, he knew he was an intruder as his riding boots clunked against cobbles. *Once,* he had lived here, belonged here, been a familiar here, but that *once* was a long time ago. There was a saying: You can never go home again. *Yes,* he thought. *Truth in that.* He no longer belonged with these manicured gardens or in that mansion.

Mausoleum, was his impression as he moved up the wide curving steps to the front door. His palms were sweaty when he reached for the brass lion-head knocker, but he only hesitated briefly before he rapped it.

He had to knock twice more before the door opened. Burkhart, the butler—older, grayer, more austere—scrutinized him up and down for a moment before he asked, "Yes?"

Sean grinned. "You're looking well, Burkhart. Don't you know me?"

The butler began, "I . . ." But then, he obviously saw past Sean's clothing. Recognition lighted his eyes, and for the first time that Hood could recall, an enormous smile split Burkhart's face. *"Mister Stormy!"*

Sean almost found himself embraced by the man, but Burkhart caught himself with an obvious effort of will. He stiffened and smoothed his demeanor back into bland indifference, though he couldn't hide the sparkle in his eyes. "Please come in, Mister Stormy."

Sean stepped into the foyer. "Burkhart, I have to ask you a question . . . did you go to school to learn that expression, the nostrils and all? That's bothered me for years."

The butler didn't smile, but said severely, "Yes, sir, I did. May I take your hat . . . and your . . . uh . . . weapons?"

"No, thank you, Burkhart, I'll keep them. Is my brother in?"

"Yes, sir. Mister Hood is holding a meeting upstairs in the library."

"A meeting? Who with?"

"His lawyers and accountants, sir. It seems Mister George received word from a Pinkerton agent this morning early that the agency had word of you. Mister George called an emergency meeting as a result."

Sean's brows rose. "Really! Well, I came at an opportune time, then, didn't I. No need to announce me, Burkhart . . . I know the way."

"Yes, sir," the butler breathed. Triumph was almost but not quite successfully hidden in his tone, and a small crease that might have been the beginning of a smile hovered beside his mouth. Silently, he watched Stormy mount the stairs leading to the second floor before he strode toward his quarters to listen at the call-pipe.

Sean paused outside the carved, polished wooden library panels to look right and left up and down the dim, quiet, carpeted hall. From behind a closed door at the far left end, he could hear children's voices—George III, Matthew, Maggie . . . by this time, there might even be another born. There was silence to his right, but from the other side of the wall in front of him came the sound of men's voices in what seemed to be heated conversation or an argument.

Very quietly, he opened the door just far enough to step through, closed it behind him and leaned back against it. He folded arms across his chest and crossed one ankle over the other, his boot toe on the carpet, while he looked and listened.

The long-retained family lawyer, Winston Knowles, and his young associate, sat to the left of a desk that had been moved into the library since Sean had last been here. Georgie crouched behind the desk, turned to face Knowles, and spoke angrily to him; nearly yelled at him. Three other men—Stormy recognized Byron O'Reilly, Hood Shipping's chief accountant, by his flaming red hair, but couldn't tell who the other two were from the back—sat in chairs pulled close to this side of the desk. Ledgers and documents were piled on the waxed plane before them.

Sean heard Georgie shout, "I don't *care* if Father stipulated that his Will was not to be read until both Sean and I were present or for five years after his death, Winston! Stormy has been gone for over two years! Who knows whether he's ever coming back! Without estate resolution, I am unable to expand Hood Shipping. I want to buy *now,* Winston, while I have the upper hand!" He shot a finger in O'Reilly's direction without looking at the accountant. "Byron's figures show we came out a hundred and ten thousand ahead this quarter . . . more than two hundred thousand last quarter! I have ample cash on hand, Winston. Mikal Theopolis isn't going to wait forever, but I can't buy his company until the Will is executed, the estate settled, and I know where I stand! I can't wait almost three more years, dammit!"

The attorney opened his mouth to retort, but Sean spoke first. He said softly, "Well, gentlemen, I'm glad to hear we're in such good financial shape. It seems I got here just in time, doesn't it."

Veracity found Liam Hardesty's home to be even more impressive than the Hoods', if that was possible, for the hansom cab stopped at the front steps of a multi-turreted graystone edifice perched well behind a lush garden even more manicured than its neighbors'. Veracity stepped down and said to the driver, "Please wait. It may be a while, but not more than a half-hour. If all goes well, I shall have another passenger for you on the return trip."

The driver nodded and settled back to view the scenery. It was a nice mid-September day, and he didn't mind being out of the downtown bustle at all. Besides, he was being well paid.

Veracity dug another business card out of her purse, then with her bag over her arm, her folded parasol in hand, and her identification ready, walked up recently scrubbed flagstone steps and rapped the heavy iron knocker.

Presently, a plump, florid-faced middle-aged woman in a black dress, white apron, and ruffled bonnet, opened the door. "Good afternoon, Miss. If yez represents a charitable organization, I must tell yez that Mister Hardesty . . ."

"No." Veracity presented her card. "I am V. L. Cooper. I have a one o'clock appointment with Mister Hardesty. Please tell him I'm here."

The maid stared from her to the card and back. "*Yez* is a Pinkerton detective?"

"Yes, I am. May I come in?"

Obviously disbelieving, the maid nevertheless stepped aside to allow her to pass; said, "If y'll wait here, please . . ." closed the door and vanished down the hallway.

While she waited, Veracity looked around. Dark wood. Brass and crystal chandeliers. Heavy mohair-upholstered furniture. Porcelain and cut glass. A tint of cigar smoke and fine brandy in the air. Old money. An established family, like the mansion, expected to last.

The maid was back. "Mister Hardesty will see yez in the east livin' room. Please to follow me, Miss."

Liam Hardesty was so big that even his stooped shoulders couldn't diminish him. In his youth, he may have been six feet four; great gnarled hands made a mockery of the maroon velvet smoking jacket he wore. Thinning red hair that white had turned to apricot bushed wildly around a long-jawed deeply-lined face. He was in his mid-fifties, but the grooves bitterness and sorrow had cut into him made him look older. Still, the hard glint in pale blue eyes told Veracity that here was a sharp, ruthless man, and that she would have to be very careful what she said to him.

He greeted her with the same astonishment the maid had shown. After she'd been seated, he

353

repeated in a gravelly voice, "*You* are a Pinkerton detective?"

"Yes, Mister Hardesty. As you are well aware, it has taken the agency over two years to locate Sean Hood. I am the third agent who has worked the case. Along the way, Mister Hardesty, we have discovered some rather . . . unexpected facets to the whole affair . . . if you will excuse my unfortunate choice of words, please."

His face had darkened. He sat in a chair opposite her, slouched and glowering, his big frame nearly hiding the furniture. "But Hood . . . you located Hood? Pinkerton indicated that your telegram to him said you were returning here, yes, but he didn't say anything about Hood's whereabouts. Where is he at this moment?"

"Sean returned with me. Would you like to see him to extend your . . . forgiveness for your daughter's . . . unfortunate demise . . . in person?"

Hardesty's blue eyes narrowed. He said very softly, "Yesssss. Where is Sean Hood now, Miss Cooper?"

No! Veracity felt her skin roughen beneath her crisp white blouse, the goosebumps raised by the chill that alarm raced down her spine. Her instincts knew that Hardesty didn't intend to *forgive* Stormy at all!

She swallowed and said, "Before this goes any farther, Mister Hardesty, I think there is something you need to see." She leaned her parasol against the chair arm to search past the Avenging Angel in her purse. She produced an envelope and offered it to her host. "I believe you should read this, Mister Hardesty."

Slowly, Liam reached for the envelope. More slowly, he extracted George Hood Senior's letter to Sean. The paper seemed to be only a note in Hardesty's huge hands; he fished spectacles from a pocket inside his smoking jacket, put them on and scowled at the words. Veracity watched color first drain from his face as he read, then flash back so intensely she thought for a moment he suffered a seizure of some kind.

He gritted, "*Sean* Hood isn't the one? It was George Junior? His brother, *Georgie?*" His tone escalated. "I have been livin' next door to that . . . All this time, I have . . ."

And a second revelation stuck Veracity as abruptly as her knowledge that Hardesty actually intended to kill Stormy on sight. She suddenly knew who had hired Oscar Pratt and his New York City dock longshore backup. She said, "You have been offering bounty for Sean's head when he is as much an innocent victim as Melissa was . . . or as you are, Mister Hardesty. I should tell you that Oscar Pratt and his men are all dead. You won't have to pay them for killing Sean."

Hardesty's mouth dropped open. "How did you . . . ?"

"I may be female, Mister Hardesty, but I am a

very good detective. It was a logical conclusion, you see. For years, the Hood family has been sending money to Sean. If he would assume blame for Melissa's . . . problem . . . they would support him. It wouldn't be reasonable for relatives who created and *maintained* a Remittance Man to also pay five thousand dollars to kill him.

"Secondly, as owner of Hardesty Drayage, I expect that you deal with longshoremen all the time. Oscar Pratt and his cronies were longshoremen." She frowned and shook her head. "But what I don't understand is why you told Mister Pratt your name was George Hood. Why didn't you use your own identity, Mister Hardesty?"

Liam brooded at the carpet for a long, silent moment before he muttered, "Two reasons. One, if Pratt was somehow caught, *I* wouldn't then be charged with hirin' an assassin. But most importantly, was it Sean Hood who captured my men an' discovered their . . . employer . . . I had hoped to . . . cause him some . . . pain the like of which I feel."

Now, Veracity nodded. "He did, and you nearly destroyed him with that ploy."

"Knowin' what I know now, I . . . regret that. Did you tell Sean t'was I who . . . ?"

"No. Until this moment, I merely suspected. I didn't want to advance unfounded theories.

Would you care to see Sean now? He is at the family home just down the street. I have a cab waiting."

"He's with Georgie? George Junior is also there?"

"I wouldn't know, Mister Hardesty. But at least you can extend your apologies to Sean."

"Yes." Hardesty lurched up and out of the chair, handed the letter and envelope back to her, and finished, "If you'll give me but a moment to put on street clothing . . ." Before she could answer, he lumbered out of the living room and disappeared into the hallway.

Shortly, he was back, his suit jacket on, a silk stovepipe hat in his right hand. He extended his left arm. Veracity rose and slipped her hand through his elbow to let him escort her out, and she was very aware of the hardness of the weapon she felt beneath his jacket.

CHAPTER NINETEEN

The tick of the library clock on the mantle was loud in the silence as men at the desk swiveled around to stare toward the doors. Sean hadn't moved; they saw a tall, slim, bearded man dressed in clean but rough clothing, his old flat-crowned western-style hat pulled low over his eyes, and in the shadows by the door, only his holstered side-arm was readily visible. Clearly, he was a stranger.

Georgie's scowl shifted from his attorney to the newcomer. He snapped, "Who the hell are you! How did you get in here! Burkhart . . . where's Burkhart! Out, or I'll call for the authorities!"

"Oh, now, you don't want to do that, Georgie." Sean unfolded his arms and stuck a thumb against the brim to shove his hat back, and when light from the high windows and desk lamps glossed his face, his brother's mouth fell open.

George gasped, "St-Stormy?"

"Only my *friends* call me that, Georgie," Sean said coldly. "To you, it's *Sean*." He pushed away from the door and approached slowly across the room to address the attorney. "Knowles, who else besides Georgie and I have to be present before you'll read Father's Will?"

Winston answered curtly, "Mister Hood Senior

stipulated that you, Mister Hood Second and his wife, Gertrude, and your butler Karl Burkhart, must attend the reading, Mister . . . are you really Sean Hood?"

Stormy snapped, "Oh, yes, that I am."

Eyes and mouth still wide, George eased out of the chair and backed away when Sean rounded the desk. Stormy kept coming. His black eyes were fixed unwaveringly on his brother's blue, and though his expression was smooth, something close to menace hung in the air around him. Still soft-toned, he finished, "If Trudy is at home, then it appears that all necessary parties are present, doesn't it." He again shoved at his hat; let it fall to hang by the chin string. "Did you happen to bring the Will with you, Knowles?" He pulled George's chair farther from the desk, turned, sat and adjusted his gun belt so the weapon grip was within easy reach before he put heels onto the desk edge and crossed his ankles. He still hadn't looked away from Georgie.

Knowles frowned, "Why, yes, Mister Hood. Mister George Hood the Second asked me to . . ."

"When was the Will written, Knowles?"

"Uh . . . the . . . the week before George Senior passed away. He called me here to make out a new document. This one . . ." he opened his briefcase and produced a large sealed white envelope, ". . . supersedes any and all previous . . ."

"Good." Sean still studied Georgie. He said into the air, "Burkhart, I know you're listening. Would you please collect Miz Trudy, bring her to the library, and then stay?"

George motioned to the call pull and speaker tube on the wall beside the fireplace behind Stormy. "Sean, you'll have to . . ."

"No, I don't."

George had recovered somewhat from his startlement at seeing his brother. He began, "Dammit all, Sean, this is *my* house now, and that's *my* chair you're sitting in!" He grabbed blindly at another and shoved it forward. "Here! Sit here! I was in the middle of a business meeting when you burst in, and . . ."

"So I heard." Sean's lips bent into a small smile that didn't reach his eyes. He took his feet off the desk and stood. "*No hay problema*, Georgie. Whatever you like . . . until the Will's read." He moved toward the wingback George indicated.

As he passed, his brother stepped back from him and lawyers and accountants glanced at each other. Side-by-side, the difference between the brothers was striking. Sean was taller by an inch than George, lean, hard, sun-browned. His raven hair and cold black eyes more than the weapon on his hip made him seem ominous in the richly-appointed library. By contrast, Georgie appeared soft and pudgy, though he was not.

"What?" Sean breathed. "No show of brotherly

love, Georgie? No 'Welcome-home-where-have-you-been-all-this-time,' Georgie?"

George kept backing away. He licked lips. His eyes darted around the room. He said, "Sean . . . now, Sean . . ."

"What? You think I'm going to attack you? *What have you ever done to me that would make you think I would attack you, Georgie?*" Sean felt rage rising and struggled to subdue it. The effort tainted his voice with bitterness.

George stiffened. His scowl made him and Sean look more like brothers when he snapped, "God dammit, Stormy, let's leave family business until we have privacy!"

"*Family* business?" Sean's grim smile broadened. "But Georgie, here are our *family* attorneys . . . certainly, they are up on all our *family business*. Here are the company accountants . . . they *run* the family business. Surely, we have no deep secrets from them, do we?

"Y'know," he pulled the hat string from under his chin and set the Stetson aside before he sat in the wingback; again adjusted his side-arm for easy access, "strange thing, here, Georgie. You are the elder brother, but somehow, I feel *older*. Why d'you s'pose that is? Could it be from my years of running from the gun slingers you hired to kill me, Georgie?"

In the dumbfounded silence that brought, Georgie's mouth fell open. "What? S-Some has been . . . *I* didn't hire anyone to hunt you down!"

"Really! Then, who you s'pose contracted with Oscar Pratt and his gunnies? Who offered five thousand dollars for my head if it wasn't you, Georgie? Before he died, ol' Pratt said someone named *George Hood* had hired him . . . y'don't s'pose it was *our father* who did that to me, do you, Georgie?"

George Junior's face had gone the color of old putty. He shook his head; stared from man-to-man among the attorneys and accountants frozen in their chairs around his desk, their mouths likewise open in shock or brows lowered over revolted expressions. He eased himself into his chair and gasped, "I didn't . . . I didn't do that, Stormy. I would *never* do that to you, you've got to believe me! Sure, after F-Father died, I stopped s-sending you money, but . . . *no!* No! I didn't hire killers to . . . no! I would *never* . . ." His voice died abruptly, killed by a knock on the door.

It was Sean who called, "Come in."

Burkhart opened the door but stood aside to allow George's wife, Gertrude, to precede him before he also stepped inside and closed the door behind him. Trudy was a big woman, tall and rawboned, whose figure motherhood hadn't rounded, yet there was a softness to her gray eyes that betrayed a gentle female trapped inside a plow horse's body. She tried in vain to minimize her appearance; her center-parted dark brown hair began severely but was caught in a mass of curls at her nape. Her long light blue full-skirted dress bore lace insets and ruffles in an effort to plump her figure into a more matronly aspect. The only thing that really saved her from plainness was her brilliant smile—it lighted like a warm evening lamp when she saw Stormy. Both hands out, she swept across the floor toward him, and he rose hurriedly to greet her.

"Sean! Oh, Stormy, how good to see you again! It's been such a long time! Are you merely passing through, or have you come home to stay?"

Sean squeezed her fingers; leaned to kiss her cheek. "Trudy, you're looking very well. Uh . . . how long I stay depends on the reading of Father's Will, and . . . other things." He glanced around at the men, handed his sister-in-law into his chair and himself moved to lean against the fireplace.

Winston Knowles said quickly, "All required parties are now present. If you wish a formal reading of George Patrick Hood Senior's Last Will and Testament, we can do it now, and . . ."

"*Yes!*" George said.

Sean looked up at the mantle clock. "We can read it, yes, but let's wait a few minutes longer. There are some other people I'd like to have present. It's one-twenty. Two more folks are arriving shortly. They should also hear what Father stipulated."

"*What* two people?" Georgie and Knowles asked simultaneously. Hood finished, "All of us that Winston said needed to be present are here."

"We'll wait," Stormy snapped.

"Dammit, I've already waited over two years to . . ." Georgie's words stopped abruptly when he found himself stared down by the round black eye of a six-shooter. Everyone in the room except Gertrude froze, gaping at the weapon Sean pointed at his brother.

Mrs. Hood gasped and cringed into her chair. She whispered, "Stormy, what are you doing! This is your *home,* Sean! You . . ."

"Please excuse me, Trudy. I apologize for this, but we will wait just a few moments longer. *Georgie, you wanted that chair, stay set!* The rest of you just keep calm and no one will get hurt."

George's face was back to pale. He stayed in his chair. His eyes flicked from the weapon to Stormy's dangerously-hard expression as he choked, "You've changed, Sean. I don't think I . . . like you anymore."

"Did you ever, Georgie?" Stormy holstered his gun, but kept it loose. "Burkhart, is someone available to answer the front door?"

"Yes, Mister Stormy. Katie is . . ."

"Ah! And even now," Sean nodded when

knuckles tapped the library doors. "Burkhart, if you please."

The butler had already begun to move. Again, all faces turned toward the hallway, this time to see who it was they waited for. Burkhart opened the door, there were murmured introductions, he stepped aside and announced, "Agent of the Allan Pinkerton National Detective Agency of Chicago, Miss V. L. Cooper . . . and Mister Liam Hardesty."

With Hardesty towering behind her, Veracity said, "Thank you, Mister Burkhart," and strode briskly across the room toward the desk. She looked briefly at Sean still leaning against the fireplace before she opened her purse and turned to stare narrow-eyed at Liam.

Georgie whispered, "H-Hardesty!" His eyes fixed on Liam, his right hand slid surreptitiously toward a desk drawer.

Sean began, "*Now,* everyone who needs to be here is h . . ."

Hardesty's hand dipped beneath his jacket. Hating eyes on Georgie, he yanked the big Colt .45 out and pointed it at the elder Hood. Accountants and attorneys hit the floor when a different pistol shot thundered in the room and Liam's weapon sprang from his fingers, sailed through the air and skidded along the rug.

Veracity held her smoking Avenging Angel dead-on him. "We Pinkerton agents are not hired gunslingers, Mister Hardesty, nor are we accomplices in murd- . . ."

"*No!*" Sean yelled. He leaped between Liam and Georgie and crouched, the tented fingers of his left hand against Hardesty's chest. His right again aimed his own iron at his brother who had frozen in the act of bringing a weapon from the desk drawer. "Hold it, Georgie! Winston, get that gun and put it up on the mantle!"

Trudy had slid down in her chair, both hands pressed over her ears. Terrified, she cried, "What's going on? I don't understand this at all! What's happening?"

Hardesty leaned against Stormy's staying hand. He growled, "Why are you protecting George after what he did to you, Hood?"

"I'm not protecting him from you, Liam . . . I'm protecting you from him. If you murder him before all these witnesses, he'll merely be dead, but you'll go to prison or hang, and you've already suffered enough. Sit down over there. *Everybody* sit. Veracity, please keep an eye on this crowd.

"Trudy, I apologize to you for this uproar in your home . . . and for . . . everything you're about to hear. For everything." He straightened, divided his attention between Hardesty sinking slowly into the chair Burkhart brought, and Georgie whey-faced and now sagged limply into his own seat. "Now, Winston, you can read

Father's Will. Burkhart, take care of that, please."

The gunshot had brought servants up the stairs. Fists pounded the doors above muffled cries of: Is everything all right in there? The butler hurried to crack the panels. He murmured assurances of well-being out into the hall, shut and locked the library doors, and returned to stand beside Veracity still keeping a sharp eye on everyone in sight. Her Angel was back in her purse, but the purse was still open for easy access.

The attorney had put George's weapon on the mantle. He frowned down at Hood. "Mister George?"

Sean snapped, "He wanted the Will read, read it, dammit."

"But these people aren't party to this. This is private Hood family business, and . . ."

"You read it, Knowles, or I'll read it." Sean jammed his iron back into its holster and started forward.

"Read it, Winston," George said dully. "For God's sake, read it and get it over with."

Knowles glanced around at the others before he nodded, reseated himself, reached for the envelope still lying on the desk top and adjusted his wire-rimmed glasses on the bridge of his nose. He unsealed the envelope flap, extracted a multi-page document, opened it and cleared his throat.

He said solemnly, "This is the Last Will and

Testament of George Patrick Hood Senior . . ."
he lifted brows at his audience, ". . . dated August
twentieth, eighteen seventy-two . . . ummm
. . . two weeks after Missus Hood Senior passed
on and the week before Mister Hood Senior,
himself, died. I'll skip all the legal verbiage;
suffice it to say this document was constructed
in this very room, dictated to me personally by
George Senior."

He looked back at the Will. " '. . . being in good
health and of sound mind,' *et cetera, et cetera* . . .
'do hereby name Winston Knowles, who has
been my personal attorney for seventeen years, as
executor of my estate. He shall see that my estate
is divided, as follows:

" 'To my youngest son, Sean Evan Hood, I
bequeath and devise, in complete and perfect
ownership wherever situated, any and all family
assets, including all my rights and property of
any nature . . .' "

"No!" Georgie cried. He looked wildly around
at Knowles, at Trudy, at Sean. "No, he *can't* have
left everything to Stormy! What about . . ."

"Mister George," Winston scowled, "you
haven't let me finish."

George waved a hand at him. "But . . ."

"Please, sir, let me finish!" The attorney again
cleared his throat, found where he had left
off, and continued, " '. . . of any nature, *with
the following exceptions* . . .*" He cast a look at

369

Georgie, but Hood didn't say anything now.

" 'To my daughter-in-law, Gertrude Wilkins Hood, I give the family home at Sixty-third Street and Fifth Avenue, including all furnishings and grounds free and clear, said dwelling to be occupied by her and any or all of her children so long as she shall desire to inhabit the residence. Gertrude Wilkins Hood shall also receive a yearly allotment of one thousand five hundred dollars for her personal use, and two thousand five hundred as maintenance compensation for upkeep of her and her children's home. Let it be known, that if Gertrude Wilkins Hood shall divorce George Patrick Hood Second . . .' "

"But why would Father even think of such a thing," Trudy gasped, "much less write it in his Will? I'm so confused . . ."

" '. . . *if* Gertrude Wilkins Hood shall divorce George Patrick Hood Second,' " Knowles repeated grimly, " 'George Second shall locate other lodgings and Gertrude and her children shall retain the house until such time as Gertrude remarries. At that moment, the house and grounds shall revert to Sean Evan Hood for his use or disposal. These arrangements will be administered for Gertrude and/or Sean Evan Hood by Knowles-Gacy Attorneys and the accounting firm of O'Reilly, O'Reilly, Kissling, and Gerrant, as long as required.

" 'To each of my grandchildren, I leave ten

thousand dollars for their education and to start them off well in life, said funds to be administered by the above-named attorneys and accounting firm, the remainder of their inheritance turned over to them on their twenty-first birthdays or, in the case of my granddaughter(s), as dowry upon marriage.

" 'To my long-time family retainer, Karl S. Burkhart, I leave the sum of ten thousand dollars and my gratitude for his many years of unswerving loyalty and service.

" 'To each of the present household staff, I leave one thousand dollars . . .' "

"Me!" George scowled. "What about me? He hasn't mentioned me at all! He's doling out family assets indiscriminately, while he seems to be ignoring me! I'm his eldest heir! He . . ."

Knowles looked up; said severely, "You are mentioned next, Mister Hood. Please be patient." He again located his place in the Will. "We were discussing the present household staff. Ummm, '. . . I leave one thousand dollars cash and also my thanks for their service.

" 'To my eldest son, George Patrick Hood the Second, I leave the full contempt I feel for myself. I know I can never be forgiven for my part in the crime I helped perpetrate against my youngest son, Sean, but should George ever find the courage to beg the pardon of his wife, Gertrude, of his brother, Sean, and of Mister Liam

Hardesty for the loss of his daughter, Melissa, perhaps in their charity, they will tolerate his presence.

" 'May God forgive him and me, for I cannot.' And it's signed, G. P. Hood, Sr." Winston folded the papers.

Trudy began, "I . . . I don't understand!" but abruptly, harsh laughter drowned her out. Everyone looked from Georgie sitting stunned and wordless behind the desk, to where Liam chuckled grimly.

"So," Hardesty grated, "disinherited and exposed, y'are, aren't you, Georgie Hood, an' the rest of your life to pay for your sins. Revenge enough, I'd say." He looked over at Sean. "But to *you,* young man, I extend my apologies and deepest regrets for hirin' Oscar Pratt to kill you—I'm grateful he failed."

Sean's brows rose. "*You* did that? You?"

"Yes, the more fool, me. But if you'll be a bigger man than I and overlook my error, I'll be delighted to do business with you."

Trudy cried, "Would someone please explain all this to me?" She leaned toward Georgie. "What . . . why . . . ?"

Sean held up a hand for silence. He looked down at George and said mildly, "I believe you're in my seat, Georgie."

Numb and disbelieving, George stumbled upright and sidled away. Stormy sat down, leaned back, again propped heels on the edge of the desk and drew his six-shooter to absently spin the cylinder. Everyone watched him curiously as he bit his lip for a long moment.

Then, he said, "Mister Hardesty, I forgive you. I can understand your feelings at the loss of your daughter. I, too, have lost . . . my whole family, really . . . with one exception, and there I gained enormously. I'd like to introduce my wife, Veracity Cooper Hood, Pinkerton agent without peer. It was Veracity who delivered your message of forgiveness to me, Liam."

Hardesty shook his head. "T'was a lie, young man. I but tried to lure you home to kill you. It was another of my mistakes."

"Perhaps, Liam. But you did me one hell of a big favor." He held out a hand. "Veracity . . ."

Quickly, she walked around the group to where Sean sat. He reached up to pull her close and whispered in her ear. She drew back, glanced around the room, studied its occupants for a moment, then said, "No, I don't."

"You're sure?"

"Sure-certain."

"It'll be a long time till we'll be back, y'know."

"I know . . . and I'm sure."

He grinned at her, again drew her close and kissed her quickly. "Done." He looked back at Hardesty. "Liam, I've forgiven you and you've forgiven me. In this forgiving mood, and for the good of your own soul, could you also forgive Georgie?"

Hardesty's expression turned to stone. "*No!* I'll give that bastard nothin'!"

"It's not for him, Liam, it's for you. Hate won't bring Melissa back, it'll destroy *you.* I know. I nearly let it kill my humanity. Besides . . ." Sean grinned crookedly, ". . . I have an ulterior motive. I want your promise that you'll allow Georgie to do business as usual here in New York City. That you won't try to ruin Hood Shipping."

"But the firm is now yours, young Hood."

"For the sake of argument, let's say it wasn't. Would you allow your lust for revenge to destroy Gertrude Hood and her children? Would you impoverish them? . . . scandalize them? . . . *and,* in the process, sully Melissa's memory in the eyes of everyone who ever knew and loved her?"

"Please . . . please . . ." Trudy whispered, ". . . what is this about Mister Hardesty and his daughter? What have they to do with us?"

Sean said gently, "Trudy, it's best you discuss it with Georgie in private after this is all over." He looked back at Liam. "Well, Hardesty?"

"I'll . . . give you my answer *after* I hear your *ulterior motive.*"

"Fair enough." Sean addressed the chief accountant. "Mister O'Reilly, as boys, both Georgie and I had personal bank accounts set up for us by our father. Is mine still in existence?"

"Yes, Mister Sean, it is, but . . ."

"But?"

"It's almost vacated, sir."

"But if I recall correctly, I believe there was nearly seventeen thousand dollars in it before I . . . left." Sean swung around to glare toward where George leaned against the bookcases as though he hadn't enough strength left in him to either fight or flee. "My *God,* Georgie, is there no *end* to your . . ."

"No, sir, Mister Stormy," Burkhart broke in. "It wasn't Mister George Second who embezzled your funds, but I."

"You! You, Burkh- . . . *ah! You're* the one who sent five hundred dollars to various places along with the cryptic notes merely saying *Come home,* and signed *George Patrick Hood!*"

"Yes, sir. I knew when Mister George Second stopped sending your remittance. You're *my* sss . . . uh . . . the . . . the son I never had, Mister Stormy. I feared for your welfare. When I . . . used up my own savings, sir . . . I apologize, but I had nowhere else to get the money but from your account. The bank was accustomed to me doing business for the Hood family. They never questioned it. I worried that you needed the funds. I h-hoped you would return . . . *hope* you do not take offense."

"Thank you, Burkhart. To the contrary, I'm grateful." Sean turned back to O'Reilly. "And how much does Georgie have in his personal account?"

From the shadows, George gathered enough gumption to flare, "That's none of your business, Sean!"

"Oh, yes it is. O'Reilly?"

The accountant opened a ledger and flipped pages. "Fifty-seven thousand, nine hundred thirty-six dollars and two cents, Mister Sean."

Stormy looked at Knowles. "You're *my* lawyer now, correct, Winston? Then, write up an agreement for me. It seems that whatever else he is or is not, Georgie is a good businessman who has run Hood Shipping well—right, O'Reilly?"

The accountant nodded, and Sean went on. "I will sell forty-nine percent of my company holdings to Georgie for fifty-seven thousand, nine hundred thirty-six dollars and two cents *and* his signed agreement that he pays me ten thousand dollars a year over and above my fifty-one percent annual profits for the rest of my life, *and* that he continue paying my wife, Veracity Louise Hood, ten thousand a year for however long she lives after me should I die first. I will retain fifty-one percent shares in the company to keep my hand in and to . . . keep Georgie honest.

"Write that up now, then I will sign, Georgie will sign, Liam Hardesty and Burkhart will witness, and it's a done deal. Agreed?"

"No!" Georgie shouted. *"I contest. I contest*

376

the Will . . . this whole thing! Father wasn't in full possession of his faculties, no matter what he said! Mother had just died . . . Sean had vanished . . . no! The company is *mine!* It's always *been* mine! I am the one who . . ."

"Georgie," Sean snapped, "if you'll shut your face and sign, the company is still yours. I don't intend to interfere at all, I merely don't want to cut myself off from the family completely. Sign the damn sales document, *now, Georgie!*"

"No! I agree to buy the shares, yes, but ten thousand a year . . . if you lived another fifty years, that'd be *five hundred thousand dollars* . . . what's all that money for!"

Sean said somberly, "You made me into a Remittance Man, remember, Georgie? Once a Remittance Man, *always* a Remittance Man. That ten thousand a year is to ensure that I stay far away from you, because the next time we meet, Georgie, I will kill you for what you did to our mother and father . . . and to Melissa, to Hardesty . . . and to me."

It was spoken so quietly that it took a moment for Stormy's words to sink in. Then, attorneys and accountants slid wide-eyed looks at each other. Beside Burkhart, Veracity tensed; like the others, she knew a solemn oath when she heard it.

So did Georgie. He swallowed; seemed to shrink even farther into the shadows by the bookcase; nodded quickly to Knowles. "Yes . . . uh . . . yes. We-Write up the . . . the contract, Winston, and I'll . . . I'll sign."

Knowles pulled himself together. He grabbed paper out of his briefcase, hurriedly wrote, Sean proofed the draft and signed. Georgie signed. Hardesty and Burkhart witnessed, and as he placed the pen back into its holder, the butler asked softly, "But where will you and Miss Veracity go now, Mister Stormy?"

"Home, Burkhart."

"*This* is . . ."

"No," Veracity cut in, "*this* is not home, Mister Burkhart. Nor would it ever be."

Burkhart tipped his head. "Wherever you go, Missus Hood, do you need a butler?"

She laughed. "Not out in Skull Valley in the Arizona Territory, Mister Burkhart. But Sean and I *could* use a good friend."

"Then, I do believe I shall retire and . . . ummm . . . see the world . . . as your friend, Miss Veracity . . . Mister Stormy? If you'll have me?"

Sean's brows rose. "Can you ride a horse, Burkhart?"

Burkhart grinned easily; it was fascinating to Sean to see a personality emerge out from under a quarter-century of butler training. "I paid my way through school by exercising horses at a local riding academy, sir."

"It's Stormy, Burkhart," Sean said. "No more

sir." He turned to Knowles. "How soon will that document be processed, Winston?"

The attorney tugged his lower lip with two fingers, cogitating for a moment. "I *can* rush it through the legal process. By Friday? Would Friday be adequate?"

"Yes. I leave it to you and O'Reilly to set things up for me." He rose, holstered his iron, and turned to his sister-in-law. "I'm sorry, Trudy. I'm so damn sorry. Good-bye."

Gertrude's expression was torn between tears and a preparation to be furious, but she managed, "Good-bye, Stormy," before she looked at Veracity. "I'm . . . sorry we . . . It doesn't seem that we will get to know each other, does it, Veracity."

Veracity shook her head. "Not yet, Trudy. But perhaps one day. If you're ever inclined to come west, we'll always have a place for you."

"Thank you." Gertrude stood abruptly and smoothed her skirt. Her head jerked up as she said, "Burkhart, my best to you in your retirement. George, you will come with me . . . *now!*"

The rest of them watched her sweep out. George started to follow, but hesitated to look at Sean and began, "Stormy . . ."

"Good-bye, Georgie."

"Yes," George murmured, and followed his wife.

"Oh, my," Veracity whispered, "does he ever have a lot of explaining to do."

Sean nodded. "We'd better leave while there's still a roof on the house. Gentlemen, Burkhart will know where we're staying. Burkhart, will you please get a carriage for us? Then, we'll see you day after tomorrow. *Now,* I'm going to take my wife back to our room, change clothes, and then . . . say farewell to city life for good."

"Not quite," Veracity laughed. "Before we go home, I'm going to introduce you to my family in Philadelphia." She sighed happily. "My, but I hope Charles happens to be there also. Oh, and Stormy, I need to buy a new dress."

His brows rose. "But you just got a complete wardrobe yesterday."

"True, but not one of those dresses is red. I need a red dress, Stormy . . . *a really red dress!*"

Burkhart leaned close to Sean to murmur, "A much better choice than Miss Elaine was, Mister . . . uh . . . Stormy. I didn't approve of that young lady, but of Miss Veracity? Indeed!"

"Speaking of Elaine . . . where is she now?"

"Wife of Lester Lathrop. Wed him less than three months after you vanished."

"Good," Sean said vaguely, listening to the shrieked invectives issuing from behind a closed door far down the hallway. "Good." As he took Veracity's arm and followed Burkhart out, he asked Hardesty, "Liam, have you made your decision?"

"Aye." Hardesty lumbered after them down the

stairs. "You still retain fifty-one percent of Hood Shipping. As far as I'm concerned, Georgie is merely your on-site manager. I'll not oppose you . . . or him."

"Thank you, Liam." Sean took Veracity's hand. "After you find your dress, Missus Hood, we're going to buy you a piano. The best piano in New York City." He grinned at her surprise. "We'll have it shipped to Skull Valley so you can play at home . . . for *me!* You're not going into the Palace Bar again, if I have anything to say about it."

She slid her arm around him. "Just as soon as I resign from the Pinkerton Agency, you'll have *everything* to say about it, Mister Hood."

"Good. *Very* good." As he handed her through the door Burkhart automatically opened for them, he took a deep breath and his smile widened. Life had just taken a definite turn for the better. Maybe being a Remittance Man wasn't all bad, at that!

Sept. 25, 1847
To: Mrs. Fredrick Cooper
    Philadelphia, Pennsylvania
My dearest Mother . . .

I do hope this missive reaches you before I do!

You may wonder who, exactly, Mrs. Sean Evan Hood is. 'Tis I, Mother, Veracity. I have recently wed the most

381

wonderful man! His name is Sean Evan Hood. His friends call him Stormy, and he is . . . Well, I shall leave that for you to discover in person!

As you see from the stationery letterhead, we are presently in New York City. Upon conclusion of Sean's business affairs here, he and I shall travel by rail to Philadelphia. We plan to leave Tuesday next (September 29th), and depending on weather, track conditions, and schedules, will arrive very early Thursday, October 1st.

I have a million things to tell you, and can hardly wait for you and my sisters to meet Stormy. Mother, should you be inclined to hostess a reception to introduce Mr. Hood to our family and to my Philadelphia friends, I would find that most pleasant!

How I look forward to sharing my happiness with you!!

Your loving daughter,
Veracity

P.S. Yes, Mother, before you ask, I suppose you might as well also invite Charles to the reception. It will serve the bounder right!

V.

ABOUT THE AUTHOR

Though born in a remote valley in Washington State, S. I. Soper relocated as a teenager to Arizona, subsequently lived and worked in California, Texas, Missouri, traveled in Europe, Africa, Central and South America, the South Pacific Islands, and has now returned to the Pacific Northwest to live and write on the shores of the Puget Sound. Soper's other Western titles include: *Home Remedy* and *Not So Innocent Bystanders*.

Books are produced in the United States using U.S.-based materials

Books are printed using a revolutionary new process called THINKtech™ that lowers energy usage by 70% and increases overall quality

Books are durable and flexible because of Smyth-sewing

Paper is sourced using environmentally responsible foresting methods and the paper is acid-free

Center Point Large Print
600 Brooks Road / PO Box 1
Thorndike, ME 04986-0001 USA

(207) 568-3717

US & Canada:
1 800 929-9108
www.centerpointlargeprint.com